10
BLIND
DATES

ASHLEY ELSTON

HYPERION
Los Angeles New York

First Edition, October 2019
10 9 8 7 6 5 4 3 2 1
FAC-020093-19228
Printed in the United States of America

This book is set in Fairfield LT Std/Monotype
Designed by Mary Claire Cruz

Library of Congress Cataloging-in-Publication Data
Names: Elston, Ashley, author.
Title: 10 blind dates / Ashley Elston.
Other titles: Ten blind dates
Description: First edition. • Los Angeles : Hyperion, 2019. • Summary: After an unexpected breakup, seventeen-year-old Sophie lets members of her large, eccentric extended family set her up on ten blind dates during Christmas vacation.
Identifiers: LCCN 2019011422 (print) • LCCN 2019015970 (ebook) • ISBN 9781368044271 (e-book) • ISBN 9781368027496 (hardcover)
Subjects: • CYAC: Dating (Social customs)—Fiction. • Family life—Fiction. • Christmas—Fiction.
Classification: LCC PZ7.E5295 (ebook) • LCC PZ7.E5295 Aam 2019 (print) • DDC [Fic]—dc23
LC record available at https://lccn.loc.gov/2019011422

Reinforced binding

Logo Applies to Text Stock Only

Visit www.hyperionteens.com

For my husband, Dean, who I met on
a blind date on Valentine's Day in 1992

and

For my brother and first cousins, Jordan, Steve,
Todd, Matt, Beth, Gabe, Katie, Jeremy, Anna Marie,
Sarabeth, Jessica, Rebecca, Mary Hannah, Emily, India,
Katherine, Madeline, Haley, Amiss, Rimes, and John.
Thank you for making my childhood magical.

Friday, December 18th

"Are you sure you won't come with us?"

Mom hangs out of the passenger window and wraps me in a fierce hug for the tenth time in the last ten minutes. The pleading tone in her voice is doing its job. I'm an inch away from the first bit of freedom I've ever known, yet I'm only seconds from caving and jumping into the backseat. I hug her back, tighter than usual.

Dad leans forward, his face washed in the soft blue light from the dash. "Sophie, we really hate leaving you here for Christmas. Who's going to make sure I get those fork marks in the peanut butter cookies just right? Not sure if I can be trusted to do it alone."

I laugh and duck my head. "I'm sure," I say. And I am. This saying good-bye part is hard, but there's no way I can suffer through the next week and a half at Margot's house staring at bloated appendages.

My parents are driving to Breaux Bridge, a small town in

south Louisiana a little less than four hours away, to be with my sister and her husband. Margot is six weeks away from having her first baby, and she's developed superimposed pre-eclampsia, whatever that means. All I know is that it's made her feet swell to ridiculous sizes. And I know this because Margot is so bored out of her mind while she's been stuck in her bed that she's sent me pics of them from every conceivable angle.

"It's not like I'm going to be by myself," I continue. "I'll have Nonna and Papa and the other twenty-five members of our family to keep me company."

Dad rolls his eyes and mutters, "Don't know why they all have to hang out in one house all the time."

Mom pokes him in the ribs. The size of our extended family is no joke. Mom is one of eight, and pretty much all of her siblings have several kids of their own. My grandparents' house is always full of people, but around the holidays it turns into Grand Central station. Beds and spots at the table are awarded based on age, so when my cousins and I were younger we always spent Christmas Eve stuffed into one big pallet on the floor of the den like sardines, and every meal was a balancing act between your plate, your red Solo cup, and your lap.

"Are you sure you don't want to stay with Lisa? It'll be quieter at her house," Mom suggests.

"I'm sure. I'll be fine at Nonna and Papa's."

It *would* be a lot quieter at my aunt Lisa's. She's Mom's twin, older by three minutes, but because of that she watches me as closely as Mom does. And that's not what I'm looking for. I'm looking for a little freedom. And some alone time with Griffin. Both are in short supply when you live in a small town and your dad is the chief of police.

"Okay. Dad and I should be back the afternoon of Nonna's birthday party. We'll open presents then." Mom fidgets around in the front seat, clearly not ready to leave. "I mean, if Brad's parents weren't already going to be there, we wouldn't have to go. You know how his mom always tries to rearrange Margot's kitchen and move her furniture around. I don't want Margot all worked up, wondering what that woman is doing while she's stuck in bed."

"And God forbid, *his* parents take care of *your* daughter," I tease. Mom is overly protective of her children. All Margot had to do was mention that her husband's parents were coming in and Mom started packing her bags.

"We could wait and go in the morning," Mom suggests to Dad.

Dad's shaking his head before she finishes. "We'll make better time if we drive tonight. Tomorrow is the Saturday before Christmas. The roads will be a nightmare." He leans forward once more, meeting my gaze. "Get your stuff and head straight to your grandparents'. Call them to let them know you're on the way."

That's my dad—all business. This is the first time in years Dad will be away from the station for more than a few days.

"I will." One more hug from Mom, and I blow a kiss to Dad. Then they're gone.

The glowing red taillights of my parents' SUV disappear down the road, and a flood of emotions rolls through me—thrilling anticipation, but also an ache that settles deep in my belly. I do my best to shake it off. It's not that I don't want to be with them—just thinking about waking up on Christmas morning without my parents has my stomach twisting in knots—but I just can't spend my entire break trapped in Margot and Brad's tiny apartment.

Once I'm back in my room, the first thing I do is call Nonna to tell her I'll be there in a few hours. She's distracted; I can hear the customers at the flower shop she owns talking loudly in the background, and can guess she's only hearing about every third word I say.

"Drive carefully, sweetheart," she says. As she's hanging up, I can hear her shouting poinsettia prices at Randy in the greenhouse, and I smother a grin.

It's six o'clock, and it's just a short drive from Minden to Shreveport, where my grandparents and the rest of my family live. Nonna won't look for me until around ten.

Four glorious hours to myself.

I fall back on my bed and stare at my slowly turning ceiling fan. Even though I'm seventeen, my parents don't like for me to stay home alone. And when I do manage to pull it off, there's usually a parade of deputies doing drive-bys—*just to check on things*. It's all sorts of ridiculous.

Feeling around on the bed for my phone, I call Griffin to let him know I'll be staying, but after eight rings it goes to voice mail. I send him a text, then wait for those three little dots to appear. I hadn't told him I was trying to convince my parents to let me stay—no reason for both of us to be disappointed if it didn't work out.

I stare at the blank screen for another few seconds, then throw the phone down on the bed and move to my desk. There's a clutter of makeup and colored pencils and nail polish bottles scattered across the surface. Almost every inch of the bulletin board hanging on the wall in front of me showcases crisp white index cards for each college I'm considering. There's a color-coded list of pros (green) and cons (red) on each card, plus all of the application requirements per school. A few sport a big green checkmark, meaning I've already met every requirement and been accepted, but most I'm still waiting to hear from. I call this my Inspiration Board, but Mom calls it my Obsession Board.

My eyes move to the first card I tacked up at the beginning of freshman year—LSU. Once upon a time, I thought it was the only school that would make the board. But then I realized I needed to keep my options open.

My phone dings and I glance back toward the bed. It's just a notification that someone liked my last post—not Griffin texting me back.

I glance at the blank cards stacked on my desk and, for half a second, consider making a Griffin list. We've been together for over a year, and school is usually our biggest focus, but with the two-week break ahead and no midterms or papers to worry about, the idea of being here alone with him is exciting. Even though we've been taking things slow, I'd be lying if I said I hadn't thought about taking our relationship to the next level.

Green: *Together almost a year*
We're seniors and almost eighteen

Red: *Haven't said "I love you" yet*
Not sure if I'm ready to say "I love you" yet

Mom would definitely have a problem if she sees that list hanging there, so I resist the urge.

My phone chimes again. I feel my heart lurch when I see the text icon, but when I check the screen, I see another pic from Margot.

I open the image and stare at it for a few minutes. Someone needs to take the phone away from her.

ME: ????? What is that???

MARGOT: That was a close-up of my toes. There is zero space between them. I can't wiggle them or separate them. They're like little sausages.

ME: What if they never go back to normal?? What if you're stuck with sausage toes forever? What if you can never wear flip-flops again because you can't get that little plastic piece between your first two toes? You're going to humiliate your kid with those feet.

MARGOT: I guess sausage toes are better than sausage fingers. Maybe I'll have to wear those really ugly orthopedic shoes like Aunt Toby used to wear.

ME: You could bedazzle them. And maybe write your name in puff paint along each side. They would be adorable sausage toe shoes.

MARGOT: Now you made me hungry for sausage.

ME: You're disgusting. And you've scarred me for life. I'm never getting pregnant for fear of sausage toes and bedazzled orthopedic shoes.

It's a few minutes before she texts me back.

MARGOT: Mom just texted me that you're not coming!!! What in the hell, Soph??? You were going to save me from the tug-of-war between Mom and Gwen. You know how those two are together!!

ME: You're on your own. I really hope they fight over who gets to clean out the lint between those sausage toes. Maybe they'll have to use dental floss.

MARGOT: You've given me a mental picture I'll never be able to get rid of. I curse you with sausage toes for the rest of your life!

ME: I'll come when the baby's born.

MARGOT: Promise??

ME: Promise

MARGOT: So has Griffin gotten there yet?

ME: None of your business.

MARGOT: Give it up. No, wait . . . don't give it up.

ME: Ha. Ha.

I scroll through all the social media sites, wasting time waiting for Griffin to call me. My phone finally rings, and his name flashes across the screen. I don't even try to stop the smile that breaks out across my face.

"Hey!" he screams over the loud music and noise in the background.

"Hey! Where are you?" I ask.

"Matt's."

I've already seen several posts from people hanging out in Matt's backyard and pool house, including Addie, my best friend since the third grade.

"Are you on the way to Margot's?" he asks.

"Change of plans. I'm staying with Nonna and Papa. But I don't have to be there for a few hours."

"What? I can hardly hear you," he says in a loud voice.

"Change of plans!" I scream. "I'm staying here."

I can hear the steady beat from the bass but can't make out which song is playing.

"I can't believe your dad didn't make you go," he says.

"I know, right? Want to come here? Or I can come to Matt's."

He's quiet a second before saying, "Come to Matt's. Everyone's here."

I feel a pang of disappointment. "Okay, see you in a few," I reply, then end the call.

The crowd at Matt's is bigger than I expected. Today was the last day of school before the holiday break, and it looks like everyone is ready to celebrate. There must be a million lights strung over his house and the bushes and trees. Really, there are lights covering anything that stayed still too long.

Most people are in T-shirts and shorts, and even with all of the decorations it's hard to feel festive. Doesn't really feel like winter break when you're swatting mosquitoes. Stupid Louisiana weather.

I park my car four houses down, the closest spot I can

find. Even from this far away, I can still hear the deep thump of bass coming from Matt's backyard. It wouldn't surprise me if the neighbors call the cops within the hour. Hopefully, we'll be gone by then; it would be hard to explain why I was here instead of halfway to my grandparents' house when one of the deputies inevitably calls my dad.

When I get to Matt's, I spot a guy and a girl sitting in the grass near the driveway, and they seem to be arguing. The drama doesn't usually get started this early. They get quiet when they notice me, and I pick up the pace, trying to give them their privacy. Following the music, I head to the backyard toward the pool house. Just as I'm about to round the house, I feel a tug on my arm.

And then I'm swallowed in a breath-crushing hug.

"I thought you weren't coming!" Addie squeals loud enough that several people turn in our direction.

"Can you believe I talked my parents into going without me?"

"I can't! Are you staying at Nonna's?" She sticks out her bottom lip in a pout. "I'm still barely going to see you!"

I laugh. "Yes, you will. I have a plan. Nonna will be so busy during the day, she won't even miss me. I'll head back here and we can hang out."

"Your parents will flip if they find out. We'll have to hide your car." Addie jumps up and down. "Oh! And bring Olivia. I haven't seen her in forever."

I nod, even though I doubt she'll want to come back with me. Olivia is one of my many cousins and the daughter of Mom's twin sister, Lisa. We're only two months apart in age and used to be super close when we were younger, but we've seen less and less of each other over the last couple of years. "Olivia is helping Nonna at the shop. I'm not sure she can get away."

Addie's eyes brighten; then she starts dragging me to the pool house. "We'll just have to find a way to break her out of there."

"Have you seen Griffin?" I ask, changing the subject away from Olivia.

"Not yet, but Danny and I just got here. Maybe he's inside." She nods toward the pool house. "Want a beer?"

"Nah, I have to drive to Nonna's soon. I'll find a bottle of water somewhere," I say as we part ways. Addie heads to the keg hidden in the shrubbery and I push through the crowd. The music is so loud once I get inside that the first few people I talk to can't hear me at all.

I finally make it through the room and find a few of Griffin's friends.

"Sophie! What's up!" Chris yells, then tries to hug me. He's already down to his white undershirt and boxer shorts. I hold my arm out to keep him at a safe distance. Chris is the guy that always manages to get one step from naked at parties. At the school Halloween dance, he came dressed as a cowboy, but by the end of the night all that was left of his costume was the pair of chaps over his boxer briefs. He got a week's worth of detentions for indecent exposure.

"Not much. Where's Griffin?" I ask, then turn around to scope out the room.

Chris waves his hand behind him. "Somewhere back there. Went looking for a beer."

I nod, then scoot around him. It's hard to make any progress through the crowd, but I finally spot Griffin just as he turns into the small kitchen in the back of the pool house. It takes me a few minutes to catch up, since I stumbled into the middle of a dance circle and Josh Peters won't let me leave without spinning me around a few times. As I'm just about to round the corner into the kitchen, where the music is actually somewhat muted, I hear Griffin say, "Sophie's on her way."

It's not the words that make me stop. It's the way he says them. Full of disappointment.

Parker, one of Griffin's best friends, is pulling two beers out of the refrigerator. Neither one of them notices me just outside the door.

"I thought she was going to her sister's house or something?" Parker asks.

Griffin's head hangs. "She was. But not anymore."

He's so bummed I'm staying, like I've ruined his break. I can hear it in his voice, that horrible feeling—the one where you were so looking forward to something, like you were about to bust out of your skin because you were so happy, only to have it snatched away. That's how I felt when I thought I wouldn't be here for the break.

And that's how he sounds after hearing I will be here.

What is happening?

Griffin starts to turn, and I duck around the corner. Why am I hiding? I should be storming in there, demanding answers. But I'm frozen. I count to five and then slowly look back into the kitchen.

"She'll be here any minute," he says, but stays rooted in his spot.

Parker pops open one of the beers and hands it to Griffin. Griffin takes a long drink.

"So what's the problem?" Parker asks. Obviously he can hear the disappointment, too.

Griffin shrugs. "This is going to make me sound like an asshole, but I was kind of glad she was going to be gone. You know, like a trial run of what it would be like if we broke up."

My heart is pounding.

"Do you want to break up with her?" Parker asks, then takes another swig of his beer.

Griffin shrugs again. My desire to scream is almost overwhelming.

"I think so."

I gasp. Parker and Griffin both turn toward the door. Parker's eyes get big, and he looks from me to Griffin and back to me.

There's a split second where Griffin tries to figure out if I heard what was said. But the expression on my face makes it obvious that I did.

I stumble back, hitting the wall before fleeing.

I have to get out of here. I can't look at him. I can't be here.

"Sophie!" Griffin follows behind me, but I duck and dodge my way toward the door. I'm afraid I won't make it outside before the tears start to fall. Then Addie sees my face and barrels through the people dancing, pulling me out of the pool house.

"What happened?" she asks once we're on the other side of the pool.

I crumple to the ground and tell her everything.

"That asshole," Addie says. She turns, like she's going to hunt him down.

"Please help me get out of here," I plead.

She moves back toward me. "Of course. Let's go."

Addie helps me off the ground and we pick our way through the landscaping. Tears are streaming down my face now, and I don't even try to stop them.

My heart is crushed.

More than crushed.

Pulverized.

He wants to break up with me.

"I can't believe him," Addie mutters under her breath. "*He's* going to break up with *you*? Whatever. He's lucky to have you!"

I don't have the words to answer her. Not sure if I ever will.

Just as we make it to the driveway, we see Griffin. He's running down the driveway, scanning the street.

"I can't talk to him right now," I croak out. Addie nods and moves me into the shadows before marching out to confront him.

"No. Just no," Addie says. "She doesn't want to talk to you."

Griffin's face is illuminated by one of the lights anchored to the eave of the house. He looks awful.

Guilty, yes, but there's also sadness swimming in those eyes.

"Please, Addie. I need to talk to her." He squints toward the darkness where I'm hiding. "Please, Sophie. Talk to me. Let me explain. I didn't mean it like that."

I take a step back, not wanting to be near him . . . not wanting to hear his excuses. Running behind a row of azalea bushes to the front yard, I trip every other step, trying to put some distance between us.

I hope Griffin doesn't follow me. There is a small part of me that wants to take what I heard, twist it around until it's something that doesn't crush me. But I can't quit hearing the disappointment in his voice. No matter what he says, he didn't want to see me. He didn't want to be here with me.

By the time I make it to my car, I'm shattered. Footsteps pound on the pavement behind me, and I brace myself.

"Sophie, please talk to me?" Griffin begs.

I'm facing the car. He's right behind me, and I know Addie is somewhere behind him.

My mouth tightens. "I was so excited my parents let me stay home because all I could think was how fun it would be to hang out with you. Just the two of us. That's what I was looking forward to. But you want a break. From me. Right? Isn't that what you were looking forward to?"

His hand lands softly on my shoulder and he says, "Turn around and talk to me."

I shrug him off. "Is that what you want?"

I can feel him struggling to find the words. "I don't know what I want, Soph. Everything is so confusing right now. Things got so serious between us. It's our senior year. We're supposed to be having fun!"

I spin around. "Well, let me make it easy for you. You want a break? You got it. We're done."

He reaches for me, but I dodge his grasp. He seems frantic, and I can't help but think it's because of how this is going down. He didn't get his trial run first.

"Wait, Sophie. Can we talk about this? I love you. I really do."

His words are like a blow. I've waited and wanted him to say this to me for months.

I can't do this.

I can't stay here.

"Please stay and talk to me," Griffin begs. I turn and get into my car.

Griffin finally retreats to the sidewalk as I start the engine, and Addie runs to the window. "Let me drive you."

I give her a weak smile. "I'm fine. I'll call you later, okay? I love you."

She reaches in the window and gives me a quick hug. "I love you, too."

Thankfully, Griffin keeps his distance.

Within minutes, I'm on I-20 headed to Shreveport.

By the time I get to Nonna's house, I'm a wreck. I check my appearance in the rearview mirror and almost scream at the mascara-streaked stranger staring back at me. My nose is red, my eyes are swollen, and I'm pretty sure there's dried snot crusted on my shirt.

Thankfully, most of the lights are off, so there's a good chance no one is here but my grandparents. At this house, it's not unusual to step over sleeping bodies just inside the door. Out of the eight kids my grandparents have, six live here in

Shreveport, four of them within blocks of this house. Though you'd think it would mean they'd go home, that's usually not the case. But tonight looks quiet.

I park my car on the street and grab my bag from the backseat, but I only make it to the front steps before I collapse. I can't go in there like this. Nonna will call my parents, and they'll be mad I didn't come straight here. But they'll also be upset about Griffin. They love him. Even with all of their crazy rules, they already treat him like he's part of the family.

Using my duffel as a pillow, I lie back on the dark steps and stare at the full moon. There's a huge part of me that wants nothing more than to curl up in my mom's lap and cry.

A year. That's how long I've wasted with Griffin. A freaking year.

What did I miss? We were both focused on school. We were both looking forward to college and making sure we got into the schools we wanted. I thought we both were happy with our relationship.

But apparently he's not having any *fun* with me.

"You going to stay out here all night, or are you going to come in and tell me what happened?"

I nearly fall off the step when my grandmother's face looms over mine.

"Nonna!" I jump up and stumble into her arms, almost knocking us both over.

She runs a hand up and down my back. I start to cry all over again.

"Oh my, come in and tell me all about it."

We walk inside, hand in hand, straight to the kitchen. Her kitchen is the heart of this house. It's a big open room with lots of cabinets and counter space. The fridge is one of those gigantic stainless steel ones that's covered in pictures, and I know if I open it, the shelves will be packed with food. There's a row of bar stools along the side of the island and a huge wood farm table stretching in front of a row of windows that look out toward the neighbor's house. And there is always a vase of fresh flowers sitting in the center.

It's my favorite room in the house.

Nonna leads me to one of the bar stools, then cuts me a piece of the most decadent chocolate cake I've ever seen. There's never a shortage of goodies here, and tonight definitely doesn't disappoint.

"I don't think you're crying about your mom and dad leaving, so I assume this is about that boy. What's his name?"

"Griffin," I mumble.

"Yes, Griffin. Tell me what happened."

I pause before taking a bite of the cake. I've always been close to Nonna, but we've never talked about my love life.

She notices my hesitation and says, "I raised four daughters. I promise you I've heard my fair share of heartbreak sitting right here in this very spot."

I let out an awkward laugh. Nonna prides herself on her ability to fix what's broken when it comes to this family—no problem is too big or small. She just can't help herself.

She pours me a glass of milk, and I watch her move around the kitchen. She'll be seventy-five in a little more than a week, but you'd never be able to tell, thanks to an inconsequential number of gray hairs and a faithful skin-care regimen. And she's still strong enough to carry the huge bags of potting soil and mulch at the nursery, even though Papa fusses at her.

I take a deep breath. "I know I told you I was at Addie's house, but I went somewhere else instead. A friend was having a party. I wanted to see Griffin before I came here. I was going to surprise him by telling him I'd be around during the holidays."

Nonna's eyebrows shoot up. "Uh-oh. That rarely turns out well."

I choke down a laugh. "You can say that again."

Nonna settles in next to me and takes a big bite out of her own piece of cake as I tell her everything. When I'm finished, she rubs circles on my back, and I fold into her. "Sweet Sophie, I know this feels like the end of the world right now, but it's not. Better to see how Griffin feels now before you waste any more time with him."

She hands me a napkin and I wipe my eyes dry. "But I thought we wanted the same things."

"Things change all the time. Maybe you thought you two were moving in the same direction when really you weren't."

Once I finish my cake, she walks me from the kitchen to the guest room upstairs. "This room is all yours until your parents get back. Tomorrow, you can help me at the shop. Busy hands will keep your mind from wandering. And Olivia will be happy to have the company. She's been pouty now that everyone else is out of school and she has to work."

I let Nonna tuck me in and baby me like she did when I was a little girl. It feels nicer than I remember.

She kisses my head and says, "It will all seem better tomorrow."

Saturday, December 19th

I hate to call Nonna a liar, but it's tomorrow and everything still pretty much sucks. My eyes are nearly swollen shut from all the crying, and I've got a headache that just won't stop.

I glance at my phone. There are thirty-two missed calls and texts.

I scroll down to Addie's name and send her a quick text: I'm okay. Call you a little later.

Then I pass over Griffin's messages and open the conversation with Margot.

ME: You awake, Sausage Toes?

MARGOT: Of course I'm awake. I'm stuck in the bed All. Day. Long. But can't get comfortable enough to sleep. How's Nonna's?

ME: Good. Have they cleaned between your toes yet?

MARGOT: STOP!!!

ME: You started it with the nasty pictures.

MARGOT: Change of subject. Tell me about the food. What did

Nonna fix last night? The moms won't let me have anything that isn't organic and non-GMO.

ME: 3 layer chocolate cake with chocolate icing and chocolate shavings on top. I had a gigantic piece.

MARGOT: You SUCK. I would give everything in my checking account for you to bring me a piece.

ME: I know all about the online shopping you've being doing, so I can guess what's in your checking account and it's not enough.

MARGOT: Well, heads-up if you talk to Dad later. He was mad you didn't call when you got there.

Crap! I totally forgot I was supposed to check in.

ME: How mad? Mad like when we broke the front window when we tried to turn Barbie's car into a rocket ship?

MARGOT: Hahaha! He wasn't that mad. He called Nonna and she said you were in the shower.

I owe Nonna one. She totally covered for me.

ME: I don't want to admit this because you'll never let me live it down . . . but I kind of wish I was there with you and your sausage toes.

I wipe at my face, brushing away the tears. I could still get in my car and drive down there this morning. Even though I'll never hear the end of it, at least I could crawl into bed with Margot and not come out until Christmas is over.

MARGOT: I wish you were here, too. But you would be miserable. I'm miserable. Brad's miserable. Even our dog is miserable. You were right to stay with Nonna and Papa.

I try not to feel disappointed. I know she would welcome me if I outright asked to come down. But my sour mood would no doubt make her more miserable than she already is.

MARGOT: Are you okay?
ME: Yeah. I'm fine. I'll text you later.

I'm not sure why I didn't tell her about Griffin. Maybe I'm afraid if I tell her about what happened it becomes irrevocably true. Or maybe I know Margot's got enough to worry about right now. She's trying to play it tough, but she's worried about the baby.

I power off the phone, ignoring the rest of my messages and missed calls, and drop it in the bedside table drawer. Can't deal with any more of that right now.

My reflection is scarier than I thought it would be by the time I make it to the bathroom. I'm not a pretty crier. The red around my eyes makes them look darker than normal, and my normally tanned skin has a sickly pale look to it. All my tossing and turning last night ruined the soft curls I spent forever perfecting when I thought Griffin would be excited to see me. Now my long black hair is a dingy, tangled mess.

Once I've showered and dried my hair, though, I feel a little better. On a scale from normal to complete disaster, I'm somewhere around pathetically passable. At last, I inch my way down the hallway, toward the chorus of voices coming from the kitchen, and prepare myself for the onslaught.

The family is here.

My family is a wild bunch. My grandfather was born and raised in Sicily. He was supposed to go back home after spending some time in the United States, but he fell in love with my grandmother. As the story goes, my grandfather's mother almost started an international incident when she found out he was staying in Louisiana. The only thing that stopped her was the fact that Nonna's family was originally from a town near his.

Dad always struggles when we come here. He's an only child and has no extended family, so sometimes he says it feels like entering a war zone. I'm not as bad as him, but since we are the only group, besides my uncle Michael, that doesn't live in Shreveport, I feel somewhat like an outsider.

I didn't always feel that way, though. When I was younger, I spent most of my summers and every holiday here, surrounded by my cousins and the neighborhood kids. It was like summer camp. I was closest with Olivia, our cousin Charlie, and Charlie's best friend, Wes, who lives next door. Uncle Bruce, Olivia's dad, even named us the Fab Four. But the older we got, the more it felt like we drifted apart. The three of them all went to the same school and were part of the same clubs and cheered for the same team. So I threw myself into my clubs and my team. It wasn't long before my visits became shorter and further apart.

Aunt Maggie Mae catches sight of me the moment I enter the kitchen.

"Well, there she is! I declare, you look more like your mama every time I see you!"

You know those people who make fun of how Southern people talk? They must have gotten their source material from my aunt. Maggie Mae, who is married to my mom's brother Marcus, was one of those true Southern belles back in the day, complete with the big white dress when she was presented to society. And she won't let you forget it.

She pulls me against her chest and I'm afraid I'm going to suffocate in her overly endowed boobs. "Bless your heart, sweetie. I heard about your heartache. That boy ain't got the good sense God gave a rock."

"Um . . . thanks, Aunt Maggie Mae." I think.

I'm passed around the kitchen and kissed on the cheek, the forehead, and even the lips (by Aunt Kelsey, who does not understand personal space at all) in a matter of minutes. I slide onto one of the bar stools as the aunts resume their argument over whose ambrosia salad is better—Aunt Kelsey's, made the classic way, or Aunt Patrice's, made with Jell-O—and which one should be served for lunch on Christmas Day.

I'm firmly in the anti-ambrosia camp, but I keep that opinion to myself.

Aunt Maggie Mae has two sets of twins—twin daughters who are close to my age and twin sons who are much younger. The twin daughters, Mary Jo and Jo Lynn, give me an awkward wave from across the kitchen, and I give them a more awkward wave back. When they were young, almost all of their clothing matched except for the monogram. Even now at eighteen, they *coordinate*. It's ridiculous. They're a year older than Olivia, Charlie, and me, but we're all in the same grade. Charlie's been calling them the Evil Joes since we were twelve, when they locked him out of the condo we were all sharing in Florida in nothing but his *Star Wars* briefs. Truthfully, he had no business still wearing those. Think: small. And tight. A group of teenage girls he had been flirting with all week saw him, and you'd have thought it was the funniest thing they had ever seen. Those girls giggled every time Charlie got anywhere near them for the rest of the week.

He never got over it.

My aunt Lisa, Mom's twin, and her son, Jake, are here, too.

"Sweet Soph! So glad to see you!" Aunt Lisa looks so much like Mom, it's hard not to cry when I see her.

"I'm happy to see you, too." I hug her a little longer than normal. She even smells like Mom. "Where's Olivia?"

"Already at the shop," she says. "I hear Nonna volunteered you to work there over the break."

"Of course she did," I answer with a smile.

Jake nudges me and says, "Dang, girl. You look like crap."

Aunt Lisa smacks him in the back of the head. "Jake, don't be a jerk."

He laughs as he hobbles off in search of an open seat at the table. Jake broke his foot doing something stupid, probably involving heights and visions of grandeur, at his fraternity house at LSU, and now he's wearing one of those boots.

Charlie weaves his way to where I'm sitting, and I hop up from my bar stool, grinning, when he gets close. I haven't seen him in forever. He pauses a second or so before giving me a halfhearted hug. I'm a little taken aback by his hesitation, but my arms go around him immediately, and I feel better than I have all morning.

"Are you okay? Nonna told me what happened with Griffin," Charlie says when I finally let him go.

Of course Nonna told him. She's probably told everyone by now.

"Yeah. I'm fine."

He sits on the stool next to me. "Other than the boyfriend trouble, how's it going?"

I shrug. "Good, I guess. Busy. How about you?"

He nods. "Good. Busy, too."

Charlie falls silent, and I'm racking my brain, trying to think of another question to ask him. Gah, since when were conversations with Charlie this hard?

Before I have a chance to come up with anything, he says, "Well, we're planning on hanging out after family dinner tonight, if you're around."

I swallow too much coffee and cough when the hot liquid goes down wrong. "Family dinner tonight?" I choke out. If word has spread about my boyfriend wanting to dump me, I'm not sure I can face all of the pity stares I'm sure to get.

Charlie smiles. "You know it. It doesn't take much for Nonna to get everyone together, and your visit will definitely bring out the extra table. We can go to Wes's after to get away from the crowd."

Wes lives next door and has been more like Charlie's brother than friend, mainly because Charlie spent half his childhood at Wes's house. Charlie's parents met when they both worked for Doctors Without Borders in the Philippines, where Aunt Ayin is originally from, and they both still donate time wherever they're needed. Charlie and Sara stay at Nonna's when their parents are gone. Which means Charlie almost always ends up at Wes's.

"We'll make Olivia come, too," he says. "The Fab Four . . . just like old times."

A nervous flutter runs through me, but I say, "Sure! That

sounds like fun." Charlie grins and grabs a muffin. He's out the door before I can change my mind.

Nonna sets down a piece of quiche in front of me and gives me a squeeze. "Feeling better today?" she whispers.

I nod as she refills my coffee.

"We'll leave for the shop in an hour, okay?"

"Okay," I answer. It's not like I have anything else to do now.

The shop is really just an old house in a neighborhood that has become more and more commercial over the years. Most of the businesses opted to tear the houses down and rebuild, but Nonna and Papa kept this cute little blue house the exact same way they found it. All of the yard out back is now mostly greenhouse space, while the inside is stuffed with gardening supplies, statues, and other yard and garden decorations. It's got that homey feel to it that totally works.

When we were younger, we would play hide-and-seek in the back greenhouse and help plant flowers in the front flower beds. The wave of nostalgia almost knocks me over as I start down the front walkway.

Before Nonna disappears through the side gate to the backyard, she nods toward the front porch. "Olivia should already be inside. Would you help her at the counter today?"

I nod and stop in front of the wide set of steps that lead to the front porch. There are red poinsettias lining each step, and a huge wreath made out of greenery hanging on the front door with a big red bow. The flames in the gas lanterns on each side of the door wink and dance, and I swear I can smell gingerbread.

There's a big part of me that doesn't want to walk through that front door, no matter how festive it is. It's been a long time since it was just me and Olivia, and I'm suddenly nervous.

I take a deep breath and open the door. Olivia is carrying a huge sack of potting soil to an old, scarred wooden table that sits in the corner. It looks like she's in the middle of repotting some rosemary into decorative containers.

"Hey!" I say. I must have startled her because she drops the sack and a cloud of dust rises around both of us. I've missed her more than I realized, and my reluctance melts away. I reach forward and throw an arm around her, hugging her close.

Like Charlie, she hesitates before hugging me back.

"Soph," she says against my ear. "What are you doing here?"

I pull away and scan her face. We both cough, and I wave my hands around, trying to clear the air around us.

"I'm staying with Nonna while my parents visit Margot. I'm surprised your mom didn't tell you."

She nods. "She did. I just didn't expect you *here*."

"Is everything okay?" I ask. So it *is* going to be awkward between us.

She looks like she's about to say something but then stops when we hear Nonna moan. "Good grief!" Nonna says, looking between us, then at the mess on the floor. "Well, don't just stand there gawking at each other. Get a broom."

And then we're both moving.

It's almost dark when I leave the nursery with Olivia. Every house we pass is covered in lights, and there's lots of traffic—people shopping or heading to holiday parties.

"Are you ready to talk about it?" Olivia asks as she drives.

For a second, I think she's talking about whatever it is that's off with us, but then she says, "Tell me what happened with Griffin."

I grimace. We worked hard today, and Nonna was right—I needed to keep my mind off Griffin. But now I force myself to replay it all in my head. "Well, I showed up at this party." I pick at my thumbnail and run through the story again. It doesn't get any easier no matter how many times I say it. And if talking to Olivia is this difficult, going back to school will be so much worse. It'll take a Christmas miracle for our breakup to be old news by the time I walk down the hall without Griffin by my side.

"Oh, Sophie. I'm so sorry," Olivia says. "He really said you weren't any fun?" By the tone of her voice, I can tell she's as surprised as I was.

I let out a groan and say, "That's what he implied."

Olivia frowns. "The Sophie I used to know was super fun. *He's* clearly the problem."

My head whips around at the *Sophie I used to know* part. What does that mean? But before I can ask, she says, "Well, you're here now, and we're not going to let Griffin bring us down. We'll find something fun to do while you're here, just like old times. There'll be a ton of parties during the break."

I nod, but somehow hanging out at some loud party where I barely know anyone does not sound appealing.

We pull in front of Nonna and Papa's. The driveway and half the block is full of cars, so Olivia eases down the street, looking for a spot. "*Everyone* is going to ask you about Griffin. News travels way too fast through this family. Nonna tells one person and then it's like some phone tree thing is activated, and within an hour everyone knows everything."

"I know. They all knew this morning at breakfast. And your mom already filled my mom in, too."

My phone was still in the drawer upstairs, but Mom had tracked me down at the nursery. That was *not* a call I wanted to get. At least she felt so bad for me that she didn't even mention my detour last night. And I had to laugh when I heard Margot in the background, yelling, "Tell her I sent more pictures!"

"Don't let Aunt Maggie Mae give you any crap," Olivia says. "She'll use any excuse to talk about how Mary Jo's boyfriend is being wooed by both LSU and Bama, and how Jo Lynn's boyfriend just got an early acceptance letter to A&M."

"It's hard to believe anyone would date the Evil Joes."

"That's exactly what Charlie keeps saying." Olivia turns off the car and we both stare at the house.

"Are you ready for this?" she asks.

"As ready as I'll ever be."

When we step inside, we're greeted with pure chaos. The younger cousins race through the halls on scooters, RipStiks, and one another's backs.

"Hey, Sophie! Hey, Olivia!" the tiny voices ring out as they lap us. The last little one to pass is one of my youngest cousins, Webb. He's flying down the hall on his scooter wearing black boxer briefs and a Superman T-shirt.

"Webb," I say. "You seem to be missing your pants."

Olivia waves him off. "He's going through an anti-pants phase. Refuses to wear them if he's in the house. Any house."

Papa and a few of my uncles are parked in front of the TV, arguing about the game. I lean down to kiss Papa on the cheek. Charlie and one of my other cousins, Graham, snuck him out of the nursery to go fishing this afternoon while Nonna was busy in the greenhouse.

"How many did you catch?" I whisper.

He chuckles and ruffles my hair. "Five, but don't tell your grandmother."

Of course, Nonna was the one who asked Charlie and Graham to come get him when she realized Papa needed a break.

"There are my girls," Nonna calls from the stove when we enter the kitchen. She's wearing her *Ciao Y'all* apron and she looks like she was doused in flour. "Why don't you both set the table? We're almost ready."

Olivia grabs the place mats and I follow behind with the plates.

"Sophie," Aunt Camille calls out. She's at the counter next to Nonna, sprinkling croutons on the salad. "What happened with your boyfriend? And who's this Paige girl? Was he cheating on you with her?"

Olivia throws me a look over her shoulder, then rolls her eyes. *Here we go.*

"There's no girl named Paige. He was talking to his friend Parker," I answer.

Aunt Kelsey, who has a daughter on each hip and one clinging to her leg, limps into the room. There's usually a fourth little girl attached to her, so I scan the area to see which one is missing.

"Where's Birdie?" I ask her.

Aunt Kelsey does a quick check and seems to notice for

the first time one of her littles is missing. She rolls her eyes and yells to her husband, "Will? Do you have Birdie?"

A muffled *yes* bounces back.

She shakes her head, then continues into the room. "I can't believe he broke up with you," she says before dropping the three attached to her one by one into the high chairs lined up against the wall.

"I think his crime is more *Intent to Break Up*, Kelsey," Nonna adds.

The problem with the phone tree is a lot of the details get mixed up.

Aunt Maggie Mae snorts. "Well, I never liked him. You could tell he was up to no good by just looking in those eyes. Not like Mary Jo's boyfriend. LSU and Bama are both just *dying* to get him. We hope he picks LSU; I just don't think I can root for Bama, even if my future son-in-law is the quarterback."

Olivia pretends to gag.

"You didn't think Griffin was too bad when he helped fix your tire last summer," Uncle Sal says.

"Pooh. Of course he helped. He had to—he was standing right there. And he was only trying to look good in front of Jo Lynn's boyfriend, who got a full ride to A&M so he can study engineering."

Charlie, Graham, and Graham's older sister, Hannah, are laughing on the other side of the room, where they're putting out the extra table and chairs. Graham is the same age as Olivia's brother, Jake, and they're both at LSU together. Honestly, I'm surprised Graham's not in a boot, too, since if Jake's doing something wild and crazy, Graham is usually right behind him.

Charlie's sister, Sara, strolls in carrying a huge gift basket. Her long black hair is almost halfway down her back, her cheeks have lost that baby fat, and she's a few inches taller than I remember. It's shocking to me how much she's changed since I last saw her.

"Nonna, this was sitting on the front porch," Sara says, then sets it down on the counter.

"Oh, how lovely," Nonna says as she reads the card. "It's from the Dethloffs across the street."

"When did Sara start looking so grown up? And gorgeous?" I ask Olivia.

"Serious growth spurt over the last couple of months. Charlie is *not* happy, now that every boy in school has their eye on her," she answers. "And she made freshman homecoming court back in October!"

"She did? How did I not know this?" I ask.

"I don't know." Olivia shrugs. "I guess you haven't been around much lately."

The kitchen door slams, and we all turn as Aunt Patrice, Uncle Ronnie, Denver, and Dallas come in wearing matching sweaters—and not the cute kind. I catch Denver's eye and nod toward the sweater. He points to his mom, shaking his head. I can't help but laugh. Those poor kids don't stand a chance, especially since Aunt Patrice loves telling everyone they named their sons after the locations in which the boys were conceived.

Ew.

Aunt Lisa wraps an arm around me. "Well, I liked him. But I'm sad things ended the way they did—you deserve better than that."

There's no way I'm going to make it through dinner.

"Don't worry about Sophie. I've got it all figured out," Nonna says, and the room suddenly gets quiet.

"Oh no. This can't be good," I mumble under my breath.

"Mama, what are you scheming?" Aunt Lisa asks.

Nonna tries to look offended, but we all know she loves getting in the middle of everyone's business. "Well, when life gives you lemons, you get right back on that saddle."

"I'm not sure that's how that saying goes," Graham says.

"She just needs a date or two, you know, to get her mind off her troubles," Nonna adds.

Aunt Maggie Mae looks way too interested in where this conversation is going. "The girls and I know some single boys her age."

Uncle Sal's head pops up. "After you set her up, I've got a nice boy in mind who works for me"

"Oh! Oh!" Aunt Patrice shrieks. "I have an idea! Let's each of us pick someone for her! I have just the thing. . . ."

And then everyone is talking at once.

"What is happening?" I ask no one in particular. Before I can stop this insanity, Nonna produces a long piece of white butcher paper.

"This will be so fun!" she says. Several aunts help clear the counter and Nonna lays the paper down. Then she grabs a Sharpie and starts writing dates, starting with tomorrow through New Year's Eve.

"Sara, come help me with this," Nonna asks.

Sara shoots across the room and helps Nonna tack it onto the bulletin board near the pantry door, and I give her a frown for being so quick to help. Sara gives me a wink back.

Movement at the back door catches my attention, and I see Wes peek his head in. Charlie motions for him to come inside.

It's been a while since I've seen him, too. His blond hair and pale complexion stand out in this household of dark-haired, tan-skinned Sicilians. He looks taller than I remember, and he's not nearly as scrawny as he used to be.

He sits down next to Graham and Charlie and points to the paper with a questioning look.

They both shrug. But I have a pretty good idea of where this is headed, and it terrifies me.

Nonna stands up next to the paper and points to it, Vanna White–style. "This is how Sophie will get over that no-good ex-boyfriend of hers."

Wes searches the room until his eyes fall on me. He tilts his head and raises one eyebrow, and I give him a small, embarrassed smile.

"There're enough of us here that we are bound to know some nice single boys. We're going to set Sophie up on a few blind dates, and by the time she goes back to school after the New Year, she'll hardly remember what's-his-name."

"Griffin," Jake supplies.

Nonna rolls her eyes. "Thank you, Jake."

Oh. My. God. I'm about to crawl under the table.

"This is a bad idea," I say from the back of the room, louder than I intended. "And I'll be home by New Year's. Mom and Dad are coming home for your birthday party. I already have plans that night!"

Obviously, those plans included Griffin, but I still can't let this happen.

Nonna waves her hand in the air, dismissing my protests. "I already talked to your mama. They're coming here for the party and staying the weekend, so you'll be here for New Year's Eve."

This is not happening.

Papa walks into the kitchen, and I run to him. "Papa, Nonna has lost her mind. She's going to make me go on dates. With guys I don't know."

Papa looks at Nonna with a twinkle in his eye. "Well, Nonna thinks of herself as a matchmaker. And I don't go against her when she's got her mind set on something."

"Don't I know it," Uncle Michael chimes in. "Sophie, run while you can. She's been trying to fix me up for years." He's the youngest of the eight kids and the only one who isn't married.

"Michael, the last three men I tried to set you up with would have been perfect if you just would have given them the chance," Nonna says. And then she spins around to me. "Sophie, this will be fun. Trust me."

"This can't be happening," I mumble. I wish I could click my heels and be at Margot's house.

"Can't never could," Aunt Maggie Mae says, then asks, "So how does this work?" She's licking her lips.

This is guaranteed to end horribly if she's involved.

Nonna chews on her lower lip. She's obviously making up this nonsense as she goes. "No dates on Christmas Eve and Christmas Day . . . so that leaves ten free days for ten dates. The boys have to be her age. Oh! And you have to post the activity the morning of the date so she knows what to expect."

"She doesn't get to know their names?" Olivia asks.

"No. Then it wouldn't be a blind date," Nonna answers.

"So we can pick *anyone*?" Jo Lynn asks.

Charlie's head pops up, his eyes finding mine. He's shaking his head fast and mouthing *Evil Joes*, over and over.

"Do I even have a say in this?" I interrupt.

The room gets quiet and everyone stares at me. Nonna's

face softens. "Step outside with me for a moment, Sophie."

I weave my way around bodies and toys and pray my face isn't as red as it feels. Aunt Lisa squeezes my hand when I pass her.

Once we're on the back porch, Nonna pulls me in for a hug.

"We don't get to see you that often, and I hate you're so sad and broken. I just thought this could be fun . . . like an adventure. It will give you something to look forward to each day. And even if the dates are a disaster, it will give us something to laugh about when they're over."

I pull away and look at her. "I feel pathetic. And I'm not ready to date anyone right now."

Nonna chuckles. "I'm not trying to find your next boyfriend. This is just for fun. Trust me."

Fun.

The thing Griffin said he wished he was having. The thing that was missing between us, apparently. The thing the Sophie Olivia *used* to know was full of. Am I not fun anymore?

"If I do this, I have a stipulation of my own," I say.

"What is it?"

"I get one free pass. If for whatever reason, I don't want to go on one of the dates, I don't have to. No questions asked."

Nonna frowns, considering this. "Done. So what do you say?"

I finally nod, and Nonna beams.

"Perfect! Let the games begin!"

She pulls me back into the kitchen, and all conversation stops.

"She's agreed!" Nonna says. My family literally cheers. "Now, let's see if we can fill the board. I'll start." Nonna walks to the white paper and writes her name under December 31st.

"Uh . . . Nonna? Do you even know a boy my age that isn't related to me?" I ask. I know she can hear the nervousness in my voice.

She bobs her head around. "Sure I do. I don't know who I'm going to pick yet, but I'll find someone!"

Great. I get to spend New Year's Eve with . . . someone.

This is definitely going to be a disaster.

Papa shuffles over to the paper and stares at the dates. "How about I pick the thirtieth, since that's the night of your grandmother's birthday party? I'll pick somebody nice." He scribbles his name.

Ten dates and two of them set up by my grandparents. Awesome.

After Papa moves away, the floodgates open. Everyone stampedes to sign up. I stand in the back of the room, watching in horror. The only other person in the room who isn't trying to claim a day is Wes.

He slides down the table closer to me. I can tell he's as embarrassed for me as I feel for myself.

"This can't be happening," I say.

He turns to look at me. "I haven't seen you in a while. How you been?"

I nod toward the board. "That pretty much says it all."

He laughs. "Yeah, I guess it does."

"How are you? Are you still with . . ." Oh God, I heard he was dating someone, but I forgot her name.

"Laurel?"

"Yeah, Laurel."

He nods, then shrugs. I'm not sure what kind of answer that is.

"She was a grade ahead of us, right?" I ask.

"Yeah, she's at LSU now."

I run my hand through my hair, antsy to see the board once everyone is done. "So y'all are doing the whole long-distance thing?"

He nods but doesn't elaborate. We're both too busy staring at the board. Actually, we're staring at Mom's oldest brother, Sal, and the pushing war he seems to be having with Uncle Michael over the final date slot.

Nonna stands beside them with what looks like pure joy on her face.

Uncle Michael wedges his body in front of Uncle Sal's and sticks his butt out, effectively pushing him away, then scribbles his name on the blank space.

Uncle Michael turns away, his expression victorious. Uncle

Sal steps up and scratches Michael's name out, then writes his next to it. Uncle Michael is too busy smiling to notice.

What a disaster.

Olivia stops next to me. "Charlie and I covered two of the dates. There are only a few you'll need to be worried about."

I let out a deep breath. "Thanks."

Unable to stand it any longer, I walk toward the chart.

12/20	Olivia
12/21	Patrice
12/22	Charlie
12/23	Sara
12/24	FREE
12/25	FREE
12/26	MJ/JL
12/27	Camille
12/28	Maggie Mae
12/29	SAL ~~Michael~~
12/30	Papa
12/31	Nonna

Charlie stops and whispers, "At least the Evil Joes have to share a day."

"Yeah, but Aunt Maggie Mae has one, so that's not much better," I whisper back. Olivia and Charlie will be fine, and

Papa and Nonna will probably pick someone from their shop. I'm mostly worried about Aunt Patrice.

She's weird.

"Okay, now that the excitement is over, let's eat!" Nonna calls out.

And there goes my appetite.

Sunday, December 20th

Blind Date #1: Olivia's Pick

Olivia ended up in the bed in the guest room with me sometime around midnight. I opted out of going to Wes's, mainly because I needed yesterday to be over. I thought Charlie and Olivia would give me a hard time when I told them I was going to bed instead of going next door, but they didn't seem surprised. I had tried not to feel annoyed.

"Thank God the shop is closed today. I never thought I'd be sick of Christmas, but I'm officially there," Olivia says as she stretches around in the bed. "Do you want me to tell you who you're going out with tonight? I won't tell Nonna we cheated."

I throw a pillow at her. "Is it anyone I know?"

Olivia stares at the ceiling. "I don't think so."

"Well, then it wouldn't matter. I'll just wait." I pause before adding, "You'll be there, too, right?" Olivia and I are in such a weird place right now and I have no idea what to expect.

Olivia sits up and throws the pillow back. "I'll be with you every step, no matter who you have to go out with," she says. I can't help the warm feeling that rushes through me.

I grab my phone and the charger, since my battery is probably dead, and head to the bathroom. While I'm waiting for my phone to charge enough to turn back on, I brush my teeth and pace. I know I'll have missed texts from Margot, along with pictures of God-knows-what part of her swollen anatomy. I'm sure Addie's called and texted, too.

But what about Griffin?

When my phone lights up and the messages start pouring in, my stomach begins whirling.

Talking to him should be the last thing I do.

Too bad my heart isn't listening.

I open my messages. The majority of the texts are from Addie and Griffin, although Margot isn't far behind. Addie's texts start out with: Where are you? and Call me! then graduate to: WHERE ARE YOU?!? and CALL ME!!!!

I tackle Margot's messages first. There are three pictures: I can't even tell what the first one is; the second might be an ankle; and the third looks like her . . . hand?

MARGOT: DO YOU SEE HOW SWOLLEN MY HANDS ARE NOW??? I'm going to need bedazzled gloves to match the shoes.

MARGOT: Okay not gloves since I can't separate my fingers. I guess mittens. Will you bedazzle me some mittens?

Okay, so that was her hand.

MARGOT: Are you getting these? I look like a beast

MARGOT: Oh Soph, Mom just told me about Griffin. That asshole. Are you okay?

MARGOT: Seriously where are you??? I know you ALWAYS have your phone!!

MARGOT: Soooooppppphhhhiiiiiieeee????

Good grief, Margot. Dramatic much?

ME: Yes your hands are hideous. And no I will not bedazzle you any mittens.

It only takes a few seconds for her to respond.

MARGOT: Oh Soph are you ok? Tell me what happened

ME: Short version—overheard Griffin telling his friend he wanted to break up with me then he chased me down the driveway and there was drama in the street when I tried to leave then Addie screamed at him after I left

MARGOT: Oh. My. God.

ME: Yeah, we like to keep it classy.

MARGOT: Why didn't you tell me yesterday?

ME: You've got enough to worry about. Have your toes fused together into one big nasty foot yet??

MARGOT: Ha, ha. You're not going to brush this off that easily. If I can share hideous body parts, then you can cough up details about hideous boyfriends.

ME: Well, that's not even the worst thing that's happened to me. Nonna made a chart . . .

I tell Margot about the dates and the rules and the complete ridiculousness of the entire thing. Not surprisingly, she thinks it's the best idea ever.

MARGOT: Okay I want details. And pictures. And live texting from the actual date. This is going to be better than the Dateline: Real Life Mysteries marathon.

ME: Whatever. I'll text you later. My stomach is growling and I'm sure Nonna has fresh cinnamon rolls, and coffee and bacon and all that other stuff you can't eat right now.

MARGOT: YOU SUCK!!!

I close out the conversation with Margot and take a deep breath before I open the messages from Griffin.

GRIFFIN: I'm sorry

GRIFFIN: I didn't want things to end like this

GRIFFIN: I want to talk about this

GRIFFIN: I didn't do anything wrong. I was just talking to Parker

GRIFFIN: I'm sorry

I swipe it closed—a little irritated that every single one of his texts is about how *he* feels—and call Addie.

"Why did it take you this long to call me back?" she huffs.

"I'm sorry. I just couldn't deal. Please don't be mad." I sit on the edge of the bathtub. "I can't take it if you're mad at me."

Addie lets out a deep breath. "Of course I'm not mad at you. Just worried. I had to hunt down Olivia's number and text her to see if you were okay."

I trace a finger along the grout pattern on the tile wall. "What happened after I left?"

She lets out a sharp laugh. "Griffin and I screamed at each other in the street until Matt's neighbor threatened to call the cops. Then Griffin left. Danny and I didn't stay much longer after that."

I smile. "Thanks for taking up for me. It means more than you know."

"Girl, I would do it again in a second. You're better off without him."

A wave of sadness rolls through me. Even though I want to believe she's right, I'm not sure she is.

"Well, you won't believe what Nonna's done now." I tell Addie about the calendar and the dates. She's dying laughing on the other end.

"Soph, that is the craziest thing I've ever heard of. What if some total psycho shows up? No telling who your aunt Patrice is going to send over."

I slide off the edge of the tub onto the floor. "I know. This is going to be the worst week and a half of my life. And we had plans for New Year's Eve! You know I'd rather be there than here."

"I know. Let's wait and see how it works out. But Nonna's probably right. You'll have your hands too full to have any time left to worry about Griffin."

I hope so, because right now, I still feel pretty broken inside.

❄ ♥ ❄

By the time I finish talking to Addie, shower, and dress, Olivia has left the bedroom. I tiptoe down the hall, praying the house is empty.

Papa is at the table by himself, reading the paper and sipping coffee. "Good morning. Did you sleep well?"

"I did, Papa. Where is everyone?" The house is unusually quiet—not that I'm complaining.

"Your nonna has gone to church, and thankfully, no one else has showed yet. Olivia ran home for clothes. She told me to tell you she would be back soon."

I glance at the whiteboard on the wall below the chart Nonna made. Olivia's name is printed at the top, and then in her handwriting it says:

Festival of Lights—Natchitoches

Be ready at 2pm

Dress warm 'cause, baby, it's cold outside!

I grin at the last line. The temperature has dropped over the weekend, and thankfully, it's actually starting to feel like Christmas.

I also notice that Uncle Sal's name is scratched out on the chart, and Uncle Michael's name is written in all caps beside it.

Papa notices me staring at the calendar. "Have you been to the festival before?" When I shake my head, his smile lights up his face. "You'll love it. And Olivia will pick out a nice boy. You should have a nice day," he says.

I fix myself a cup of coffee and refill his. "Don't you think this whole blind date thing is weird? I mean, who does this?" I sit on the stool next to him.

He laughs. "This is exactly what I would expect from your grandmother. She is such a romantic. And she just wants everyone around her to be happy. Her heart was as broken as yours when she found you on the front steps."

I swallow the lump in my throat and stare out the kitchen window.

"Have I ever told you how your grandmother and I met?" Papa asks.

He has. In fact, I've heard this story so many times I might tell it better than he does.

I smile and turn toward him. "No, sir." He knows I know this, but he loves telling this story as much as I love hearing it.

He leans back and his eyes glaze over, like he's gone back in time. "It was Valentine's Day. I was supposed to take this girl to dinner and then out to the movies. *Ocean's 11* was playing . . . and I'm talking about the original one—not that one with the Clooney fellow. The girl . . . oh, what was her name . . ."

Louise.

He snaps his fingers a few times. "Louise!" He seems pleased to have remembered this detail. "Well, Louise came down with the flu just that morning. I wasn't worried about missing the dinner—in fact, I was glad to save the money. But I had been waiting for that movie for weeks. So I decided to go by myself."

I love this part.

"So I get my popcorn and find a quiet spot in the back. And then I hear it. A soft sniffling sound. It was dark in the theater, but I grew up with three sisters, so I knew that sound—it was a girl, and she was crying. She was close by, only a few seats away."

Nonna.

Papa sits up straighter in his chair. "Well, I felt so bad for her. Why would a girl be crying in the movies on Valentine's Day?"

He pauses, waiting for me to guess the answer.

I shrug, like I don't know.

"So, I asked her. She had been stood up. I mean, who would do such a thing? And on Valentine's Day! I offered to share my popcorn and we talked the entire movie, not once looking at the screen. We've been together ever since." Papa pushes my hair out of my face. "If your nonna hadn't been in the theater with her heart broken, we might never have met. Just have fun with this and things may surprise you."

I don't expect to meet the love of my life but maybe, just maybe, this will help heal the pieces Griffin broke.

"I'll try, Papa."

Olivia is touching up her lipstick in the mirror in the foyer while I pace. The guys should be in here in less than ten minutes and I'm super nervous.

Papa is in his chair in the front room watching the Saints game while Nonna rearranges a perfectly arranged vase of flowers that sits on the table by the front door. I know she's just looking for an excuse to get to the door before anyone else has the chance.

The kitchen door opens. I jump at the sound. We hear a "Hello? Where is everyone?" then Aunt Lisa and Uncle Bruce stroll down the front hall. "There y'all are!" Aunt Lisa says. "We thought we'd come check on things."

"Mom's been trying to get me to tell her who I picked for you all day, but my lips are sealed." Olivia smacks her freshly painted lips in the mirror.

"Okay, yes, we're curious. And I told Eileen I'd be here, then call her with details. And Bill made Bruce promise he'd make sure Soph's date was okay."

I roll my eyes. I'm not surprised my parents sent spies to check things out.

And then we hear the door again. Charlie and Sara skid into the front hall, out of breath. "I told you we wouldn't miss it," Sara says, then punches Charlie in the arm. She turns to us. "He made us run here."

"Oh, I'm glad I put that roast on earlier! After the girls are off, we'll have dinner," Nonna says.

"We really don't need an audience for this," I say, then look at Olivia, my eyes pleading with her.

"Yeah, y'all are going to scare him off if everyone is hovering by the door."

The doorbell rings, and this time we all jump. There's no way anyone is leaving the front hall now that the guys are on the other side of the door.

Just before Nonna opens the door, Uncle Michael stumbles down the stairs. "Wait! Let me get down there before you open the door."

And of course, Nonna waits.

Thankfully, Olivia grabs my hand the second the door opens and we barrel through. The guys waiting outside jump back.

"Be back later," Olivia shouts at the family. She pulls me

to the car waiting at the curb. Luckily the guys catch on and are right behind us.

I've met Olivia's boyfriend, Drew, a few times, but it's not until I'm in the front passenger seat that I get a good look at my date. He is *super* cute. He's wearing a football T-shirt from his high school and a worn pair of jeans. He looks good in a relaxed sort of way.

"Hey, I'm Seth Whitman."

I smile. "Hey, I'm Sophie Patrick."

Olivia and Drew climb in the backseat, and Seth cranks the car but doesn't put it in drive. He looks back toward the house, where everyone is standing on the front porch. Waving.

He waves back while I lean my head against the seat and groan.

Seth turns in his seat wearing a firm expression. "I'm about to ask you to do something and I need you to take this very seriously."

I can feel my eyes widen. *What on earth*?

"What is it?" I ask.

And then his top lip twitches. "You're the DJ." He hands me a long aux cord that's plugged into the car stereo. "We've got almost an hour drive and the only good road trip is one with good music. Are you up for the challenge?"

"Yes!" I plug the cord into my phone and start scrolling through my playlist. Suddenly, I feel pressure. Even though he was teasing me, this first song needs to be a kickass one.

My finger hovers over "Perm" by Bruno Mars. I take a big breath and tap the screen. It only takes a few seconds before everyone in the car recognizes the song.

Seth looks away from the road and gives me a perfect smile. "That's a good one."

I smile back. "It is."

Being DJ is more fun than I thought it would be, and I love seeing their expressions when I jump around from Beyoncé to Tom Petty to Nicki Minaj to Bon Jovi. Olivia and I sing at the top of our lungs. Judging by the boys' muffled laughs, we must sound like drowning cats, but I don't care.

I can't help that Griffin pops into my head more times than I would like, but mostly I'm thinking this would have never happened in his truck. He only likes country music, and no one is allowed to mess with the dial.

By the time we get to Natchitoches, I'm actually looking forward to the rest of the date.

The festival takes place downtown, along the Cane River. Every building, light post, tree, and bush is covered in lights, and string after string hangs above the crowd, zigzagging down the street. There are also huge lighted pieces, like nutcracker soldiers and a Santa being pulled in a sleigh by a team of crawfish, lining the bank across the river.

"There are over three hundred thousand lights at the festival," Seth murmurs in my ear. I believe it.

The streets are packed as we weave through the crowds,

stopping at booths for candied pecans and hot meat pies. We pass under a banner showcasing the reigning Miss Merry Christmas, splendid in her bright red dress and crown. Christmas decorations cover every possible inch, and they are gaudy as hell but perfect at the same time.

My phone buzzes in my back pocket for the tenth time, so I take a quick peek at the screen while the guys play a basketball throw game.

I should have known it was Margot.

MARGOT: I'm dying to know how it's going. I'm bored out of my mind. The moms are cleaning out every drawer in my house and I'm terrified my underwear is going to wind up in the silverware drawer.

ME: Maybe the moms think the thongs and the tongs belong together.

MARGOT: Ha. Ha. Seriously, how's the date going???

I take a quick pic of Seth and send it to Margot. It's a profile shot as he's poised to shoot the basketball.

ME: It's going good! He's cute. And fun.

MARGOT: He's hot! Have fun!

ME: Thanks!

When the boys are done with the game, Seth pulls me

through the mass of human traffic. "We've got to do the Avalanche Slide!"

I look to where he's pointing and do a double take. Off to the side is a huge structure covered in man-made snow. The temperature is chilly but nowhere near freezing, so I have no idea how the whole thing hasn't turned into a pool of water. On top of the structure is a cartoon cutout of Frosty the Snowman.

"Oh, I don't know," I mumble, and Olivia gives me a horrified look. "What?" I ask her.

She looks up at the slide and back to me. "Are you seriously not going to try it?"

It's Olivia's face that gets me. It's almost like she wants to throw in *The Sophie I used to know wouldn't think twice . . .*

So why am I hesitant?

I grab Seth's hand. "Let's do this."

We race up the steps with Olivia and Drew close behind us. At the top, the guy working the event gives us each a round plastic platter and simple instructions: Sit on the disc and let it fly.

I touch the snow and it feels slushy, like it's only a few degrees from melting completely. I've never been to the mountains, and the only snow I've ever seen before is the small dusting we get every other year or so that somehow manages to shut the South down.

Seth lines his platter up with mine and holds them in place.

"Are you ready?" he asks. He's grinning from ear to ear. It feels good, being around someone who's this excited to be with me. I don't think I realized how much I missed that feeling until now.

"Yes! Let's do this!"

We both scream the entire way down. It's not a long ride—just enough to get my heart pumping. We slide into the rubber stoppers and fall over laughing.

Olivia and Drew crash into us, giggling like crazy. An attendant takes our platters, but no one seems concerned about getting up out of the fake snow.

Olivia crawls over and we lie side by side. "So what do you think?" she whispers, nodding toward Seth and Drew, who are busy throwing watery snowballs at each other.

I smile. "He's really nice."

"You've had that smile plastered on your face for the last three hours," she says, nudging me.

I grin even bigger. "Okay, okay, I'll admit this is the most fun I've had in a while."

"You know, we'll never hear the end of it when Nonna hears you had a good date."

I scoot in closer. "Then let's not tell her. After what she did, we should make her sweat a little."

We both laugh. Out of nowhere, a huge clump of snow hits me square in the face.

Once I brush the mess from my eyes, I see Seth backing away from me, guilt all over his face.

It feels like time is frozen. I let him squirm until I can't hold the laugh in any longer. "Oh, you're going to get it now!" I scoop up a handful of snow and start pelting him. Before long, we're in a full-fledged snowball war—boys against girls.

It only ends once we've been shooed off by the attendant working the event. At this point, we're all wet, a little cold, and tired from all the laughing.

Drew pulls Olivia inside a photo booth while Seth buys us two hot cocoas from a pushcart.

"Let's sit here," Seth says.

We plop down on a bench near the edge of the festival.

"I can't believe I've never come to this before," I say. I was worried we'd be fumbling around for conversation, but I'm surprised how easy the entire afternoon has been.

"We come every year. The whole thing's sort of cheesy, but it's fun getting out of town and doing something different." He waits a second before continuing. "Olivia told me about your ex-boyfriend and your grandmother's solution."

I feel my cheeks turn red. I hope he thinks it's from the cold. "Yeah, leave it to my grandmother to make things interesting."

Seth chuckles. "Well, it sounded crazy at first, but I'm glad Olivia picked me for your first date." He sits up a little taller. "I'm hoping to make everyone else look bad."

I smile. "Yeah, it will be hard to compete with a snowball fight in Louisiana."

"Let me give you my number," he says. "Seriously, when

this thing is over, maybe we can go out again. I've had a lot of fun today."

When I take out my phone to add Seth's number, I see a string of notifications from Griffin. Seth sees it, too.

"Is that your ex?" he asks.

I nod. "Yeah. We really haven't talked since we, um, broke up."

Seth takes my phone but instead of adding his contact, he opens the camera, and flips it so we're in the frame.

"Okay, smile," he says.

I smile but Seth crosses his eyes, and puckers his lips. He snaps a picture as soon as I start laughing, then adds his number to my phone, assigning the image to his contact. He sends a text from my phone to his.

"I'll get us some more hot chocolate," he says. I look at the picture, which is cuter than I thought. I feel my cheeks heat up. I really *have* had fun tonight.

But then Griffin's face steamrolls over those warm and fuzzy thoughts. When I see another notification from him, it's like a bucket of cold water was just poured over me. I can't help but open the messages.

GRIFFIN: I guess you're just going to keep ignoring me

GRIFFIN: I want to talk to you. I want to see you

GRIFFIN: Can I see you tomorrow? I'll meet you anywhere

GRIFFIN: Sophie please

My heart is thumping by the time I finish reading his messages. I'm so confused. Does he miss me? Is he regretting what he said? Or does he just feel guilty about how it all went down?

I send back a quick message:

ME: Not ready to talk to you yet

Then I power the phone off before I can see his reply. There's no reason I should feel guilty—we broke up—but it's there, underneath everything else. I've had a great day and I hate that Griffin is making me feel bad about it.

I watch Seth as he balances two hot chocolates, a funnel cake, and a bag of cotton candy. He gets tangled up in a group of toddlers, then nearly drops everything when some kid who's texting and walking bumps into him. A few steps later, he and an older woman start some awkward dance when he tries to step around her but she meets his every move. He finally gets in the clear and stops, looking at me in amazement.

"Did you see that?" he yells across the short distance.

I'm laughing when he closes the gap with a little dance in his step.

Griffin may make me feel guilty, but Seth makes me smile.

I take one of the drinks and pinch off a piece of the funnel cake. Olivia and Drew emerge from the photo booth, laughing at the strip of pictures, and that's all it takes for Seth to drag me in for pictures of our own.

When we finally pull up in front of Nonna's, Seth has just told us about when Drew was in kindergarten and gave his teacher a tampon as a gift because he thought there was candy inside. Olivia and I can't stop cracking up.

"This story is going to haunt me for the rest of my life," Drew says, then pulls Olivia in for a good-bye kiss. I look at Seth so I'm not staring at them, and he shrugs, clearly feeling as awkward as I do.

Olivia gets out of the backseat and I give Seth a quick wave before opening the door. "I had a great time," I say.

He smiles and says, "We'll have to do it again."

Nonna is waiting up for us when we get back, ready to gloat.

"So . . . how was it? You can't hide that smile from me forever, Sophie," Nonna says.

I lean against the kitchen sink, where she's washing the last of the supper dishes. "You got me. We had a good time," I reply. "But it doesn't make this any less weird! And there's still nine more dates to go, so, you know, there's still the potential that this is going to be a disaster."

Nonna hands me a tied-up garbage bag. "I think you're going to surprise yourself. Add this to the can at the curb for me, please."

I run down the front porch steps and drop the bag in the trash. On my way back to the house I see Wes pull into his driveway next door. I wave and wait for him to get out.

"Hey," he says. "How was your first date?"

"Not bad, actually."

We walk toward each other, meeting right at the property line. "Where'd y'all go?" he asks.

"That festival in Natchitoches. Ate funnel cake, had a snowball fight—you know, typical Sunday night," I say, laughing.

He nods, then cocks his head to the side. "I think Nonna was right."

My face scrunches up. "Right about what?"

"This dating thing. You look good."

I can feel my cheeks warm. "Well, I must have really looked like crap earlier."

Wes laughs. "I didn't say that. I'm just glad you're smiling."

He heads toward his house and I walk back into Nonna's, each of us waving to the other when we go through our front doors. Just as I enter the kitchen, I hear Olivia say, "Uh-oh." She's staring at the date board.

Aunt Patrice has filled in the details for my next date:

The Living Nativity—Eagles Nest Middle School
Be ready at 4:00 p.m.
Your outfit is in the laundry room.

I'm terrified.

Beyond terrified. Living Nativity? At a middle school?

"The date is supposed to be with someone my age, Nonna! If she set me up with a middle schooler, that's an automatic forfeit for her."

Nonna is wiping down the counter on the other side of the kitchen. "Oh, I'm sure he's old enough, Soph. Patrice understands the rules."

Olivia disappeared inside the laundry room as soon as she finished reading Aunt Patrice's note, and her squeals of laughter make me want to run and hide. Finally, she comes back to the kitchen carrying what looks like a wadded-up piece of fabric.

"Are you ready for this?" she asks.

"No."

She holds the hanger up high, letting the fabric unfurl.

"What in the world is that?" Nonna asks as she moves closer to it.

"It's a robe. I think Sophie is going to be a part of the Living Nativity," she says, pointing to the note pinned to the top that says: *Mary, mother of Jesus*. "And it looks like she's got a starring role!"

Monday, December 21st

Blind Date #2: Aunt Patrice's Pick

The sun is barely up when Olivia and I get to the shop. With only four more shopping days until Christmas, today is going to be a nightmare.

Since Olivia has worked here for a while, she handles helping customers looking for a last-minute gift while I'm stuck at the register. Nonna has put together quite a few gift baskets that include small potted flowers, plants or herbs, books on gardening, small tools like shears and spades, and other cute gardening things. She can't make them fast enough.

During my midmorning break, I hide in the kitchen just to get away from all of the people. I kick back on the small couch that is older than me and text Margot.

ME: I've only got 10 mins before Nonna chains me back to the register at the shop so if you're going to send me any gross pictures, do it now.

Margot sends me a close-up of her face. I haven't seen her in a while and I'm surprised by how different she looks.

MARGOT: My face is swollen. Especially my nose. My nose is huge. Like, it's the biggest nose I've ever seen

ME: You're better than birth control. If there was even a chance I was going to be having sex anytime soon you've completely scared me off.

MARGOT: Good! Mom keeps saying I'll forget how bad this part is but I'm telling you—I WILL NEVER FORGET THIS NOSE

ME: So what does your doctor say? Is this normal?

I've been trying to keep things light with Margot ever since she got put on bed rest, but I can't stop the lick of fear that blindsides me every time she sends me a picture.

MARGOT: It's not abnormal. And they're watching me closely. I have another appointment this afternoon. Don't worry about me. Worry about who Aunt Patrice is going to set you up with.

ME: Did you hear what I have to wear?????

MARGOT: Haha. Yes. Mom talked to Nonna this morning. I definitely need a picture of that. And the date. Instead of Mary they may have to call you Mrs. Robinson.

ME: Who's Mrs. Robinson?

MARGOT: Ugh. Now I feel old. Google it.

ME: Ok whatever gotta get back to work. Text me after the doctor's appt.

Charlie and Wes come into the kitchen carrying snacks and drinks to refill the old refrigerator. Nonna has them doing odd jobs—or as she likes to put it, "doing all the crap no one else wants to do." Next on their agenda is changing lightbulbs and air filters, so I really can't complain about being stuck behind the register.

"Are you researching hairstyles of the early Bethlehem period?" Charlie asks. I throw a magazine at him.

"You're hilarious," I say, and snag a Coke Zero from the box.

Wes tosses me a package of Nutter Butters, which happen to be my favorite cookie. "You know we're going to have to be there when you get picked up for your hot date. There's no way we're missing this."

"If y'all really loved me, you'd feel sorry for me and offer to work my shift for the rest of the day." I give what I hope are really pathetic puppy-dog eyes.

Charlie and Wes look at each other a few seconds like they're considering it. Then they both say, "Nah!"

Charlie drops down beside me. "Hey, while you're on break . . ." He whips his phone out of his back pocket, pulls up something on the screen, then shoves it at me. "I need you to take this quiz."

Wes groans. "Seriously? We're doing this again?"

I stare at the screen, which reads, "Which Character from *The Office* Are You?" then look to Wes for clarification. He drags a chair away from the small table and sets it next to the couch, then takes a seat. "You know Charlie is obsessed with *The Office*. He's watched the whole series like twice by now."

"Three times, actually," Olivia says when she comes into the room. "Is he making her take the quiz?"

Wes nods, and I look back at Charlie's phone. I sort of remember Charlie liking this show, but I definitely wasn't aware it had moved to this level.

"So why am I taking this quiz?" I ask.

Wes opens his mouth to speak, but Charlie throws a hand up and shushes him. "Let her take it first."

So I get busy. The multiple-choice questions are kind of weird. What kind of paper do I like? What's my favorite condiment? And on and on.

"Okay, I'm done. It's calculating my results."

"You probably got Erin. Or Kelly," Wes says. "Or maybe even Pam."

"Would that be good?" I ask.

Wes smiles and nods. "Yeah, they're cool."

"Who'd you get?" I ask Charlie.

Wes's mouth twists, and he looks at Olivia. They both bust out laughing.

"It's not funny," Charlie says.

I don't get it. And I can't believe how much I *hate* that I don't get it. But then I remember this is what it was like the last several times we were together—always some inside joke from school or a club that I wasn't in on.

Olivia finally explains. "Charlie has taken every quiz ever made with the sole hope of getting Jim because Jim is the coolest guy on the show. Everyone loves Jim."

She's giggling so hard she can't speak, so Wes finishes for her. "But he gets Dwight. Every time."

"I've even answered every question purposefully wrong and I still get him!" Charlie yells. He points to Wes. "He's rigged it somehow!"

I look at Wes. "And let me guess. You get Jim?"

He nods. "Yep."

I look down at the phone, where the results have loaded, and say, "I got Carol Stills, the real estate agent."

Now all three of them are staring at me.

"What? Is that bad?" I ask.

Olivia finally looks away from me to Charlie. "Who's Carol?"

Charlie looks surprised. "She was the woman who Michael dated a little while. She wasn't on many episodes. Maybe five?"

My forehead scrunches. "How many episodes are there?"

"Two hundred and one," they all answer at the same time.

It's like the world is trying to make sure I remember I'm the outsider here. I roll my eyes and say, "I gotta get back to the register. See y'all out there." I don't even wait for their reply before I leave the room.

"I'm using the 'get out of date free' card," I say as I take one final turn in the mirror. As expected, Olivia and Charlie are on the floor laughing. Literally rolling around on the floor. Wes at least has the decency to stay upright while he dissolves into hysterics. After the weirdness at the shop, I want to be annoyed at them, but it's hard when I'm distracted by my growing horror at this upcoming date.

Since I have three different layers on (regular clothes, some tunic-looking thing, and then the robe), I'm burning up. And itchy. And the musty smell tells me this thing hasn't seen the light of day since last Christmas.

"But what about the Evil Joes' date?" Olivia says. My hands are still on the belt I'd started unwrapping. "Or Aunt Maggie Mae? I would totally save the pass for one of those."

"No telling what the Evil Joes have in store for you," Charlie says, then shudders. "Save the pass."

"You think it's going to be worse than that?" Wes asks Olivia and Charlie, pointing at me.

Olivia cocks her head to the side. "I think tonight will be weird but harmless. I would be more worried about the Evil Joes, too."

Charlie nods in agreement. "Evil Joes are evil."

I throw my hands up in the air. "Have you taken a good look at what I'm wearing? The possibilities of how tonight can go horribly wrong are endless!"

"How about we come rescue you? Nonna said you had to go out on the dates—she didn't say you had to stay the whole time," Olivia adds.

I stare at them with what I hope is a menacing expression. "Do you all swear to come get me?"

Olivia says, "Yes."

Charlie looks up toward the ceiling, his finger tapping his chin. "I don't know. That would be really going against the spirit of the game, Sophie. Especially after Aunt Patrice has gone to such lengths to take your personal interests and likes into account when she planned this very thoughtful date."

I throw my shoe at him. Turning to Wes, I say, "You'll come get me, right?"

He shrugs and says in a quiet voice, "I can't help you tonight. I have plans."

Of course he does. I shouldn't have forgotten he's got a girlfriend.

"Oh yeah. With Laurel?"

Charlie turns to Wes, one eyebrow cocked. "Dude, really?"

"Really," Wes says in a voice that discourages any more questions about it.

Nonna walks in carrying a stack of towels and mutters, "Oh my."

I hold my hands out. "This is all your doing, Nonna."

She drops the towels on the bed and then walks around me in a slow circle, clicking her tongue. She runs her hand down my arm. "There's something sewn into the seam," she says. Dropping to the floor, she lifts the hem and rummages around for a few seconds. "Aha!"

The next thing I know, I'm blinking.

Blinking.

As in there are tiny, blinking lights sewn under the seams of the robe.

"Oh. My. God," Olivia says, then bursts out laughing again.

Charlie and Wes stare in disbelief. "Why are there lights? I don't understand," Wes says.

Nonna stands up. "It's festive!"

"It's a fire hazard! Nonna, you've *got* to get me out of this one!" I say frantically.

She cocks one eyebrow. "Are you using your one free pass?"

I glance at the others. Wes is nodding, vigorously, while Olivia and Charlie are shaking their heads and mouthing *Evil Joes*.

"I guess not," I mumble, and drop down on the edge of the bed.

Nonna squeezes me quickly and says, "This date can't last long—that Nativity thing shuts down around nine."

"And her date's bedtime is probably close to that," Charlie says under his breath.

Nonna throws him a look over her shoulder, then turns back to me. "I'll have some fresh beignets ready and we'll all meet here after your date. It will give us something to giggle about."

Awesome. I'm going to be stuck in this getup for up to five hours just so we have something to giggle about over beignets later.

Nonna leaves the room. Olivia and Charlie just keep staring at the blinking lights like they're mesmerized by them.

"We'll come through the tour. Several times," Charlie says once he snaps out of it. "And make sure we get pictures. You do need a new profile pic now that you and the dumbass broke up. Do you think everyone will be lit up or just you?"

I throw a pillow at him. "No pictures!"

Wes picks up the last piece of the costume that I've been avoiding: the headpiece. He's trying really hard not to laugh as he plops it on my head. "Wait, I think this has lights, too." I hear him flip a button and I turn to the mirror. Sure enough, there's a ring of light around my head just like a halo.

Wes's face appears next to mine in the mirror. "This just keeps getting better and better."

I push him in the chest, knocking him off-balance, and he falls back, laughing.

"All of you suck," I say as I pick up my robes with as much dignity as I can muster and walk out of the room, trying not to trip.

I check the clock as I walk into the kitchen. I stuffed my phone and enough cash for a cab into the pocket of my pants so I can bail if I need to. And I'm pretty sure I'll need to.

Papa is in the side yard, supervising a couple of guys as they unload a cord of firewood near the back door, while Nonna is writing a check and talking to another guy who looks my age at the kitchen counter.

I back into the hall to hide. My blinking lights bounce off the white walls and make me feel dizzy.

"Thanks so much for your business, Mrs. Messina."

"You're welcome. Thanks for getting to us so quickly."

I peek around the corner. The guy is just about to turn away when Nonna puts her hand on his arm, stopping him.

"How old are you?" she asks.

Oh God. What is she doing?

"Um, I'm eighteen," he answers, confusion laced in his words.

"Are you single?"

I drop my head back against the wall and let out a groan.

"Um . . . No, ma'am. I, uh, I have a girlfriend."

Nonna lets out a *humph* and says, "Well, drat."

I wait until I hear him leave the kitchen before I move away from my hiding spot.

“Seriously, Nonna? Were you really going to set me up with someone you don’t know for New Year’s Eve?”

She shrugs. “I know him.” She picks up the business card he left on the counter and reads it quickly. “His name is Paul.”

“Paul, huh. Without looking back at the card, tell me his last name.”

I can tell she’s itching to take a glance. But she’s saved from answering when we hear the door open again.

“I forgot to give you your receipt,” Paul says, coming back into the kitchen. His eyes widen as he stares at me, trying to process the blinking robe and halo veil.

“Oh, thank you, *Paul*,” she says with a quick glance to me. “And it’s too bad you have a girlfriend. I was going to set you up with my granddaughter Sophia.” Nonna gestures at me with a huge smile on her face.

Paul is speechless. He nods and sputters and basically runs from the house like it’s on fire.

“I cannot believe you just did that,” I say.

Nonna laughs, then turns toward the front door when she hears it open. “You better prepare yourself, I think Patrice is here.”

“I’m just telling you now, if my date is in middle school, it’s a forfeit.”

A small crowd has gathered to witness my humiliation. Mom's spies, Aunt Lisa and Uncle Bruce, are sitting in the front room with Nonna and Papa, but they have their chairs turned toward the foyer. All they're missing is a tub of popcorn. Of course, Olivia, Charlie, and Wes wouldn't miss this. Uncle Michael is staying in one of the other guest rooms, so I'm not surprised he's here, but Jake and Graham stopped by and acted like they were looking for Graham's sunglasses, even though Papa pointed out his glasses were perched on the top of his head. Oh, and Uncle Sal and Aunt Camille were "just walking the dogs" and thought they'd pop in.

Yeah, right.

Aunt Patrice and Uncle Ronnie are standing in the foyer, flanking a very young, very short boy who I assume is my date. He's dressed in robes similar to mine, but no one has turned his lights on yet.

Or—oh God. Maybe it *is* just mine that blinks.

"Sophie, I would like to introduce you to Harold Riggs. He's a freshman at Eagles Nest High School."

A freshman.

You've got to be kidding me.

I turn to Nonna, throwing her a pleading look, but she moves to Harold and scoops him up in a hug.

"So nice to meet you, Harold!" she says, way too enthusiastically.

He nods and then looks at me. "Hi," he says. I don't think his voice has changed yet. "What grade are you in?"

"I'm a senior," I mumble. I can hear Olivia, Charlie, and Wes snickering behind me, so I throw a death glare over my shoulder at them. All three of them are red in the face and have tears in their eyes from holding back laughter. Jake and Graham are just as bad on the other side of the room.

Harold's eyes light up. "A senior! That's so totally cool!"

I want to dissolve into the floor right now.

Turning to Nonna, I say through clenched teeth, "You said the dates had to be my age. He is clearly not my age."

She waves a hand in front of me. "You're both in high school. Close enough!"

I hold up a finger to the group in the front hall and say, "Can you give me a minute?" I pull Olivia to the kitchen, Charlie and Wes following behind us.

I spin around once we're out of earshot.

"One hour. You will pick me up from this middle school in one hour." I point to all of them. "None of you will take pictures, or mention this in any way for the rest of our lives or I will murder you in your sleep."

Olivia and Charlie can't even answer me through their laughter. Wes gives me a salute and says, "Whatever you say, Disco Mary."

I push past them and head to the front door. As we walk

down the front path, Uncle Michael yells, "You kids have fun tonight!"

Aunt Patrice is driving because, of course, at fifteen, Harold Riggs doesn't have a license.

We're in the backseat, and Uncle Ronnie is up front with Aunt Patrice. I'm as close to the window as I can get, and Harold sits as close to me as his seat belt will allow. There are precious few inches separating us.

Aunt Patrice looks at me in the rearview mirror. "Sophie, you should probably turn your lights off until we get there. I'm not sure how long the batteries will last."

That's what I'm hoping for. I nod, but don't click them off. I keep staring at my watch. If my rescue team isn't there by five, I'm calling a cab. This middle school is out in the middle of nowhere. God, I hope Olivia can find it, or it's going to cost me a fortune to get back to Nonna's.

I glance down at my costume and then at my date. It will be worth every penny.

We pull up out front and there's a group of people all dressed like me, except I'm the only one blinking. There are several wooden structures lined up along the sidewalk in a row in front of the school, and a roped path I'm guessing the people who show up to see us will follow. The manger seems to be right in the middle, if the wooden crib is any clue.

"We're here!" Aunt Patrice calls from the front seat.

I scoot out of the car, Harold close on my trail. He makes several attempts to hold my hand as we walk toward the school, but luckily I dodge him each time.

"Hey! Check out my date! She's a senior. In high school!" Harold announces to the crowd. I want to dig a hole and die in it. Everyone else dressed in robes seems to be in middle school—Harold and I are clearly the oldest ones here.

I turn to Aunt Patrice. "I don't really understand this date. I mean, we're at a middle school."

Aunt Patrice smiles and pats my arm. "I know! This is going to be so fun. When the two kids that were supposed to play Joseph and Mary got sick with the flu, Harold stepped forward to be Joseph. His little brother goes here—that's him," she says, and points to a mini version of Harold dressed like a sheepherder. "We just needed a Mary! So when Mom came up with that crazy idea for you to start dating again, it seemed like the perfect fix for our Mary problem."

You have got to be kidding me.

"It'll be fun!" she says in a high-pitched voice.

She herds Harold and me toward the center of the manger, where a woman with a clipboard positions us.

A girl who looks about twelve moves close to me. She's dressed all in white with wings bigger than she is. She whispers,

"Have you ever been out with him before?" and nods toward Harold.

I shake my head. "No."

Her forehead scrunches up. "Well, watch out. They don't call him Hundred Hands Harold for nothing."

Before I can even process what she said, Aunt Patrice drops a real live baby in my arms. "This is why we needed you. The other Mary was in high school, too. This baby's mom didn't want anyone younger than that to hold him. See, it all worked out!"

Oh my God.

The baby—who can't be older than a few months—looks up at me. We stare at each other for a few seconds, and then he opens his mouth and lets out the most earsplitting scream I've ever heard.

And that's saying a lot, considering how many babies I've been around.

I try to hand him back to Aunt Patrice, but she moves away.

"We want this to be authentic, so it's okay if he cries a little bit."

Authentic? I'm wearing a robe that has blinking lights sewn into it. I bounce the baby around on my shoulder, I pat his back, I do everything I know to quiet him down. I'm sweating so bad at this point that my halo keeps slipping off my head.

After ten minutes, the baby finally quiets down. If I keep jiggling him just like I'm doing, maybe he'll stay quiet. It doesn't help that I have to swat at my date about every thirty seconds. Hundred Hands Harold is a very appropriate name.

I get into a rhythm: jiggle baby, elbow Harold, send a death glare to Aunt Patrice. As it gets closer to five, I think I might actually be able to hold out until Olivia gets here.

And then they bring in the animals.

When Olivia and Charlie finally come through the line, the goat next to me has eaten about three inches of my robe and shows no signs of stopping.

"You're late!" I say between clenched teeth.

Charlie holds up his phone, and before I can throw myself behind Harold, he snaps a picture.

"I will kill you, Charlie Messina. Dead. You are a dead man."

He taps out something on his phone, then holds his hands up in surrender. "I'm sorry but Margot texted me and offered twenty bucks for a picture. I couldn't pass it up."

Harold takes this moment to stake his claim. He puts his arm around me and says, "We need to ask you to keep moving down the line."

I shove my thumb toward him and look at Olivia. "This is

what I've had to put up with." I turn to Harold and ask, "Who's we? Do you have a mouse in your pocket?"

His arm slips down my back and I know his hand is going straight for my butt. Again.

I free one hand from the baby and grab him by the front of his robes, yanking him up until he's on his tiptoes. "If you try to touch my butt one more time, I will hold you down while I let this goat eat your pants, starting at the crotch."

Harold's eyes get big and his hands fall to his sides. "Understood."

And then we hear a god-awful sound coming from the goat just a second or two before the lights on my robe go out.

"I think . . . the goat just got electrocuted by the lights on your robe," Olivia says, stunned.

Charlie laughs so hard it seems like he may pee in his pants. "This is the most awesome thing ever."

I drop Harold and turn to look at the goat. It couldn't have been too serious because he's already back chomping away on the end of my robe.

Before Charlie can see it coming, I hand him the baby.

"Whoa! Whoa! What are you doing?" he shouts as I storm off.

"I'm getting out of these robes before the goat takes a chunk out of my leg. That baby's mom is the one in the blue shirt over there. Give him to her and then be ready to go."

People going through the line are whispering and pointing,

but I don't care. I can't take another minute of Harold. Or the goat.

I duck around the back of the manger, take off the costume, and hand it to some woman who's trying to keep the chickens from running off.

"What's this?" she asks, confused.

"Mary's costume. It's going to need some repairs before next year's event."

When I meet up with Charlie and Olivia close to the parking lot, I hear Harold scream, "You were the best date I ever had, Sophie. Call me if you want to go out again."

"Well, that's just adorable," Charlie says.

Olivia puts her arm around me. "You're on a streak. First, Seth wants another date, now Harold does, too!"

We're almost to the car when I hear feet pounding the concrete behind us. It's Aunt Patrice in hot pursuit.

"How are we going to have a Nativity scene without Mary?" she calls across the parking lot.

"Don't stop," I whisper to Olivia and Charlie. We pick up the pace until we're running. By the time we reach Charlie's truck, we've put some distance between us and Aunt Patrice.

"Get in," Charlie yells.

Within seconds, we're in the truck, pulling out of the parking lot.

"So how many times did that kid try to grab your butt?" Olivia asks once we're back on the main road.

"Too many times to count! His nickname is Hundred Hands Harold. Some little girl warned me about him when we first got here."

"Hundred Hands Harold!" Charlie howls. He glances at me from the rearview mirror. "I've laughed more today than I have in a long time. And you look a whole lot better than you did a few days ago."

My cheeks actually ache from smiling right now. I remember that's almost exactly what Wes said to me last night.

"I agree, you do look a lot better," Olivia says. "We've missed you."

It's the first time any of us have mentioned out loud how distant we've become.

"Me too. Thanks for coming to get me. I'm sure y'all would rather be doing anything other than rescuing me from this date."

Olivia throws me a confused look. "Please. I'm glad you're stuck with us for the next week."

"I'm just glad Ol' Griff's out of the picture," Charlie says. "This week wouldn't be nearly as fun if you were ditching us to go see him."

I lower my eyes. That had been exactly my mission before the breakup. Anytime Mom wanted to come to Shreveport for the day or the weekend, I usually opted to stay behind with Dad or at Addie's so I could be with Griffin.

"It has been a long time since we've hung out like this,"

I say. And, for the first time since I've been back at Nonna's, things finally feel normal with us. "If Wes was here, it would be just like old times."

Charlie snorts.

"What do you mean by that?" I ask.

He shakes his head. "Nothing. Just not a fan of Laurel's."

I'm dying to know more, but instead I lean my head against the window and enjoy the Harold-free ride.

✻ ♥ ✻

Nonna and I are cleaning up the huge mess in the kitchen from the post-date beignets when a knock on the back door startles us—mostly because no one ever knocks before coming in this house.

"It's open!" Nonna calls out.

Wes sticks his head in, his eyes scanning the room. "Don't tell me I missed them."

I give him a small smile. "Sorry, Charlie and Olivia left about ten minutes ago."

He lets out a quick laugh. "Not them! The beignets. Please tell me there are a few left."

Nonna puts the plate with the few remaining treats on the table. "Help yourself, honey."

Wes sits at the table and I plop down across from him.

"Your date ended early," I say.

He shrugs. "So did yours, I hear."

I drop my head to the table and groan. "You have no idea how horrible it was. Between Hundred Hands and the hungry goat, I wasn't sure I was going to make it out alive."

"Charlie sent me a play-by-play." He pauses. "And a picture."

My head pops up. "No, he didn't."

A small, powdered sugar smile plays across his face. Wes turns his phone around and there I am, sweating and red faced, holding that crying baby. The lights are glowing around me, and my halo hangs off to one side of my head. Harold is cuddled up next to me, smiling as big as he can.

It's Wes's new home screen.

I groan again.

He puts his phone down and eats the last beignet in one bite.

"So you know why my date ended early, but why did yours? It's barely nine o'clock."

He shrugs again. "We had this dinner thing to go to and now it's over."

I wait for more, but he's busy brushing powdered sugar off his fingers.

"Charlie has tomorrow's date. Any idea who he's set me up with?" I ask.

Wes sweeps up loose powdered sugar that found its way off his plate and shakes his head. "I asked but he wouldn't tell me."

I prop my elbows on the table and drop my head in my hands.

"He'll pick one of our friends. You'll have fun," he says.

We watch each other a few seconds, until I finally say what's been on my mind. "I realized tonight I've really missed hanging out here . . . with you and Charlie and Olivia."

He gives me a look I haven't seen before, part smile, part smirk. "We've missed you, too."

And for the first time since all of this started, I'm really glad I'm here.

Tuesday, December 22nd

Blind Date #3: Charlie's Pick

I can't get to the board in the kitchen fast enough. No matter how hard I begged Charlie yesterday, he wouldn't give me the slightest hint as to who I was going out with or where we were going.

Ugly sweater party
6:30 p.m.
(And yes—you have to wear an ugly sweater)

"You're going to have so much fun at that party," Nonna says. She's pulling a tray of cinnamon rolls out of the oven. The room smells delicious. And I laugh when I read the words on her apron: *I put the Pro in Prosecco!*

"You know where we're going?" I ask, then pull out a knife so I can help her put on the icing.

"Yes, it's at the Browns' just around the corner. Their first party was about five years ago and now it's a tradition in this neighborhood. Amy gives prizes for the ugliest sweater and there are lots of other games. Her sons, Alex and Brandon, go to the same high school as your cousins, so there'll be plenty of kids there your age."

Nonna moves the iced rolls to a platter, and just like clockwork, family starts pouring in from the back door.

"I know some of the family usually drops in for breakfast, but are there always this many?" I whisper to Nonna.

She cocks her head. "It's the holidays. Plus everyone is just so excited you're here."

My forehead scrunches up. "They aren't here to see me."

Nonna gives me a soft smile. "Well, of course they are. This is a real treat to have you here, all to ourselves."

Aunt Lisa puts her arm around me and gives me a kiss on my forehead. "'Morning, Sophie. I hear last night's date was interesting."

I grimace. "I'm not sure *interesting* is the right word for it."

Uncle Sal and his group take up almost the whole table. Not only is he the oldest sibling, he and Aunt Camille have the most kids, with five. They also have the most animals, since Aunt Camille has never met a stray she didn't adopt. Charlie pops in a few minutes later with Sara right on his heels. They pull up extra chairs and wedge themselves in the few open spaces at the table.

I throw a couple of cinnamon rolls on a plate and drag one of the stools closer to the table. "So where am I going to find an ugly sweater for the party tonight?" I ask Charlie.

"Make one. And seriously, the uglier the better. I've got a side bet with Olivia that my date's going to be better than hers."

Sara nudges him in the side. "I'll get in on that bet. I've got tomorrow and I *know* my date's going to make your date look like Aunt Patrice planned it."

I let out a groan. "I guess everyone knows about last night?"

"Yeah, we all got the picture, too. How old was he? Twelve?" Uncle Sal asks.

I shoot daggers at Charlie. "I guess you sent that picture to everyone?"

He holds his hands up in front of him. "I couldn't help it! Once I started I couldn't stop."

"Is there no privacy in this family?"

Everyone at the table answers, "No."

Charlie turns to his sister. "Why do you think your date is going to be better than mine? You're fifteen. What do you know about dating?"

"I'm good just as long as there are no farm animals," I say. "Or babies."

Sara gives us a smug smile. "You'll see. It's going to be awesome."

Aunt Patrice, Uncle Ronnie, and the boys burst through the back door, Patrice's eyes searching the room for me.

Once she finds me, she barrels through the crowd.

"The Nativity was ruined once you left. It all just . . . fell apart. Harold was so depressed you left that he didn't want to be Joseph anymore. The goats got sick and threw up on everything. Baby Jesus just cried and cried."

Olivia sneaks in during Aunt Patrice's outburst and drops down in the seat next to me, nudging me under the table.

"I'm really sorry, Aunt Patrice," I say with the most sincere voice I can muster.

Her frown persists. "I know you still haven't gotten over Dave, but that's still no reason to ruin everyone's fun."

"Griffin," Charlie says.

"Who's Griffin?" she asks.

"The guy Sophie can't get over," he answers.

I throw a piece of cinnamon roll at him.

Aunt Patrice looks confused. "Then who's Dave?"

Charlie shrugs. "I have no idea."

Aunt Patrice finally walks away, still pondering who Dave is. At least she's not chewing me out anymore.

Uncle Michael walks in and says, "The new sheet is up."

This dating thing has turned into something like the NBA finals. Apparently Nonna got wind yesterday that my uncles, a few of my aunts, and some of my older cousins are betting on what time I get home from my date. Their basic strategy is to weigh who picked the date, what the activity is, and how long they think I can put up with him. All bets have to be finalized by the time I get in my date's vehicle.

Nonna acts like she's annoyed, but I suspect she's in on it. How else would they know what time I walk through the door?

"So there's an actual sheet where you can place a bet now?" I ask Olivia.

"Yes. The group message was getting out of control."

"How many people are in the group? And why can't I be in it?"

Olivia's mouth forms a weird grimace. "Pretty much everyone. I wanted to add you, but Graham said the only way to keep the competition pure was to make sure you weren't influenced by the bets. Then Uncle Ronnie hijacked it with pics of his dog, so Charlie made another group text without him where we took a vote to see if we should kick him out. In the end, Uncle Michael decided to make a betting sheet."

Banks, Uncle Sal's son, leans forward and says, "It's like one of those betting squares you do for the Super Bowl."

I look at Olivia. "This has gotten out of control."

She nods toward Uncle Sal. "I mean, I didn't know if he even knew how to text, and then he was blowing my phone up."

Uncle Sal laughs. "I'm glad we've moved on to the sheets. I couldn't take one more picture of Ronnie's dog licking his butt."

My phone vibrates on the table and I turn it over. My heart skips when I see Griffin's name there. It's like he knew we were just talking about him.

Charlie turns up behind me and glances at the screen. "Oh no. No jackasses on my day." He tries to grab the phone, but I hold it just out of reach.

I scoot back in my chair and swipe open his message. It's a picture of me with Seth and Olivia and Drew from my first date. We're all huddled together in front of a giant cardboard snowman. The picture was taken right after our snowball fight.

GRIFFIN: Someone sent me this. This guy you're with posted it and said "Hoping all of her other dates suck"

Before I can even think of a response, Griffin sends another text.

GRIFFIN: I guess I didn't expect you to go on a date so soon. I know I screwed up. And I'm sorry. It kills me to see you with this guy

"Hell no," Charlie says from over my shoulder. He succeeds in taking my phone this time. "He's not going to lay some guilt trip on you when he was the one who wanted to break up."

Charlie starts tapping something on my phone. I try to snatch it back.

"What are you saying?" My shrill voice echoes through the kitchen, but no one gives me more than a glance.

"I'm telling him what you should have days ago."

By the time Charlie gives me back the phone, I know his message has been sent. And when I read over what he wrote, my cheeks get pink with embarrassment. Charlie was *very* descriptive about what Griffin should stick into certain body parts.

I'm staring at my phone when Nonna pushes me toward the hall. "Go get dressed. You're riding to the shop with me, since Olivia has some stuff to do for her mother this morning. We'll stop at the store and see if we can find you something to wear tonight."

Most of the family scatters from the kitchen once they're done eating. Charlie stops at the back door and hollers, "Be ready at six thirty!"

I'm still staring at my phone by the time I enter the guest room, but not surprisingly, Griffin doesn't respond.

Nonna and I are on the way to the store when Mom calls.

"Hey, sweetie, how are you? I guess you survived your date last night?" she says. I can tell she's trying to be upbeat, but she sounds tired. And worried.

"It was horrible, but what else would you expect from Aunt Patrice? How's Margot?"

Mom's quiet on the other end. "She's okay. Hanging in there."

I try to speak, but it feels like something is lodged in my throat. Finally, I ask, "What's going on? What are you not telling me?"

"Well, her blood pressure is a little higher than the doctor would like, and then there's the swelling. She's having a few contractions, but they're giving her some magnesium, so that should take care of that. No need to worry! We're all keeping a close eye on her!"

Mom sounds overly enthusiastic, which makes me doubt her. "Is she going to be okay? Is the baby?"

"Yes, honey. They're both okay. Are you? If I need to, I can put an end to this blind date thing. I hate to think you're up there miserable."

Gah, the last thing I want any of them to worry about is me. "No. It's fine. It's a good distraction. I keep telling myself this is going to make for a good story later."

Mom lets out a soft laugh. "Well, we love you. Very much."

"Love y'all, too. Tell Margot to text me if she feels up to it."

"I will, sweetie. She's sleeping right now, but I know she loves hearing what's going on with you. She got the biggest kick out of that picture Charlie sent her last night."

At least there was some good that came out of that.

We say our good-byes, and I hang up just as we pull into the parking lot.

"How bad is it?" Nonna asks.

"Huh?" I ask, scrunching up my forehead.

"Margot and the baby. Your mother acts like I didn't have eight children of my own. She thinks I'm too fragile to know what's happening down there."

I sigh. "Her blood pressure is too high and the swelling is bad. Some contractions, but they're trying to stop them."

Nonna nods. "Well, good. It's amazing what those doctors can do! I know everything will be just fine!"

And now I see where Mom gets her fake enthusiasm.

We wander through the store and head to the craft section, debating what we need to make the tackiest sweater ever. Nonna found an old red sweater in her drawer this morning, so all we need are decorations.

She holds up a package of silver tinsel. "How about this? We could hot-glue it down the arms of the sweater."

Oh God.

She sees the look on my face. "Sophie, the key here is tacky."

I nod and she starts throwing everything from bows to colored pipe cleaners to fuzzy cotton ball–looking things into the basket. She's got a twinkle in her eye. "When I'm done with this sweater, there's no way you won't win."

I drop my head back and stare at the ceiling. "That's what I'm afraid of."

We head to the checkout when the basket is almost full,

but she stops suddenly. "Oh! I almost forgot. Gigi needs a few things." She pulls out a piece of paper from her purse and I recognize the small scrawl of my great-grandmother. "Could you go grab these? I'll go ahead and get in line. We'll drop them off at the nursing home on the way to the shop."

I read the list and blanch at items like adult diapers. Once I find everything, I run through the store carrying all of the items on the list as discreetly as I can. Nonna is unloading the stuff for my sweater on the conveyor belt and talking to the guy checking her out.

I walk up just in time to hear her ask him, "Do you have any plans for New Year's Eve? I'm looking for a date for my granddaughter!"

What.

Is.

She.

Doing.

"Well," he says. "I think my friends might be having a party, but we're not sure yet . . ."

His eyes move from her to me and then to the items in my arms. He zeroes in on the hemorrhoid cream.

"Oh, there she is! This is my granddaughter Sophie," she says, then looks at his name tag. "Sophie, this is David."

I drop all of the items on the conveyor belt and look at Nonna. "I'll be waiting in the car."

Just as I'm about to leave the store, I hear her say, "Well, if the party with your friends doesn't work out, call Greenhouse Flowers and Gifts and ask for Sophie."

Olivia and I are hiding out in the back greenhouse on our lunch break, eating some sandwiches Aunt Lisa packed for us. She's texting back and forth with Drew, a dimpled smile on her face, and I hate to admit I'm jealous.

I've heard from Seth a few times, but we're in that new, awkward phase of communicating. I miss having a deeper connection with someone. I've already talked to Addie twice today, once this morning to fill her in on last night's date and then again after that picture of Seth and me was posted.

So instead of giving in and texting Griffin, I text Margot.

ME: How are you?

MARGOT: Good!

ME: You're full of it. Mom called me this morning.

MARGOT: Fine, then. It sucks right now. Not only am I worried about the baby but Mom and Dad and Brad's parents are DRIVING ME CRAZY.

I want so much to tell her how scared I am for her and the baby. But that's not what she needs to hear from me right now.

ME: Tell Mom you want some of her vegetable soup. You know that takes her hours to fix. And doesn't Brad's mom sew or something like that? Tell her you want her to make something special for the baby. You have to keep them busy.

MARGOT: You're right. Hold on, I'm on it.

I eat half my sandwich before Margot texts me back.

MARGOT: IT WORKED! Dad's driving Mom to the grocery store although the soup is probably going to suck since my diet is so restricted right now. And Bill is driving Gwen to the store to get some material for a blanket, even though she's already made a dozen.

ME: See! I'm a genius

MARGOT: What's up for tonight's date?

ME: Ugly sweater party with someone Charlie is setting me up with.

MARGOT: Send me pics! And don't make me bribe Charlie to do it.

We text back and forth, me telling her about the horrible date with Harold and how Nonna keeps trying to set me up with random guys that I always manage to look ridiculous in front of. Just before our lunch break is over, I text:

ME: I'm trying really hard not to be scared for you and the baby

MARGOT: Me too Soph. Me, too.

✻ ♥ ✻

The crowd tonight at Nonna's is at an all-time high. It would be faster to list the family members *not* in attendance. Olivia's wearing what can only be the most ridiculous thing I've ever seen; it's as if she took a small, fully decorated artificial tree (including lights), sliced it straight down the middle, then glued it to the front of her sweater.

Aunt Lisa and some of my cousins are helping Nonna put the finishing touches on my own hideous sweater. Whereas Olivia's sweater has a definite theme, mine is chaos. There are bows and tinsel and streamers and ornaments and God knows what else hot-glued to every available space. This sweater probably weighs a good fifteen pounds.

"Are you ready?" Charlie calls from the hall just before he walks in. We all stare at his sweater.

"Charlie, is that reindeer . . . vomiting?" Nonna asks.

Charlie struts into the room, arms spread wide, and models his outfit. Near his right shoulder is a piece of brown felt cut out in the shape of the front half of a reindeer with its mouth wide open. All different types of candy are hot-glued to the rest of the sweater as if the reindeer is projectile vomiting it.

"Isn't it awesome?" he says. "Wait until you see Judd's."

"Who's Judd?" I ask at the same time Olivia screeches, "Tell me you didn't set her up with Judd!"

“What?” Charlie says, a confused look on his face. “Judd’s fun.”

“Judd’s obnoxious. And an idiot,” Olivia says.

I sink down on the edge of the bed and look at Olivia. “Like, I should use my ‘get out of date free’ card obnoxious?”

Nonna straightens and looks at me. “After all the work we’ve put in the sweater?”

Charlie moves farther into the room. “Judd is cool, and I’m telling you, save the card for the Evil Joes.”

Nonna clucks her tongue. “What have I told you about calling them that?”

“Not to,” Charlie answers her, then pulls me up and drags me out of the room. “Judd’s downstairs. Come meet him.”

With my entourage following, we all march into the kitchen, where Judd is waiting. He’s got his back to us, but he’s looking over his shoulder mischievously, waiting on Charlie. Charlie stands next to him like they’ve rehearsed this, and they slowly turn around together, making sure their shoulders never lose contact.

Nonna lets out a surprised gasp while the rest of us just stare at them. Where Charlie has the head and front end of the deer who is vomiting, Judd has the back half of the reindeer. Let’s just say there’s an equal amount of candy flying out of that end as well.

They jump around the kitchen, pounding their hands in the air. “We’re going to kill it tonight!” Judd yells.

"No way we're not winning this!" Charlie yells back.

The only good thing about this date is that it seems Judd will have to stick pretty close to Charlie all night.

Even though the party is down the street from Nonna's, we pile into Charlie's truck so we can pick up his date, Izzy, who lives across town. Judd sits in the backseat with me, making it look like Charlie is chauffeuring us.

He clicks his seat belt, then turns sideways to face me. "So, Sophie, do you have plans for college yet?"

Charlie laughs, and I say, "Yes, I do."

"Have you made a choice as to where you would like to go, or are you keeping some options open?" Judd asks in a formal voice as if he prepared icebreaker questions in advance.

"I've applied to twelve different schools," I answer.

Charlie whips around to look at me and says, "Twelve?" in a horrified voice. "There are twelve different schools you might want to go to?"

"I want to keep my options open!" I say back.

"What twelve?" he asks.

"You should be paying attention to the road," I say. Good grief, how far away does Izzy live?

I turn my attention back to Judd. He asks, "What twelve schools are you considering?"

Ugh.

"Well, I'm thinking about Texas A&M—" I stop when I hear Charlie grunt. "What's wrong with A&M?" I ask him.

"Nothing. But there's like a million people that go there. And you get freaked out by big crowds."

"No, I don't," I say, but he's right. I really don't like big crowds.

"Where else?" Judd asks.

"Well, I'm waiting to hear back from a small liberal arts college in Massachusetts."

"Massachusetts!" Charlies howls, and swerves when he tries to look back at me again. "You realize the winters there last all year and it stays below zero for most of it."

"You're exaggerating and you know it," I say.

Charlie pulls up in front of a cute two-story house and throws the truck into park. He twists around until he's facing us. "I'm going to get Izzy. Don't say anything until I get back."

And then he's gone.

Judd watches Charlie walk up the front path of Izzy's house and then looks back to me, his forehead creased in confusion. "Wait, I thought Olivia told me all of y'all were going to LSU together."

My stomach twists. "Well, we used to say that, but I don't know . . ."

But Judd doesn't stay in the truck long enough to get my full answer. The second he sees Izzy, he jumps out so he can match his sweater up with Charlie.

Izzy seems equally horrified at Charlie's and Judd's sweaters. She took a different approach to dressing up, and instead of wearing an ugly sweater, she's wearing the skirt that usually fits around the base of a real Christmas tree as an actual skirt.

Once everyone is back inside, Charlie makes introductions, and thankfully talk of colleges is forgotten.

I had been worried about walking into the party wearing this monstrosity, but it only takes a few minutes for me to realize I'm almost underdressed. People have gone all out, and it's impossible not to just stand there and stare at every person who walks by.

The main living area of the Browns' house is a huge open space. Most of the furniture has been pushed against the walls to allow room for all of the guests. There's a giant Christmas tree in one corner, the dining room table is filled with food, and there's a bar set up on the kitchen island. There's a man dressed as Santa making the rounds, passing out Jell-O shots. I'm sure he's supposed to give those only to the adults, but since it looks like he's been sampling them himself, he's giving them out freely to anyone he passes.

As they predicted, Charlie and Judd are a huge success. And as I predicted, Judd isn't much of a date. He's currently competing against some twelve-year-old girl in one of those dance-off video games.

Not that I'm complaining!

Olivia and Drew arrive, and she introduces me to everyone there. Sometime later, Wes walks in with Laurel. His T-shirt has the words *This is my Christmas sweater* written in duct tape. But Laurel's the one who has me crossing my arms across my chest when I see her sexy Mrs. Claus outfit.

And I thought Halloween was the only time of year where they turned every costume known to woman sexy.

"Hey, Sophie. You remember Laurel," Wes says when they get near the couch where Olivia and I are sitting.

We both nod at each other, but then her attention drifts, no doubt trying to find someone else to talk to.

"Cammie!" she yells, and then scampers toward the kitchen. Wes drops down next to me on the couch, and I scoot closer to Olivia to give him some room.

"Have you seen Charlie and Judd?" Olivia asks, leaning across me to talk to Wes.

Wes laughs. "Yeah, they sent me a picture this afternoon." Then he looks at me and asks, "Are you here with Judd?"

Before I have a chance to answer, Judd pulls me up from the couch and says, "Sophie, it's our turn!"

"Our turn for what?" I ask as he drags me away, but my question goes unanswered. That is, until we stop in front of a karaoke machine.

"Oh no," I say, and start to walk away.

Judd latches on to my hand and pulls me back. "This is going to be so fun!"

Charlie sees us and starts clapping and cheering our names.

The music starts up, and I stare at the small screen. Maybe if I keep my eyes glued there instead of on the crowd, this will be okay.

Just when I think this can't get any worse, the title of the song flashes across the screen.

"We're singing 'Grandma Got Run Over by a Reindeer'?" I ask in a horrified voice.

"Yes!" He points to his sweater. "It's perfect!"

The song starts and we sing along. At some point I manage to look up and see Wes. He's leaning back on the couch and I'm pretty sure he's crying from laughter. I look at Olivia, and she's not any better.

"At the scene of the attack . . ." we sing.

Then Judd gets louder. *"She had hoofprints on her forehead and incriminating Claus marks on her back."*

I drop the mic and look at Judd. "This is really the worst song ever."

He gives me a confused look. "Really? You think so?"

I hand Judd my mic and walk back to the couch while he continues to sing.

The song draws to a close just as Mrs. Brown, the party's

host, walks in the room, clapping to get everyone's attention. She's a cute, bubbly woman and she's got that strong south Louisiana accent that makes some words unrecognizable.

"Time for the games!" she yells over the music.

I turn to Judd. "What games?" I ask.

His grin tells me I should be scared. "Fun games," he says, then pulls me to the center of the room.

"Okay, it's the young versus the old," Mrs. Brown says. "I need two lines—the young on my left, the old geezers on my right, boy—girl—boy—girl."

I watch as the room divides into the two groups. Judd steps in line next to me and seems super pumped up about this game. Wes is behind me with Laurel.

Mrs. Brown stands in the front of the room holding two really big oranges, one in each hand. "Here's what we're going to do. I'll put an orange under the chin of the first person in each line, then you have to turn and pass it to the person behind you, but you can't use your hands!"

Oh. God.

Someone cranks up the music while Mrs. Brown puts the oranges in place. Of course Charlie is at the front of our line and he wiggles his eyebrows at Izzy.

I'm going to have to get the orange from Judd, then give it to Wes. I guess it doesn't matter that my hands are sweating, *since I can't use them!*

Mrs. Brown calls "Go!" and Charlie throws himself at Izzy.

There's no way to pass the orange without being extremely close to the person you're trying to give it to. The adults drop theirs and have to start over. They've all been hitting the egg-nog pretty hard and can't stop laughing long enough to move the orange.

Before I know it, Judd's got the orange and turns to me.

"I'm coming in, Sophie!" he says, then pulls me close. I turn my head to the side and try to get my chin close to the orange. Judd is a big guy and with all the stuff on my sweater and his sweater, it's hard to get close. I finally bring my chin down on the orange. Judd pulls away slowly and I spin toward Wes.

And then I hesitate.

His eyebrows shoot up and his head cocks to the side, almost daring me. Why am I nervous about getting close to Wes? I've known him forever.

Charlie is chanting my name, and I just go for it. My arms wrap around his shoulders, pulling him close as I tilt my head. His arms go around me and we're pressed against each other. I feel Wes grip the orange and I start to pull away. But it's too soon. The orange comes loose. Wes presses against me, stopping the orange just below my collarbone, where it's wedged between a red glitter bow and a Santa ornament.

"Well, this is awkward," he says. He's looking up at me, holding the orange against me with his cheek.

He looks ridiculous. Laughing, I look across the room, where the adults' orange is moving rapidly down the line, and then look down at him. "We can't let the old folks win!" I say. "Get the orange!"

He starts moving the orange around with his face, trying to get it under his chin. It rolls toward my shoulder, then down my arm. Wes is crouched around me, since he's so much taller than I am, and I'm on my tippy toes, trying to raise my shoulder toward his chin.

"Stop wiggling!" he says.

"You suck at this!" I reply.

Charlie is next to us, trying to give Wes directions, but all Wes manages to do is roll the orange around my arm, then back to my shoulder until he gets really close to my boob.

"You need to get the orange and move along," I say.

He finally manages to catch it in the right place. Wes squeezes me close one last time and then he's gone.

It's a clean pass to Laurel and then she turns to the guy behind her.

Wes looks at me over his shoulder and my heart is pounding. We stare at each other a few seconds before he turns away.

When we beat the grown-ups, Judd picks me up and swings me around.

Mrs. Brown gets our attention for the next game. "I'm going to pick six from the youngsters and six from the oldsters." I become one of the lucky ones; Judd jumps around like a maniac and points at me until Mrs. Brown picks me.

She hands me a rectangular tissue box that has a long ribbon attached to the bottom. I shake the box and it rattles. It's full of Ping-Pong balls.

I can't even imagine what this means.

"Now, everyone, tie the ribbon around your waist so the box is sitting right above your behind with the opening pointed out."

Olivia helps me get mine tied on just right. I notice Charlie and Wes were also picked to do this challenge. I glance around for Laurel, but she's nowhere to be found.

Wes is standing with his hands up so Charlie can get the box tied around his waist. His T-shirt fits a little snugger around his biceps than I remember—it looks like he's been working out. He looks . . . good.

I brush the thought away immediately. Why am I noticing Wes's arms?

Mrs. Brown claps her hands several times. "Okay, when I yell *Go!* you dance around and shake what your mama gave you until all the balls are out of the box."

I shake my head at Olivia and mouth the word *No!*

She laughs, nods her head, and mouths the word *Yes!*

The music starts again and Mrs. Brown screams, "Go!"

And then we all start moving. I find out quickly that up and down isn't doing the job, so I start moving side to side. Basically I look like I'm stuck in the washing machine spin cycle.

I should be humiliated, but for some reason I'm not.

Charlie is doing some sort of crazy motion where his hands are on the ground and his butt is in the air and he's bouncing it from side to side. His Ping-Pong balls are flying out everywhere. Wes seems to be having the same trouble I am. He moves toward me while shaking his hips back and forth.

"Aren't you glad you came?" he shouts over the music.

"I'm still not sure!" I shout back.

"We'll help each other out. Give me your hand. I'll dip you and hopefully, they'll all come flying out."

I put my right hand in his and lean back. He keeps his arm around my shoulders while I shake my hips. "That's cheating," an older woman says. She's jumping up and down like she's on a pogo stick.

"She said to dance, and we're dancing!" Wes says.

Charlie comes up beside us and yells, "Say 'cheese!'"

More pictures.

"Margot's going to love these," Charlie says.

I roll my eyes and Wes laughs.

When my box is empty, I say, "Okay, your turn."

We change positions, and within seconds, I'm standing over Wes.

We keep spinning around and around and we're both getting a little out of breath.

"We owe Judd one for this," I say to Wes. Judd had managed to get Wes nominated, too.

His eyebrows shoot up and he pulls me in close. "When we're done, slip my phone in the back pocket of Judd's pants."

I look quickly at Judd before turning back to Wes. "Why?"

"You said we owe him one. I've got just the thing."

After a few more turns, the last of the Ping-Pong balls are out, but an older couple already beat us. While I untie the box from my waist, Wes holds out his phone. "Just drop it in."

I shake my head. "No. No way."

Wes rolls his eyes. "Come on!" He puts his hands on my shoulder, then spins me around until I'm facing Judd, who is busy taking to Mrs. Brown's son Brandon. "Those pants are so big he'll never feel it."

It's been a long time since I've been part of a prank. I take a deep breath and move toward Judd.

"Hey," he says when I stop next to him. "Have you met Brandon?"

"Thanks for letting me crash your party," I say. I move close to Judd and put one hand on his shoulder, like I want to tell him a secret. As I hoped, he leans in close to me.

"Do you know where the restroom is?" I ask. I slip Wes's phone in his back pocket just as he twists around and points to a hallway on the other side of the room.

"Just down that hall, second door on the right."

I nod, a ridiculously big smile on my face, and head in that direction, detouring once he's focused his attention on Brandon again. By the time I get back to Wes, Charlie and Olivia are standing there with him.

"Okay, what next?" I say.

Wes grins. "Pull out your phone and call me."

I can't tell if Olivia and Charlie know what's happening. Pulling up my contacts, I tap on Wes's name.

"So what's going to—" I'm interrupted by the loud sound of an air horn. Most everyone around Judd is startled, but Judd jumps like one of those cartoon cats that leaves its fur behind.

It's unbelievable, really, how high he went.

The air horn keeps going off. Judd grabs his butt, trying to figure out what's going on.

"You can probably hang up now," Wes says, laughing.

"Oh, right!" I look at the screen and hit the red END button. I can't stop giggling as I watch Judd.

"That never gets old," Charlie says, and I'm guessing this isn't the first time they've pulled this particular prank on him.

Judd gets the phone out of his pocket and looks at the screen. He walks toward us, waving Wes's phone back and forth, and says, "Nice one, Sophie!"

Olivia leans over my shoulder and taps Wes's name on my phone. The air horn goes off again, nearly sending Judd to the floor this time. We double over with laughter.

"What are you doing?"

We all turn around to find Laurel standing behind us, arms crossed.

"We're just messing with Judd," Wes says.

"Yeah, it's too easy to resist," Charlie adds.

Laurel rolls her eyes. "I don't know why you have to act like a little kid."

Olivia and I exchange sideways glances. I mean, is it a little childish, what we're doing? Maybe. But it's funny. And Judd isn't afraid to give as good as he gets, so no harm done.

Wes doesn't answer her.

"Are you about ready to go?" she asks him.

Mrs. Brown is already setting up the next game. The room is still full and the music is still playing and the table is still full of food. This party isn't close to being over.

He shakes his head. "Not really."

She gives him a look. "Mia texted me. She's at a party downtown, and a ton of people we know from school just showed up. She wants us to come down there."

Wes throws a glance at us before turning back to her. "I don't really want to go hang out with a bunch of people I don't know."

"Well, I didn't really want to come back and hang out at some high school party."

Wes's shoulders stiffen. I don't have to look at him to know he's pissed. Charlie, Olivia, and I should really walk away, but none of us is moving.

"Yeah, it sucks that you have to hang out with the same *friends* you hung out with five months ago," Wes bites back.

Laurel cocks one eyebrow at him. "I guess I'm going alone, then."

He nods. "I guess you are."

They stare at each other for a few seconds. Then she spins around, not stopping until she's out the front door.

Wednesday, December 23rd

Blind Date #4: Sara's Pick

My head is foggy when I wake up. Bits and pieces of a very realistic-feeling dream linger, and it takes me a few minutes to separate fact from fiction. In it, all of these guys had shown up at Nonna's, ready to pick me up for a date. It was like a zombie apocalypse, except the guys weren't dead.

I shudder and throw off the covers, hoping a shower will chase the nightmare away. Walking down the stairs, I hear the noise coming from the kitchen. But I don't feel the usual fingers of dread that would normally start clawing their way through me. Instead, I find myself wondering if my cousin Frannie managed to convince Aunt Kelsey to let her watch the *Nightmare Before Christmas*—she couldn't stop talking about it at breakfast yesterday. And do Olivia and Charlie know what's going on with Wes and Laurel?

Yeah, I really want to know the answer to that one.

Judd is the first person I see when I enter the kitchen.

"What's up, Sophie?" he yells from where he's sitting with Charlie at one of the extra tables. Other members of my family mill around the kitchen and living room with coffee mugs and breakfast plates. Judd's still wearing his sweater from last night, but it looks like someone ate all of the candy, leaving behind the wrappers that are still flying out of the reindeer's butt.

I walk over and point to his chest. "Looks like you got robbed."

He glances down, then throws his head back in a laugh, loud enough to get the attention of my very loud family. "Nah. Just got a little hungry in the middle of the night. There's literally no food at Charlie's house."

Charlie thumps him on the shoulder. "Dude. We have food."

Nonna has set up breakfast buffet style, so I grab a plate and wait in line for my trip down the counter. Whiffs of bacon, cinnamon, and coffee have my mouth watering.

Aunt Kelsey's four daughters are sitting in chairs against the wall, and all of their faces are covered in icing.

"Hey, Fran," I call out. "How was the movie?"

Fran's eyes get big. She leans forward in her chair and says in a serious voice, "It was so scary." Her *r*'s sound like *w*'s and it's honestly the cutest thing I've ever heard.

Just as I'm about to fill my plate, I see Sara creep in the back door and start writing on the board. Everyone in the room gets silent, even the babies, as if they've been waiting all morning for this very minute.

They probably have.

Sara finishes and spins around to face us. "I'm so winning this," she says.

Underground Christmas
8:00 p.m.
Formal attire
(I'll totally go shopping with you!)

"There's no way you got her a date to Underground Christmas," Uncle Michael says. "Hell, I've been trying to get tickets to that since I got to town!"

"What is Underground Christmas?" Aunt Patrice asks.

I'm somewhat relieved that Aunt Patrice has never heard of it, but all I can think about right now is: FORMAL ATTIRE.

"Tell everyone what Underground Christmas is, Sara," Nonna says. Today, she's sporting an apron that has a picture of a spatula, whisk, spoon, and rolling pin with the words *Choose your weapon* written below them.

Sara rubs her hands together, clearly loving the attention. "Well, Underground Christmas is just the biggest, baddest party this town has ever seen. The Regional Arts Council puts it on, and it only happens every other year because there's so much planning involved. My friend's parents' restaurant is just one of the local restaurants catering it, and, Soph, it's going to blow your mind."

"That's a pretty wild party, Sara. How old is her date? Are you sure that's the right event for your cousin?" Uncle Charles gives his daughter a serious look.

Her hands go to her hips. "Dad, she's almost eighteen. Aunt Patrice set her up with a freshman and so did I. A freshman in college."

My eyebrows shoot up. Wild party? And my date is a college guy?

Everyone starts talking at once. I drop down next to Charlie, Judd, and Olivia.

"Dude, Sara's got you beat," Judd says.

Charlie hits him in the shoulder again. "Dude, you were the date I set her up with, so you're ripping on yourself!"

Judd winks, and I can't help but smile.

Olivia picks up her plate and heads to the sink. "Sophie, what are you going to wear?" When we were younger, the two of us used to play in Aunt Camille's closet, which was filled with hats and party dresses and gloves and heels and everything else you could imagine. We would dress up and Aunt Camille would serve us tea and cookies. I enjoyed it, but not as much as Olivia.

"No clue," I reply.

"I'm just bummed I can't go, too," she says.

And then it dawns on me—no backup on this date.

"So no one in the family will be at the party tonight?" I ask.

No one speaks up, and I drop my head on the table. Sara passes by, her hand running through my long hair. "Don't worry, Soph. Your date is super hot. You're going to have a blast."

"Super-hot date who just happened to be available for one of the hottest parties of the year." Charlie snickers. "He sounds like a winner."

Sara grins. "Just wait. You'll see."

I call Addie the second the house clears from breakfast. She sounds as excited to dress me up as Olivia did.

"I have the perfect dress. Gabby wore this gorgeous gown to Cotillion last year, and I just know it will fit you. And if not, Maryn will have something you can wear. She's always going to parties for her sororities." Addie is one of three sisters, so there's never a shortage of clothes at her house.

"Okay, I may drive over if I can catch a break from work."

We talk a few more minutes. I'm dying to ask about Griffin, but I don't. I promise to call her later, then I jump in the shower. When I get out, Margot is blowing up my phone.

MARGOT: UNDERGROUND CHRISTMAS!

MARGOT: I'm not sure you're prepared for this party

MARGOT: There will be naked people there. Lots of skin. And nakedness.

I barely get my hands dry enough to text her back.

ME: What do you mean, naked people???

MARGOT: NAKED. As in little or no clothes. Brad and I went to one of those parties a few years ago and I thought Brad's eyes were going to pop out of his head. And the naked people usually have food on them. That you're supposed to eat!

ME: ???????????????

ME: What!?!?!?!?!?!

Olivia knocks on the door and I almost drop my phone. "Hurry up," she calls from the other side. "Nonna's letting us have the morning off to find you a dress!"

I clutch the towel tightly around me and swing the door open.

"Did you know there will be naked people at that party tonight? With food on them?"

She lets out a giggle.

"I can't even right now. Just give me a minute," I say, and then shut the door. I dress quickly and dry my hair just enough so it won't be dripping down my back.

Olivia is stretched out across the bed when I come out.

"Tell me about the naked people," I say.

She rolls over and looks at me. "From what I've heard, there are guys and girls walking around in costume. Teeny tiny costumes that match whatever the theme is. And then some of them are draped across tables with food on them like they're the platters. It's all to shock everyone there. Very scandalous."

"Oh, I'll be shocked, all right," I say. "Moving on. Addie says her sisters have dresses I can borrow for tonight!"

She hops off the bed. "Perfect. Let's grab Sara and hit the road."

Minutes later we're in my car headed back down I-20 to Minden.

Olivia starts laughing at something on her phone. "This picture Charlie posted is priceless!"

Sara leans forward from the backseat. "Y'all look so cute!"

Olivia holds the phone up where I can see it, and I almost swerve off the road. It's the one Charlie took last night when Wes and I were dancing, trying to empty the tissue box of Ping-Pong balls. Except you really can't tell that's what we're doing. It just looks like Wes has me dipped back and we're both laughing hard.

"And so far, four people have tagged Griffin in the comments," Sara says.

Olivia laughs. "Good!"

I want to beat my head against the steering wheel. I had another string of texts from him this morning, all saying the same thing: "I made a mistake" and "Please talk to me." I'm guessing this picture is what stirred him up.

"Griffin wants to get back together," I say. "He keeps saying he made a mistake and he doesn't really want a break."

Olivia twists in her seat and looks at me. "Is that what you want?"

I stretch my neck to one side, then the other, trying to work out the tension I'm feeling. "I just don't know if he really means what he says or if he's reacting to seeing me with other guys."

Olivia chews on her bottom lip. "Are you going to see him when we get to Minden?"

I shrug. "I don't know. Part of me thinks—go ahead and get it over with. Have it out with him one way or another. But I'm not sure I can handle it yet. I can't quit thinking about how bummed he was when he heard I wasn't going to Margot's. I mean, why would that have changed so quickly?"

"Well, I think you have your answer," Olivia says.

"You have to finish the dates, Sophie!" Sara adds.

We ride in silence a few minutes, and then my phone starts beeping.

"Oh God, is it Griffin again?" I ask as Olivia checks my phone.

She laughs. "No. It's Seth. He wants to know if you can go to lunch tomorrow, since it's your free day."

Before I can give her an answer, she unlocks my phone and runs her finger down my screen, scrolling through my conversation with him. "He's been texting you, but you're ignoring him."

"I'm not ignoring him. There's been a lot going on!" I throw her a look. "Also, ever heard of privacy?"

She rolls her eyes. "You're ignoring him."

"Whatever. Tell him I'd love to go to lunch." I know that wouldn't have been my reply if Olivia hadn't made me feel bad about ghosting him, though.

Olivia texts back and forth with him a few minutes and then she laughs again.

"What's he saying?"

"Well, Judd's texting you now. He's issued a challenge."

"Reindeer-pooing sweater Judd?" Sara asks.

"Yep, same one," Olivia says.

"What's the challenge?" I ask.

"He has a list of things he wants you to do while you're at Underground Christmas. But you have to have photographic proof. He said it would be like a scavenger hunt."

Judd is officially nuts. "Let's hear the list."

Olivia almost can't stop laughing long enough to read it. "Okay, first, and I quote . . . 'A video of you eating a piece of food that was sitting on the naked skin of someone else. Bonus points if it was on the buttocks.' His words, not mine."

I lean my head back against the headrest. "The fact that these things are even possible is freaking me out."

"Man, I wish I was going with you," Olivia says.

Sara lets out a sigh. "Me too."

"You look stunning," Addie says as I spin around in front of the mirror attached to the closet door. The dress is incredible. I don't know what kind of material it is, but it's soft and fits me like a second skin. The dress is long, skimming the floor, and the pewter color has a little bit of a shine to it so it sparkles when the light hits it.

"But quit pulling at your top," Olivia says. The dress is strapless and I have the never-ending feeling that it's two seconds from slipping down. "It's not going anywhere."

Addie hands me a pair of heels and I slip them on. She came back with us to Nonna's to help me get ready. I hadn't realized how much I missed her until she opened the door. There had been a half-dozen dresses for me to choose from in her sisters' closets, but the second I laid my eyes on this one, I knew it was the one.

"Are you sure Gabby won't mind if I borrow this?" I ask.

"No, not at all."

I hear the sound of a picture being taken and spin around. Olivia holds up her hands. "Settle down. I'm just sending it to Margot."

"And then every other member of our family will have a copy within ten minutes."

"Well, at least this outfit doesn't blink," Olivia says. "Okay, my bad, I may have accidentally posted it." The way she's smiling tells me it was no accident.

"Olivia!" I grab her phone. The photo shows the dress from the back, which is almost as pretty as the front. We decided to leave my hair down and Olivia curled it into loose waves. In the picture, my face is turned to the side and I'm looking at the mirror so you can only see my profile. The light from the window is pouring in, making the dress really shine.

"See how beautiful you look," she says.

I can't help but smile. Then I see the caption—*Cinderella getting ready for her big night out!*—and groan. "Really, Liv? Cinderella? Does that make y'all the mean stepsisters?"

"Only if that means we get to go to the ball, too," Addie says.

And then the comments start coming in. Most of them are about how pretty I look, but I notice Griffin has been tagged twice already. I groan again.

When my phone starts dinging, I'm not surprised. I swipe it open and see his latest text.

GRIFFIN: I don't know what's going on but I have to talk to you. I have to see you.

My finger hovers over the keyboard, but I have no idea what to say to him. Would he be texting me like this if I was sitting at home, crying over him? That's the part I can't get past.

So instead of texting him back, I throw the phone in the small chair by the window.

"I bet Nonna has a necklace or bracelet that would go perfectly with that dress," Olivia says, then heads to the door.

Addie bounds off the bed, following her out. "Oh, I want to come see."

For the first time all day, I'm alone. I glance at the phone and realize I haven't heard from Margot since this morning.

I sit down in the chair and pull up our conversation.

ME: What's up? You've been ridiculously quiet today

She doesn't respond immediately, which worries me. Leaning back in the chair, careful not to mess up my hair, I stare at the phone until a constant thumping from outside gets my attention. I peek through the blinds and look down on the driveway that runs in between Nonna's house and Wes's.

And there he is, dribbling a basketball. He looks like he's been at it awhile, because his shirt is off and his hair looks damp with sweat. Wes bounces the ball a few times, then shoots. It swishes through the net. Rinse, repeat. He's got a pretty good average going, only missing one out of every four or five shots. Every time he shoots, I can't help but stare at the muscles in his back.

What is happening to me? I'm just now feeling like I'm part of the Fab Four again. I can't screw it up by thinking about Wes like that.

Our group went down that road before, and it ended disastrously. Olivia and I both decided at the beginning of freshman year that we had a crush on Wes, but sincc she swore hers was stronger, I backed off. They tried to date for a few weeks, but it just didn't work. Then they didn't speak to each other for months, which was horrible for all of us.

Charlie brought us all together and told them to get over it. We all agreed our friendship was too important to risk it, and we decided that we would all only be friends. And that's all we've been ever since.

But the thoughts floating through my head while I watch him are *not* the way you think about a friend. Seriously, when did he get all of those muscles?

Sara pops in the room and lets out a squeal. "Sophie! You look perfect!"

I almost fall out of the chair. I close the blinds so she won't know I've been practically drooling over a half-naked and sweaty Wes. Grabbing the small beaded bag, I check my phone once more to see if Margot has texted me back before dropping it inside. "Thanks, Sara. I'm trying not to be freaked out about this party. Or the college guy you set me up with."

She's so excited she's practically shaking. "Well, he's here! Are you ready?"

I want to sink down to the bed. I'm not sure I've ever been so nervous for a date, especially since I have Judd's list scrolling through my brain.

Then Olivia and Addie are back, armed with necklaces, bracelets, and earrings. Once they think I'm finally dressed and ready, Addie says, "Okay, let's go check this guy out."

The house is packed, like I knew it would be. Everyone wants to be a part of this date thing. I don't know the guy I'm going out with, but I feel sorry for him already. I can't imagine what it's like to pick up a girl for a date and have twenty people staring at you.

At the top of the stairs, I take a deep breath. The foyer is crowded, but I didn't expect to see the betting sheet taped to the wall next to an old family portrait. Graham's standing next to it holding a couple of pens, and he's acting like that guy at the fair trying to entice anyone who passes by to stop and play.

How embarrassing.

I get to the bottom of the stairs, and a guy in a tux takes a couple of steps toward me.

Pleasantly surprised doesn't even cover it. Sara was right. He's *hot*.

"Hey, I'm Paolo Reis." He holds a hand out to me and I take it. He's tall with big brown eyes, and his black hair has a slight wave to it, just enough to give it a little body. "You look gorgeous."

Okay, Sara won. And from the looks Charlie and Judd are throwing from across the room, they know it, too.

"Thank you. You look really nice, too."

Sara is beaming. And so are Olivia and Addie. Of course, Olivia is capturing all of this with her camera, so I'd better prepare myself for the posts to come.

Paolo turns toward Papa and shakes his hand. "I won't have her out too late."

Papa shakes his hand back and then leans forward to kiss me on the forehead. "You look just like your mother did at your age. Have fun, sweet girl."

I'm not going to cry. I'm totally not.

A couple of my uncles walk over to Graham and start arguing over one of the boxes. I guess after getting a good look at Paolo they want to change their bet.

"Can't give you that one," Graham says. "Aunt Kelsey already claimed it."

I try to ignore their ridiculousness.

With my hand still in his, Paolo pulls me through the foyer and out the front door. We're headed down the brick path to where his car is parked on the street when I look toward Wes's house. He's still in the driveway—and still has his shirt off—but he's holding the ball against his hip, watching us.

His eyes catch mine and he gives me a small nod. I nod back and then slide into Paolo's car, where he's holding the door open for me.

"So that's probably the most nervous I've ever been picking up a girl in my life," Paolo says once he's in the car.

"Seriously? It didn't show," I say. If that was him nervous, I can't imagine what confidence must look like.

He looks at me, just before he cranks the car. "There were just so many people."

I laugh. "Welcome to my world."

We pull away from my grandparents' house. I refuse to look back to see if Wes is still watching. Instead, I turn toward Paolo. "Okay, I'm just going to ask. Why on earth did you not already have a date to this party? I mean, is there something I should know?"

He laughs. "Straightforward. I like it."

I don't think he's going to say anything else, but then he clears his throat.

"There's this girl," he starts.

"There always is," I say, and he laughs again.

"I moved here halfway through high school, but I didn't meet her until we were at LSU, even though she's from here. Things are complicated. I thought that maybe when we were both back on break, some of the issues we're having might work themselves out, but it's not looking too good."

"I'm sorry," I say. I want to add, *I'm sure it will work out!* but it sounds lame. And I'm certainly not in any place to give anyone relationship advice. I stare out the front window, and Paolo glances at me once, then twice. "So what's this Sara was telling me about all the blind dates?"

I say, "It's complicated," and he laughs again. "I overheard my boyfriend telling his friend that he wanted a break from me because senior year is supposed to be fun."

"Ouch. What a dick."

"Yeah. So this was Nonna's idea of cheering me up."

Paolo slows at a red light and turns toward me. "Is it working?"

I cock my head to the side. "It's been different. And I've had some really weird and some really fun dates. My ex keeps seeing pics of me dating on social media, and since I'm not curled in a ball, bawling my eyes out, he's begging to see me, to talk to me. So I guess it's working."

The light is still red and Paolo leans a little closer. "Then this is what we're going to do. We're going to flood his timeline with pictures of us having fun tonight."

A car behind us honks as the light turns green, and Paolo returns his attention ahead. I'm glad he misses the ridiculous smile stretching across my face.

"Okay, but I don't want to do anything that makes things more complicated for you."

"Don't worry about me. The ball's in her court. She knows I'm ready when she is. I'm just glad I didn't have to go to this thing alone."

I've decided whoever this girl is, she's a dummy. He's cute and nice and genuine, and she's an idiot. "So where did you move here from?"

"Cabo Frio, which is a small town near Rio in Brazil."

"Oh wow. Do you like it here?"

He shrugs. "There's things I like and things I miss back home."

I turn sideways in my seat so I can see him better. "Out of all of the places your parents could pick, why Shreveport, Louisiana?" It's the same thing I've wondered about my grandfather.

Paolo laughs. "We had some family who moved here a few years before us. One of my cousins got accepted to physical therapy school at University Health. My parents kept hearing about how nice life was here, so we moved. They opened a restaurant similar to the one they had back home, and it's done well. Mom got involved with this Christmas party when we first got here as a way to get to know people, and she's now on the board or something like that."

My phone beeps and I scramble in my purse to pull it out. "Sorry, I'm expecting a message from my sister. She's a few weeks away from having her first baby and she's on bed rest."

"Is she okay?" he asks.

"I think so," I mutter as I open her message.

MARGOT: Olivia sent me a pic of you. You look so beautiful
ME: Are you ok? Haven't heard from you all day!
MARGOT: I'm fine. Had to go back to the doctor. But I'm home now. Just tired. Send me some pics tonight. And have fun.
ME: I will.

I'm just about to put my phone back in my bag when it dings once more. But it's not a message from Margot.

JUDD: Don't forget about the challenges.

I roll my eyes and slip my phone back in my bag. Turning to Paolo, I say, "So there is one other thing you can help me out with."

❄ ♥ ❄

Paolo told me the theme to this year's party was "Feel the Beat," so I'm expecting something music-related, but I'm not expecting the group of singing Elvises that are on the curb next to the valet stand. We're barely out of Paolo's car before it's whisked away. There's a desk to one side with a woman dressed like Madonna from her early years. She squeals when she sees Paolo.

"You made it!" And then she looks at me and squeals again. "Sara said you were adorable and she was right!"

Paolo turns toward me. "Sophie, this is my mom, Riya."

"But you can call me Madonna tonight!" She slaps some wristbands on us and hugs Paolo across the table. "Y'all have fun!"

We walk past the Elvises, who are belting out "Hound Dog," and stop in front of a small—*very* small—building next to a large group of people. It's not really even a building. It's more like a box with a set of double doors on the front. And we're all just standing in front of it.

"What is this?"

Paolo laughs. "The elevator."

I look around, but there's nothing else. "Where does the elevator go?"

Paolo squeezes my hand. "You'll see."

When it opens, there's man inside who's a dead ringer for the lead singer of Aerosmith. He holds the doors open and says, "Going down?"

I giggle and we load as many people inside as possible. As soon as the doors shut, the Steven Tyler look-alike starts belting out "Love in an Elevator." He sounds just like the original.

"This is wild," I stage-whisper to Paolo.

"We haven't even gotten inside yet."

The elevator doors open up and I scoot in close to Paolo, afraid of getting swept away with the crowd. It's packed, but the ceilings are so high and the space is so big that it's not claustrophobic.

"There was a building that stood here years ago, but it got torn down," Paolo tells me. "This space was the basement someone refurbished about ten years ago."

There's so much going on at once that I almost can't take in what I'm seeing. The space is divided in sections, like big rooms. Each section has a musical theme.

"Let's check it out," Paolo says, and pulls me along. I think there are as many people working the different areas as there are guests. There's a fifties area complete with girls in poodle skirts dancing with guys in leather jackets, a hall with enormous masks of the painted faces from KISS, a room that's purple from top to bottom with a Prince look-alike belting out "Little Red Corvette" . . . It goes on and on. By the time we get to the back of the space, we've gone through ten different staged areas. And roaming through each space are entertainers: a girl on stilts, acrobats, and even a man swallowing fire and then blowing it back out.

But it's the main room that blows me away. It's basically a carnival. Everything glows in the dark neon lights, and there are girls hanging from swings suspended in the air and guys jumping from pole to pole above us. I've never seen anything like it.

I follow Paolo to a round dessert table. A woman is lying across the top of it on her stomach, wearing only a red thong and tiny bikini top. She's acting as a human serving tray for miniature cupcakes. The cupcakes are sitting on her back, her legs, and even her butt cheeks. She's got her chin resting in her hands, and she turns to look at Paolo and me.

"I recommend the red velvet ones. They're sinfully delicious," she says, blowing us a kiss.

Paolo laughs, then pushes me toward the table. "Looks like we can knock out one of those challenges!"

He holds his phone up while I take baby steps toward the table. People all around me are snatching cupcakes off her and posing for pictures. It's just a cupcake, I tell myself. And it's in one of those paper wrappers, so it's not actually touching her skin.

As awkward as this is, I'm glad Judd issued the challenges, since it's giving us something to do. But of course, I'll never tell Judd that.

I turn around to make sure Paolo is getting this. He gives me a thumbs-up. I quickly grab a chocolate cupcake from the small of her back. All of the red velvet ones are on her butt, and I just couldn't bring myself to touch them, bonus points or not.

I hold up the cupcake and smile at the camera, then shove it in my mouth. I may not want to do these challenges, but there's no way I'm losing. Judd said if I don't complete them all, I have to go on a second date with Hundred Hands Harold. Olivia, who was texting on my behalf, made Judd promise to streak down Nonna's street wearing nothing more than a Santa hat and a smile if I finished his list. Truthfully, we're all losers in this challenge if I have to witness that.

"One down, nine to go," Paolo says, laughing. "Seriously, the one I'm looking forward to is watching you spin around a pole. I think I saw one in the heavy-metal room."

"I'm glad you're enjoying this," I say as he drags me into another area.

The girl on the table calls after us, "You can come back for seconds anytime!"

❄ ♥ ❄

Before the night is over, I complete all of the challenges, including participating in a limbo competition, singing onstage with the backup singers in the Motown room, and swing dancing with one of the Elvises. We've also filled my timeline with a ton of pics. I have twelve unread messages from Griffin.

We drop down on a bench at the street level, waiting for the valet to bring Paolo's car back. It's blissfully quiet up here compared to the party downstairs.

Paolo nudges me with his shoulder. "That was more fun than I thought it would be. Hundred Hands Harold must have been a pretty bad date if you don't want a repeat."

I nudge him back. "You have no idea. I can't believe I agreed to do all of that. It's so unlike me."

"I think it's awesome. And maybe your ex was the one holding you back. Keeping that fun side locked down. I was worried when my little sister's friend said she wanted to set me up on a date, but this was great."

My phone dings again and both of us look at the screen. Message thirteen from Griffin.

"And mission accomplished," Paolo says.

I nod, then look at him. "None of this is going to mess things up with the girl you like, is it?" I really don't want her to get upset if she sees pictures of us together.

"No, she was here tonight, actually. We talked while you and the Supremes were singing 'Stop! In the Name of Love.'" He laughs again. "I explained what was going on, and I think I actually got some brownie points from her for helping you out."

"Good! I'm glad I could help," I say. And I mean it. Paolo is a really cool guy. I just hope the girl comes to her senses and snaps him up.

By the time Paolo drops me off at Nonna's, I'm exhausted. And my feet are killing me.

What I'm not expecting is for Charlie, Wes, and Judd to jump off the porch and break out in a rendition of the song I sang with the Supremes cover band.

"Please don't tell me I sounded that bad," I say when they're done.

Charlie checks his watch and pulls out a piece of paper

from his back pocket, then lets out a groan. "Ugh. Uncle Ronnie won the pot tonight." He starts texting.

"You were awesome," Judd says. "Especially when you rode that bull sidesaddle. I mean, awesome."

"Glad I could entertain you," I say. Truthfully, the challenges made my night.

"Not sure why you're excited, Judd. This means you lost," Wes says.

"Seeing me run naked down this street is a win for everyone," he says.

"Just make sure we have plenty of notice so I can make sure I'm not here," Charlie answers.

"Me too," says Wes.

I raise a hand. "Me three."

Charlie and Judd wander back inside the house, arguing over the logistics of the run, but Wes drops down on the front steps, and I sit next to him.

His shoulder nearly touches mine. I stretch my legs out and kick off my shoes. "God, that feels good."

"You look really pretty," Wes says, nudging his shoulder against mine.

"Thanks," I say, nudging him back.

Wes rests his elbows on the step behind him. "So if you had to, rank your dates so far—best to worst."

I twist around until I'm curled up on the step, facing him. "Clearly, Harold was the worst. And not just him but the whole date. I mean, any date where goats are eating your clothes has gone downhill." Wes laughs while I continue, "For first place, hmmm . . . I had a lot of fun on the first one with Seth. And tonight was a blast, too."

Wes has a fake outraged look on his face. "You mean the date with Judd isn't in the running for first? I'm shocked!"

"Yes, shocking, I know."

"So which date is the best kisser? My money's on Hundred Hands."

I duck my head so he doesn't see the blush.

He leans forward and lowers his head, trying to catch my gaze. "Don't tell me you've had all these dates but no good-night kiss."

I straighten, and then he's so close. I push his shoulder playfully, but my hand lingers there. Before I can pull it away, his hand covers mine. We're both surprised, but neither of us moves. His eyes go to my lips and he squeezes my hand. I catch myself leaning closer to him.

Warning bells blare through my brain, but I can't stop.

The sound of the door opening behind us is what does it. I push back, nearly falling off the step I'm sitting on. We both look shocked at what almost happened.

I glance to the door and see Nonna, alarm etched on her face. I jump up. I can feel Wes behind me.

"It's not what it—" I begin, but Nonna interrupts me, her face softening.

"I just got off the phone with your mother. They've admitted Margot to the hospital. The contractions haven't stopped, and her swelling is getting worse."

My stomach drops, and it takes a few moments for me to process what she's said. "Is she okay? Is the baby okay? This is too soon. She's not supposed to have the baby for another six weeks!"

Nonna wraps me in her arms.

"It's not the best situation, but she's okay. The baby's okay."

She doesn't say it, but I feel like she left off the words *for now.*

Thursday, December 24th

Free Day

I barely slept last night. There's been no chance to talk to Margot, but she did send me a text telling me not to worry. I talked to Mom for a while and she kept assuring me the same thing: Everything is going to be fine.

Olivia is asleep in the big guest bed with me. The room is still mostly dark with only a faint yellow light filtering in through the blinds, which highlights the rows of framed pictures on the opposite wall.

My grandmother has a portrait done of every grandchild when they turn two years old. We're all dressed in really fancy little outfits that have our name monogrammed across the front as if she knew in advance how full this wall would get. My eyes scan from one side to the other, stopping once I find Margot. Her dark hair is short and she's got these little ringlet curls all over her head. Her smile is big and her eyes are dancing. I wonder if Margot's baby will look like her when he or she is two.

My throat clenches. I can't stay in this bed any longer.

I slide out, careful not to wake Olivia, and tiptoe from the room. The house is quiet as I pass a pallet in the den full of my younger cousins, and I smile as I notice the tangle of arms and legs. I miss those uncomplicated days when our biggest concern was who was going to get stuck on the edge, where you were likely to end up off the pallet, onto the hardwood floor without a pillow or a blanket. Just like my little cousin Webb is right now.

I pull two blankets off the back of the couch, covering Webb in one and taking the other with me out to the front porch. Wrapping the blanket around me, then dropping down on the front steps, I lean back against the top step and watch the sky go from a deep blue to a warm yellow-orange and finally see the first edge of the sun peek out from the horizon. The air is just cold enough that I can see my breath when I exhale, but I'm warm, wrapped up in the thick blanket.

I glance at the house next door.

It's probably a good thing that we were interrupted before we did anything stupid, I think. He's got a girlfriend, and I'm in the middle of a nervous breakdown and dating half the town. But I can't help but feel a small pang of regret.

The morning has been so quiet that it's jarring to hear an engine barrel down the road and even more disturbing when a familiar truck pulls up to the curb.

Griffin has just parked in front of my grandparents' house.

I'm frozen on the step as I watch him get out of his truck

and walk up the brick path. His head is down, and he seems to be mumbling to himself. I take these few seconds to stare at him. His brown hair is a little too long, and it looks like he slept in the clothes he's wearing. The pang in my chest is still as painful now as it was last Friday night at Matt's party.

When he finally raises his head, he's so startled that he jumps back and yells loud enough to wake the neighbors.

I can't help but stare at him. Even after everything that happened, my heart starts beating faster and my palms get sweaty.

"What are you doing here?" I finally ask.

Griffin takes a few steps toward me but stops when he's a foot or so away. "You wouldn't talk to me. So I waited as long as I could. I have to talk to you."

I tug the blanket even closer. After hearing about Margot, I feel like I'm about to fall apart, and seeing Griffin here is not making it any better. Half of me knows it would be so easy to close the distance between us; let him wrap his arms around me and chase away the sadness that seems to have settled just under my skin. It's easy to ignore him when he's thirty miles down the road, but seeing him here, looking at his sad face is harder than I imagined it would be.

"I told you, I'm not ready to talk to you yet."

Griffin puts one foot on the bottom step, but I hold my hand out, stopping him before he can come any closer.

He digs his hands in his pockets and lets out a deep breath. "Please, Sophie. Give me ten minutes."

"You can say what you want to say, but say it from down there." I stand and walk to the top of the steps. I need some distance to sort through the tug-of-war going on inside of me right now.

"I screwed up, Sophie. I knew it the second I saw your face."

I spin around to face him. "I heard you. You were so bummed I wasn't leaving town. But you're telling me that feeling changed ten seconds later?"

He throws his head back and his hands come up in front of him. "I'm saying that I'm going crazy. That I have been since you left Matt's. That I see these pictures of you out with other guys and I want to rip their heads off. I mean, what is going on? There was a picture of you riding a mechanical bull in some formal dress. And then some crazy picture of you with . . ." His hands flail in front of him like he's trying to come up with the words. "Lights!" he finally bursts out.

"So you've been bothered by seeing pictures of me?" And then I add for emphasis, "Having fun?"

He blows out a deep breath and starts pacing the width of the sidewalk.

I sit down on the top step and say, "I think you only want me back because you've seen me with other guys. Would you want me back if I had been tucked away in a room upstairs, crying for the past five days?"

His forehead scrunches up. "I texted you I wanted to talk before I saw the first picture of you with someone else."

"But what about what you said that night? About how senior year should be fun?"

He runs a hand through his hair. "I don't know. I mean, we've both been so focused on school, and everything else came second. But the closer we get to graduation, the more I wonder about what we've missed. This year is almost over and everything is going to change and I just don't know . . ."

It's hard to hear what he's saying. But it's even harder to realize there is some truth behind his words. Being with Olivia, Charlie, and Wes this week has reminded me that I used to be different. When we were the Fab Four, things were fun and easy. And then somewhere along the way, schoolwork and clubs and making sure my transcript was perfect took over. I went from one extreme to the other.

And while I think Griffin may miss me, I don't think what he was feeling has really changed.

"Hearing you say what you did was hard, but it made me start thinking, too," I say. "I guess we both have a lot to figure out."

He moves up one step. "I hate seeing you with the other guys, but it's more than that. Don't throw what we have away. We can figure it out together." His voice has gotten louder, and I can't help but glance back at the front door.

It would be so easy to get back with him. I could say yes and it would be done. But how long would he be happy? And can I go back to how things were before?

"Is everything okay?"

We both turn to see Wes standing in the grass just a few feet away. He's in gray pajama pants with little Santa hats all over them, and a bright red T-shirt. Even with the thick tension hanging between Griffin and me, I want to giggle at his festive attire.

His eyes go from me to Griffin and back to me. "I heard yelling," he says.

Griffin rolls his eyes. "Yeah, man, it's fine. We're just talking."

Wes is still looking at me. I give him a small nod.

"Can we get a little privacy?" Griffin asks.

"If you wanted privacy, you shouldn't have been yelling loud enough that I could hear it from next door."

Griffin looks confused. "This isn't one of your cousins?"

Gah, I know I have a big family, but we've been together a year. You'd think he'd know my family by now.

"No, Wes is an old friend."

And then I see recognition on his face.

"The picture of you dancing. With him."

I nod and look at Wes. "It's all good. We're just talking."

Wes stands there a few more seconds. He starts to walk away, then stops and asks, "Any word on Margot and the baby?"

Griffin's head pops up. "Did something happen?"

"She's in the hospital," I say, then turn to Wes. "I haven't heard anything new. They're trying to control the swelling and stop her contractions."

Wes gives me a small smile. "She's tough. I know they're both going to be okay."

And then he's gone.

Hearing about Margot takes some of the fight out of Griffin. He drops down on the bottom stair.

"I'm sorry, Soph. I know how worried you must be."

I mumble a thanks, and we're back to awkward silence. Finally, Griffin says, "All I'm asking for is another chance. I don't want things to be over for us."

"You're going to have to let me think about it. There's so much that's happened in the last few days, I can't think straight."

He nods. "Do you plan on having any more dates while you're here?"

I picture the board in the kitchen. I could put an end to it. Tell Nonna that Griffin and I are trying to work things out. But something is holding me back. So instead I tell Griffin about Nonna's plan.

And it's clear when I finish that Griffin isn't happy. "So even though I'm here, telling you that I want us to get back together, you're still going to go on six more dates?"

I look him in the eye. "I feel like I've learned more about myself in the last four days than I have in the last four years.

And it's not like I'm really looking forward to the upcoming dates. But I need to finish what I started."

This is the moment. Either he'll get what I'm saying or he'll be gone. I'm not sure what it says about us that I can't decide which way I want it to go.

He gets up quickly, almost falling back down before righting himself. He paces up and down the front walk like he's trying to wrap his head around my words. Finally, he stops and turns toward me.

"I think we both got lazy. If you go back and look at early pics of us, I think you'll find you were as happy then as you look in the ones being posted now. And I think we can get back to that place. At least, that's what I want."

I start to say something—what, I'm not even sure—but he holds a hand up, stopping me.

"But I agree you should finish what you started, because you need to be one hundred percent sure I'm what you want."

He spins around and gets back in his truck. He's driving away before his words have even completely registered.

Is he right? I keep thinking about how different these last few days have been, but what if it's because I'm not really remembering what things were like with us in the beginning? Is it fair to compare the excitement of a first date—or four first dates—to the familiarity of a long-term relationship?

It's only when I get up to head inside that I notice Wes sitting on his front porch steps, staring at the empty street.

❄ ♥ ❄

The day drags. My phone is glued to my hand, and I've almost worn a path across my grandmother's kitchen floor.

She's watching me from her spot at the counter but doesn't say anything. Both of us were supposed to go into work for a few hours, but neither of us could stand the thought of being there while we're waiting on news about Margot. Instead, Nonna continues measuring ingredients and whatever else it takes to prepare tomorrow's massive meal, and I continue pacing.

This new radio silence is killing me. I've already talked to Mom a few times, but all I've gotten is that there's "nothing new."

"Didn't you have a lunch date today with Olivia's friend?" Nonna asks.

"I did. But I canceled. I can't go to lunch today."

Nonna lets out a humming sound but doesn't look at me. "I need you to run to the store for a few things," she says finally.

I spin around. I can't go to the store. I need to stay here and wait for Mom's call. "What do you need?"

"For you to get your mind off things."

I roll my eyes and start pacing the room again. "I'm not leaving right now."

My phone rings an hour later and it scares me so bad, I drop it. It takes forever to find it underneath a side table.

Mom's name flashes across the screen.

"Hello?" I say, almost out of breath. It feels like my heart is beating out of my chest.

"Soph," she says. "They've rushed Margot in for an emergency C-section. They should have the baby out in just a few minutes."

Mom's voice sounds gravelly. Nonna has stopped moving.

"Is she okay? Will the baby be okay?" I can barely squeak out the words.

"They told us it's safer for Margot to deliver than to try to stop it from happening. There's a neonatal doctor and nurse waiting to whisk the baby to their unit, and plenty of doctors and nurses caring for Margot, so there's no reason to think that everything won't be just fine."

Except the fact that the baby is coming early and, until this morning, the goal was for Margot to get further along before delivering. I mean, is the baby ready?

Even though I'm scared as hell, a sudden thrill runs through me. I can't believe Margot is about to be a mom. And I'm going to be an aunt!

"Will you call me as soon as you know something?"

"Of course. I'll call you soon," Mom says.

"Okay. Tell Margot I love her and can't wait to see the baby!"

"Oh, sweetie, I will."

And then the line goes dead.

I catch Nonna up. "Is it possible to be terrified and excited at the same time?"

She comes up behind me and pulls my hair back, twisting it around her hand, just like she used to do when I was little. Her voice is soft when she answers. "It's how I've felt every time one of my children or grandchildren was born . . . and now a great-grandchild! It's amazing what doctors can do nowadays. Six weeks is early but not unheard of."

"I know," I mumble. "But we haven't even had her baby shower yet. She wanted to get past Christmas first."

"Well, then, once we know if it's a boy or girl, we'll just have to go shopping."

I swore I'd never step foot in a store on Christmas Eve, but for this, I'm willing to change my mind.

Nonna is back at the stove and I continue to stare at my phone.

"This will be the first time you're a great-grandmother," I say. "I didn't realize it until you just said it. How does that feel?"

Nonna turns to face me. "It feels pretty fantastic." Her face is beaming. "And you'll be Aunt Sophia for the first time!"

"Aunt Sophia sounds too formal. She can just call me Sophie."

"I had an Aunt Judy growing up and we all called her Aunt Ju-Ju. So maybe you can be something cute like Aunt So-So!"

Sounds kind of silly but it makes me smile thinking of a chunky little baby looking up at me with arms outstretched asking for Aunt So-So to pick her up.

My phone dings and I jump in my seat.

I swipe open the message. "It's a girl!" I squeal.

Nonna clasps her hands together and I can see tears in her eyes. "A girl! How wonderful!"

"Mom says the baby was rushed to the neonatal unit, so she'll send a pic as soon as she gets one."

"Does she have a name yet?" Nonna asks. I text the question to Mom.

Those bubbles jump around and then her reply comes.

I'm so choked up I can barely get the words out. "Anna Sophia."

I'm gutted. That sweet baby has my name and I don't even know what she looks like.

"What size are you looking for?" the saleswoman asks me. Olivia and I are at a small baby store downtown. Thankfully most of the people shopping on Christmas Eve are not shopping here. Well, good for us, I guess.

"She was born today, but she's small. Barely five pounds."

The woman's eyes get big. "Follow me over here. We have a preemie section that will have something in the size you need."

Olivia and I hold up tiny little gowns. "I could seriously take the clothes off some of my old dolls at home and they would probably fit her."

"I know," I say. "These little bloomers barely cover the palm of my hand."

Then she gets distracted by a stand of breast-feeding products. "Think Margot will need some of this nipple cream?" she asks with a laugh.

"That's something she'll have to buy on her own. And seriously, after all this, it will be a miracle if I ever decide to have a baby."

"Well, it will be a miracle if Jake ever finds anyone willing to marry him, so you may have to share Anna and let me be her aunt, too. It might be my only chance."

I look at Olivia. "I can definitely share her with you."

We're close enough that she throws her arm around me and squeezes me close. "We'll be the best aunts ever. Not like Aunt Patrice."

I lean my head against hers. "Or Aunt Maggie Mae."

She laughs. "Definitely not like her."

In the end, we pick out three soft gowns that have an elastic opening at the bottom and a super-soft pink blanket.

"Want me to wrap these?" the saleswoman asks.

"Yes, please," I answer.

While we wait, Olivia picks up a miniature LSU cheerleader outfit. "I forgot to ask how things went with the college guy last night," she says, and wags her eyebrows.

"That party was amazing!"

"I saw all the pics, but did you like him? Did he say he wanted to go out again?" she asks.

I shake my head. "No, he's kind of talking to someone else."

Olivia looks bummed. "Well, that stinks."

I open my mouth to tell her about Wes but shut it again quickly. What would I say? I'm glad we're finally getting back to normal, but now let me screw it up by bringing up my almost kiss with Wes? And let's not forget he has a girlfriend . . . I think. And I'm super confused by my ex-boyfriend.

Yeah, probably best to keep all this to myself right now.

The woman returns with my wrapped gifts and we leave the store. Once we're back in the car, I stare at the picture Margot sent me. As much as I've been dying to get a look at my niece, it's hard seeing her like this. Before I got this picture, I pictured her swaddled in one of those white blankets with the pink and blue footprints on it, sleeping peacefully with rosy cheeks and full lips. The image Margot sent makes me want to cry.

The blanket is there, but Anna is lying on top of it in just her diaper. She's on her back, her arms and legs sprawled out, and there are tubes and wires and God knows what else attached to her. There's even a thin clear tube stuffed in her nose, for oxygen I'm guessing, and there's tape across one cheek to keep the tube in place. An ID bracelet circles one ankle while an impossibly small blood pressure cuff circles the other.

I zoom in on her face and smile when I see the dark hair covering her head. Margot's husband is blond and pale, and I was secretly hoping she would look like our family. Her eyes are swollen shut and her whole face looks sort of puffy, but she's gorgeous.

I can't wait to see her.

Margot didn't say much in her text, other than she's tired and sore and Anna seems to be doing "okay," which is not the word I wanted to hear when describing the health of my newborn niece. Mom told me they've been in to see the baby once so far, but they're hoping to see her again soon.

Olivia leans over to look at my phone at a red light, and I tilt it in her direction.

"She looks so small," Olivia says. "I mean, she barely takes up a third of that plastic tub she's in."

"I promised Margot I would be there when the baby was born," I tell her. Then I say the thing that's been on my mind ever since I got the text from my mom. "I'm thinking about going down there."

This gets her attention. "Today? Right now?"

I shrug. "I just feel like I need to be there." I've actually already floated this idea past Mom and she shot me down.

Olivia's left eyebrow rises—just the left one—and she gives me that look.

"You know I'm jealous you can do that and I can't," I say.

"Sounds like you've got a plan brewing?" she says.

I shrug. "Maybe." I'm quiet a moment before adding, "My parents don't want me to come because the traffic is dangerous on Christmas Eve, and the baby is in the NICU, so it's not like I could hold her anyway, and on and on . . . but I think I can get in, see Margot and Anna, and get out without my parents seeing me."

Olivia's eyes are huge. "Hold up," she says, her gaze darting from the road to me. "Let's talk this through. They're in a hospital in Lafayette, right? So it's three hours down there and three hours back. And if you stay like, an hour, that's seven hours you're not here. And that's if nothing goes wrong! How are you going to hide from Nonna that long? And what if when you get there your mom is in Margot's room? You could get down there and never see her. Or be in massive trouble."

I've thought about all of these things. But I'm not deterred.

"If I leave at nine, I'm there by midnight. I won't stay long. Just long enough to see them. Mom and Dad won't be there, because Brad will stay with Margot tonight. Then I'll head back. I'll be here before anyone wakes up."

I can tell she's going to try to talk me out of it, so I add, "You can cover for me. The house will be packed and you can run interference. No one will even miss me."

She lets out a deep breath. "You can't go alone. It's not safe. You'd be driving all night." She picks up her phone and calls Charlie, the call connecting over Bluetooth.

"Hey," he says, his voice filling the car.

"Your dumb cousin has a dumb plan and needs our help," Olivia says. I roll my eyes.

"I'm not doing anything for the Evil Joes and you know it."

We both laugh. "Not them," Olivia says. "And hold on. I'm adding Wes to this call."

I start to say no, but before I can get any words out, Charlie says, "He's right beside me. I'll put you on speaker."

"So," Olivia continues, "Soph's hell-bent on sneaking out tonight and driving to the hospital to see Margot and Anna and back. I'm just letting y'all know that we're all going with her so she won't kill herself by falling asleep at the wheel in the middle of the night."

"No. Wait, you don't have to do that," I say, but Olivia waves me off.

"Only if I can control the music," Charlie says. "And the temperature in the car. I don't want to sweat all the way down there. And you'll owe me a favor that I can cash in whenever I want. No questions asked."

Olivia and I share a look.

"What time are we starting this journey?" Wes asks.

"Around nine. After we've eaten so Nonna won't have any reason to be looking for us."

"I'll be ready," Wes says.

"Me too," Charlie says. "This plan is something the old Sophie would have done. I like it."

While Christmas Day tradition means we'll sit down to a formal meal at noon that includes all the traditional foods you expect—turkey, dressing, green beans, sweet potato casserole—Christmas Eve is the complete opposite.

Nonna loves to celebrate our Sicilian roots, so the buffet stretched out across the kitchen island includes several different pasta dishes, eggplant, stuffed artichokes, and panelle. There's an assortment of salami and cheeses, dried fruits and olives. There are also fig cookies, almond cookies, and cannoli. The tables are covered in red tablecloths and small white poinsettias sit in clusters in the center. Christmas music plays in the background, but all of the songs are in Italian and seem like they were recorded in the 1950s.

Jake and Graham wander into the kitchen and stop next to where Olivia and I are sitting at the table.

"So I heard that jackass showed up here this morning," Jake says after swallowing a bite of cookie.

First thing Wes did was tell Charlie that Griffin came by. Then Charlie told Nonna, and that's all it took to activate the phone tree.

"Yeah. He wanted to talk."

Graham rolls his eyes. "I never liked him."

"Please," Olivia says. "You barely knew him."

"Let's just say it didn't take long for me to form my opinion," Graham says.

"Don't let him guilt you into getting back together, if that's not what you want," Jake says with a pointed look. Then they move on to the cookie trays.

Most of my family have been heaping unwanted advice on me all day. I could strangle Wes for telling them Griffin showed up here.

Charlie slides into the chair next to Olivia. "We can't take my truck. I'm almost on empty."

I shush him and scan the room. But everyone is laughing and talking and not paying us any attention.

"We're taking my car," I say.

Our cover story is that Charlie, Olivia, and I are going to Wes's to binge-watch Christmas movies. We talked Sara into distracting anyone who comes looking for us. It's not a great plan, but with the house filled to capacity—and hopefully all of the adults being overserved—it's not likely anyone will be hunting us down. In fact, I'm expecting them all to fall into a food coma within the hour.

Twenty minutes later, the three of us head to the street where my car is parked. Wes is sitting on the hood, waiting for us.

"Who's driving?" Charlie asks.

"It'll be safest if we switch off every hour and a half," Wes says as he jumps off my car. "So two of us will take turns on the way down and two of us will get us home."

"You should've been a Boy Scout," Charlie says.

"I *was* a Boy Scout," Wes replies. "And so were you."

Wes and I reach the door to the backseat at the same time. I know we're both trying to do the same thing—save our turn for the worst shift, the one that will bring us home in the early hours of the morning.

"You drive first," I say.

He shakes his head and smiles, his hand reaching for the handle. "No. I'm beat. I really need to nap right now, and then Charlie and I can take turns driving us back."

Charlie moans.

I try to push his hand away, but he's latched on tight. We're close—not as close as last night, but still closer than we should be.

"That's not right. This was my idea. There's no reason for you to be up all night."

His head tilts, but he doesn't say anything. His hand is still firmly in place.

"Uh," Charlie mumbles from the other side of the car. "If

y'all are going to stand here all night, I'll go back in for another slice of Nonna's cassata."

"You drive first," Wes whispers.

I take one last look at my grandparents' house, every light blazing, before moving away from him and sliding into the driver's seat.

"Charlie, in the back," Olivia says. "We're driving first."

"How am I going to control the radio from back here?" he asks as he opens the backseat door. "This is not the trip I was promised."

Wes looks at me in the rearview mirror as I put the car into drive. "We'll nap on the way down. And I'll let Charlie listen to whatever he wants. We're good."

Charlie squirms around in the small backseat, trying to find a somewhat comfortable position, while Wes slouches in the corner of the seat and the door. Every time I check the rearview mirror, he's right there.

Not distracting at all!

I pull away from the curb while Olivia tries to find something other than Christmas music on the radio. She doesn't have much luck.

"It's a straight shot down I-49. Watch for cops going through Alexandria. It will be hard to explain a ticket to your dad," Olivia says.

I nod and try to focus on the road. This is going to be the longest night of my life.

We're only on the road for about ten minutes before Charlie starts complaining. "It's too hot back here, and this song sucks."

Olivia rolls her eyes and stretches the aux cord to the backseat. "Play whatever you want."

Charlie plugs it into his phone, and within a few minutes, some old, twangy country song blares from the speakers. The rest of us groan.

"What?" Charlie asks. "This is a great song."

"No, it's not," I say. "You have terrible taste in music."

"You do," Olivia says to Charlie. "You love those Lifetime movie songs."

"What does that even mean?" Charlie asks.

Olivia holds out her hand for his phone and he passes it to her. "The ones that could be the soundtrack for any Lifetime movie." She takes a minute or so; then a familiar tune fills the air. Olivia talks over the music. "See, this one is a rags-to-riches story with a hint of prostitution. It's about a poor mom and two daughters. One daughter is too young and sick, but the oldest is just old enough and she's pretty. So the mom thinks the only way for her to get out of the poorhouse is to put on a red dress and find a sugar daddy. Poor Fancy."

Wes and I crack up.

She skips to another song before the first one finishes. I recognize it the second I hear the words.

"And this one is a typical survivalist story. If the world

ends, all of the city folk are toast, but if you're a country boy, you'll survive. Not only will you be able to put food on the table but you'll use your manners while doing it."

She skips to another one. "And this one is a typical learn-from-your-elders bit. I mean, it's literally about an old gambler teaching a young gambler how to be a better gambler. There's smoking. And drinking. And they're on a train."

Now she's even got Charlie laughing.

"Okay, okay," he says. "But they're still really good songs."

We spend the next thirty miles going through Charlie's playlist and trying to match overused tropes to each one.

Charlie finally unplugs his phone from the cord. "You think you've ruined those for me, but you haven't."

Olivia flips on the radio, and we're back to Christmas tunes.

"What's up with Uncle Ronnie?" I ask. "He basically ran out of the kitchen when Nonna brought in the cannoli."

Olivia lets out a laugh. "He refuses to eat them."

"Why?" I ask. "That's like the best thing she makes."

"Because of us," Wes says. I glance at him quickly in the mirror, and he's watching me right back.

"Us? What did we do to him?" I ask.

Charlie leans forward and answers. "Remember when we found that powder in Papa's medicine cabinet that makes you go to the bathroom?"

"Oh my God!" I squeal.

"Yep," Wes says.

Freshman year, we were trying to get the Evil Joes back for something—I can't even remember what it was—so we thought it would be hilarious to put some of that powder in their drinks. Except we poured it in Uncle Ronnie's glass instead. And because we're poor communicators, we all took a turn adding it to his drink, not realizing the other three had done the same.

Needless to say, Uncle Ronnie was stuck in the bathroom for a while.

"But that was only one time! Three years ago! And the cannoli had nothing to do with it."

"But, remember, she made a huge batch that night. And he stuffed himself with them. That's what he thinks did it," Olivia says.

"Oh, that's terrible." But I can't help the giggle that escapes.

Charlie shrugs. "More for us."

Wes leans forward. "Charlie and I have been trying to get him to eat one for the past year, but every time we mention it, he turns green." Wes turns to Charlie and says, "Remember when we bet him the Saints would beat the Cowboys and when we won, we told him he had to eat a cannoli?"

"Yes, and he made Aunt Patrice eat it for him."

Wes's eyes meet mine in the mirror. "We have been trying to get him over it, but the guy won't budge."

"He *was* in the bathroom for a really long time," Olivia adds.

"Speaking of pranks," I say. "Anyone ready to fess up about who faked that love note to me from Ben from down the street?"

"Olivia!" Charlie shouts.

"Charlie!" Wes shouts.

"Wes!" Olivia shouts.

"Someday, I'm going to figure out who did it!" I say with a grin. "Y'all knew I had a crush on him. And I made a fool of myself when I rode my bike to his house with a platter full of those Key-lime-pie cookies to tell him how much I loved his letters." I had helped Nonna make some cookies for Ben's mom's book club the week before, so when I got a letter saying how much he loved those cookies, I made a double batch and raced them to his house. "He looked like a deer in headlights!"

They're all cracking up.

"That's okay. I'll figure it out and get you back."

"Since you'll have to hang out with us to get us back, I welcome your revenge," Charlie says, then begs us to change the station.

Friday, December 25th

Free Day

"Olivia, we're here."

I'm nudging her awake and she keeps pushing my hand away from her. She fell asleep about an hour and a half ago, about thirty minutes after Charlie and thirty minutes before Wes. She pries her eyes open and tries to figure out where we are.

"Sophie, why didn't you wake me up?" she asks in a groggy voice.

I pull into a spot near the emergency room entrance. "You weren't out that long," I answer.

Charlie stretches in the backseat and yawns loud enough to wake Wes. It's still dark out, but there's a glow coming from the dash that lights up the interior.

"Sorry," Olivia mumbles. "Hate you were up all by yourself."

I shake my head. "Don't be. Glad everyone got some sleep."

Olivia twists around from the front seat. She points out of her window and says, "Guys, looks like there's a Waffle House down the street. Want to get something to eat while we wait on Sophie?"

They nod, still disoriented. I get out of the car and Olivia comes around to slip into the driver's seat.

"I'll be right here in one hour," I say through Olivia's open door.

She's busy readjusting the driver's seat. "Call us if you need us to get you earlier," she says.

Wes rolls down his window. "Are you good to go in on your own?"

"Yeah. Get me some food, please?"

"Of course. What do you want?"

"Anything. I don't care. And some coffee."

Olivia hands me the bag of wrapped gifts we bought earlier. "Don't forget these."

"Thanks," I say, then walk toward the entrance. I stop when I remember to tell Wes to get some creamer for my coffee, and I pull out my phone. They've just driven away when I tap on his name.

I can hear the air horn from here, even with their windows up. Olivia hits the brakes so hard the tires screech on the pavement.

Oh God. I guess he forgot to change my ringtone.

"I forgot to change your ringtone," he says when he answers.

I can't stop laughing. "Creamer . . . too . . . please," I manage to get out.

"No problem. Anything else?"

"That's it." I hang up.

Charlie rolls down the window and sticks his head out. "We're up now! Thanks!"

"Sorry!" I yell across the parking lot as they drive away.

It's just after midnight, and there are only a few people in the waiting room. It's really depressing thinking about spending Christmas in the hospital. The woman sitting at the check-in desk looks like she'd rather be anywhere else in the world than right here.

"What's your emergency?" she asks in a bored voice.

"I'm just trying to see my sister. She had a baby today. What's the best way to get to the fourth floor?"

She points me in the direction of the elevator, then gives a complicated list of turns. When I get off of the elevator, there are two signs. One points in the direction of Margot's room and the other points in the direction of the NICU. I don't hesitate.

Two turns later, I'm standing in front of a giant plate-glass window, staring at several plastic tubs just like the one Anna was in for the picture.

A nurse notices me. She walks to the window and says, "Who are you looking for?" Her voice is muffled through the glass.

"Anna Sophia Graff!"

She nods, then rolls one of the plastic tubs close to the window, and I get my first look at her. The tubes and wires are all still there, but they fall away when I stare at the beautiful little face. She's tiny, even tinier than I expected.

"Is she okay?" I ask loudly.

The nurse gives me a small nod before walking away to tend to one of the other babies.

The only movement Anna makes is the rise and fall of her little chest. I don't know how long I lean my head against that glass wall and stare at her. After a while, I realize my forehead has gone numb.

"Bye, sweet baby. I'll be back to see you soon," I whisper, and blow her a kiss.

I backtrack the way I came, then turn left toward the other hall.

Margot's door is closed, and I hesitate before pushing it open. It's the moment of truth. Hopefully my parents stuck with the plan to stay at Margot's.

As quietly as possible, I slip into the dark room. Brad is asleep upright in a chair, a blanket thrown over him, and he's snoring loudly. Margot is in the bed, buried under a mountain of covers. There are several machines surrounding her, numbers lighting up the area.

I tiptoe to the bed and whisper, "Margot?"

Her head turns toward my voice, but her eyes remain closed. She looks really pale, and there are dark circles under her eyes. I decide it's not worth waking her. I came to see Anna and I've accomplished that.

I turn and head toward the door, but her voice stops me.

"Sophie? Is that you?"

I spin around and within seconds I'm at the side of her bed.

"Yes. I'm here," I whisper, then glance at Brad. He hasn't moved a muscle.

"What are you doing here?" Her voice is groggy, and it looks like it takes a lot of effort to open her eyes.

"I promised I would come see the baby when she was born."

She stares at me a moment, then slowly scoots over, patting the space next to her. Gently, I crawl into the bed next to her and lace my fingers with hers.

She squeezes my hand. "Dad will kill you if he finds out."

"That's why we won't tell him I was here."

We lie there in silence and I think she's fallen back asleep until she asks, "Did you see her?"

"She's perfect," I answer. "Totally worth the sausage toes."

Margot laughs, then moans as if it hurts.

"Are you okay?" I ask.

She nods. "Yeah. Everything is sore, especially where they opened me up for the C-section."

"Thank you for giving her my name. I'm going to be the best aunt ever."

Margot tilts her head until her forehead rests against mine. "I know you will."

There are so many things I want to say to her, to ask her, but she looks exhausted.

"I so wish I could have seen you dressed as Mary." Her voice is sleepy and her eyes are closed.

"Margot, that was the worst."

"So which one was the best?"

Of course my mind goes straight to Wes, when he asked me this same thing on Nonna's front steps.

"Olivia's was fun. So was Sara's."

"Oh yeah, Underground Christmas. I need pics."

"All you have to do is scroll through my feed. It's full of them."

She smiles, her eyes still closed.

"I'm dying to tell you something, but you have to promise me it stays between us. Like serious promise," I whisper.

Her eyes open. "Tell me."

"Promise you won't tell."

"I won't. You know you can tell me anything."

I take a deep breath and say, "Okay. I think Wes almost kissed me the other night and I'm bummed it didn't happen." And then I bury my face in her shoulder.

All I hear for a moment is the rise and fall of Margot's breath. I peek up at her. "So? What do you think?"

She sighs and leans her cheek against my forehead. "I love the idea of this, but I'm worried about you. He's one of your oldest friends. It's super hard to go back to that if things don't work out. Just be smart about it, okay?"

I pull away and look at her. I should have known she'd say this. Her senior year, she started dating one of her close guy friends. It only lasted a couple of weeks, and they weren't able to go back to normal after their breakup.

"This isn't like you and Ryan," I say.

She shakes her head. "I'm not saying that. And you probably shouldn't be listening to me. My hormones are all over the place. I cried when Uncle Sal sent me a text that said 'good luck' with the thumbs-up emoji. If you like Wes and Wes likes you—go for it!"

But that's the thing. I don't know how I feel about Wes, and certainly don't know how Wes feels about me. I'm stressing over something that I think almost happened. I blame Nonna for getting my brain all twisted up. Maybe it would have been better to spend this week crying it out rather than getting all tangled up with all of these boys.

We lie in silence, and I'm pretty sure Margot has fallen back asleep. Eventually, I kiss her on the forehead and slip out of the bed.

"Where are you going?" she mumbles.

"I have to get back."

"You're not driving back this late, are you?" She pries her eyes open.

"Olivia, Charlie, and Wes are in the car. We're napping and taking turns driving."

"Text me when you make it home," she says.

I nod and point to the floor. "There's a bag here with a couple of gifts from Olivia and me. Don't tell Mom where they came from."

"I'll play dumb. Be safe. I love you."

"Love you, too."

I'm tempted to take one more peek at Anna before I leave, but the clock on the wall shows we're already a little behind schedule.

My car is exactly where it was when they pulled away, and Wes is in the driver's seat. I get in the backseat and glance up at the rearview mirror.

"Good visit?" he asks.

"Perfect," I answer.

Charlie hands me a white plastic bag. "Food," he says. It looks like he's still half-asleep, and Olivia is already sacked out in the seat next to me.

I eye Charlie. "If you need me to, I can stay up and keep Wes company."

"Nah, I'm good. Eat and then get some rest."

I open the bag and find a Styrofoam container of pancakes. "Thanks. I'm starving."

Charlie nods and turns down the volume of the radio. "How're Margot and the baby?" he asks.

I recap my visit in between bites while Wes gets us back on the interstate.

"I'm glad we did this," Wes says, his eyes on me.

I smile at him. "Me too."

❄ ♥ ❄

I'm shifting around, trying to get comfortable, when I hear Griffin's name.

"Do you think they'll get back together?" Wes asks.

I glance around the car, but all I can see is the upholstered ceiling. Olivia and I have somehow ended up lying side by side, her balancing on the front edge of the seat while I'm pinned between her and the back of the seat.

"What?" Charlie mumbles.

Wes repeats his question. "Do you think they'll get back together?"

Is he asking because we almost kissed the other night? Is he regretting it even though it didn't happen?

Charlie must be distracted by the radio; I hear snippet after snippet of music filter through the speakers.

"Who knows? I hope not," he finally answers.

Charlie finally settles on a modern remake of "The Little Drummer Boy." Wes says, "I heard them talking this morning. It sounded like he wants her back."

"Of course he does. Soph's a cool girl and he's an ass. And he's been seeing all those pics of her having a good time without him."

I can't help the smile that breaks out across my face. No matter how much time passes, Charlie and Olivia will always have my back.

"She did look amazing in that dress the other night," Wes says.

It takes everything in me not to squeal.

"And he had the nerve to say that maybe they had just gotten lazy," Wes adds. "That if they tried hard enough, they could get back to when it was fun. I mean, of course people get lazy when they're with the same person for a long time, but that doesn't mean they're not still happy. Or having fun. If lazy is enough to ruin a relationship, then maybe there's more wrong than just being lazy."

They're quiet a few minutes. Then Charlie asks, "Is this about Laurel?"

Wes sighs. "I feel like we both worked hard to make this long-distance thing work, but it's not working. We're in two totally different places."

"I told you it was a horrible idea," Charlie says.

Wes lets out a quiet laugh. "Yeah, you did. More than once. I thought it would be easy once she was home on break, but I don't think either of us wants it anymore. All Laurel wants to do is hang out with people she met at school, and I'd rather hang out with you three. The last week has been good. Really good."

"So are all these deep thoughts about Sophie? Because

me, you, and Olivia are always together. She's the only thing that's new about this week."

I don't think Wes is going to answer. Then he finally says, "Yeah, I'm glad she's here."

Charlie lets out a deep breath. "Look, I know I made a big deal out of you not dating either of them because it might ruin our group, but we lost Sophie anyway. What I *am* worried about is that it feels like we're just now getting her back. I don't want anything to happen that pushes her away again. You know what I mean?"

Charlie's words hit me in the gut. *They feel like they lost me.*

"I know. I'm just saying I'd rather be doing nothing with the three of you than anything with Laurel."

They don't say anything else, and even though I didn't think it would be possible, it's not long before I drift back off to sleep.

Charlie, Olivia, and I part ways with Wes in Nonna's front yard about an hour before sunrise. I wanted to hug him and thank him for driving us home, but after the awkward conversation I overheard in the car, I didn't trust myself to get near him. I settled for a wave from the driveway.

The three of us tiptoe quietly inside the back door and

come to a dead stop when we see Nonna standing at the kitchen counter, baking ingredients spread out in front of her.

"How are they doing?" she asks.

We all start talking over each other, each with a different excuse, but Nonna just shakes her head.

I look at her with what I hope is reassurance. "Anna is so tiny. And so, so beautiful. But those tubes and wires look worse in person. Margot seems good but really tired and sore."

Nonna starts cracking eggs in a bowl. "I'm feeling full of Christmas spirit, so I'm going to be happy you all made it home in one piece and send you off to bed. You can find a few blow-up mattresses in the game room. But I expect you to be bright-eyed and bushy-tailed when it's time to line up."

"Yes, ma'am," we all mutter, then silently trudge upstairs to the game room in the attic. There are several bunk beds positioned around the large room, all of which are already taken. Christmas Eve is the one night everyone in my family tries to sleep under one roof so that we're all together when we open gifts. The larger our family has gotten, though, the harder it has become.

We each pull a mattress from the pile Nonna keeps on the shelf in the corner. While Charlie pulls out the electric pump to blow them up, Olivia and I hunt down some blankets and pillows. I'm out the second I lie down.

When my little cousins come screeching through the room

to wake us up two hours later, I feel like I've only slept for five minutes. It's going to be a long day.

There are cinnamon rolls and blueberry muffins and coffee cake spread across the counter when Olivia and I squeeze into an open spot at the bar, pouring coffee down our throats and trying to wake up. The mood is chaotic. The littles are running around, their sticky fingers touching everything and everyone they pass while my aunts and uncles mill around the kitchen. Everyone looks ridiculous in our matching Christmas pajamas. Nonna finds a design she likes sometime in August and every group is responsible for each member of their family. Olivia and I only remembered to throw ours on just before we came downstairs.

This year's theme is Santa on skis against a light blue background. Most of my aunts are wearing the long nightgown version while the uncles got pj bottoms and tops. Olivia and I are wearing sleep shorts with the T-shirt. The worst was the year she picked the onesies that made us all look like reindeer, including a hood with antlers attached. There are more than a few members of our family who should *never* wear onesies.

Once breakfast is done, it's time for our next Christmas-morning tradition.

Last night, just like every other Christmas Eve, each branch picked their spot in the family room and stacked their gifts into small piles. Once the gifts were sectioned off, and notes and milk and cookies were left for Santa, the door to the family room was shut until morning.

Here's where the brutal part comes in: No one is allowed in the room on Christmas morning until Nonna has two cups of coffee. And she drinks them slowly. So right now, all of the kids under the age of ten, lined up from youngest to oldest, are melting down in the hallway.

Olivia and I have moved to the table next to Nonna, where she's sipping her coffee. Charlie still hasn't gotten up, even though Uncle Charles keeps yelling his name from the bottom of the stairs.

"Is this decaf?" Aunt Patrice asks. She chose the pj's that look like thermal underwear, and they leave nothing to the imagination. It was a bad choice.

"Heavens to Betsy, why would we make a pot of decaf?" Aunt Maggie Mae answers. Aunt Maggie Mae is dressed in black slacks and a green sweater—she'll wear the pj's to bed but refuses to stay in them—and her hair and makeup are perfect. She brings the Evil Joes each a cup at the other end of the table, where they're sitting with their noses buried in their phones.

"We're going to have to start renting out the banquet room of the Hilton, Nonna," Olivia says. There's not one inch of space in this kitchen that isn't occupied with a human body.

"Oh, there's plenty of room," Nonna says, loving every minute of this.

Uncle Michael, who just walked down the stairs, makes a production of inching the door to the family room open and squeezing his head through the tight space. He stays like this for a few seconds, then pulls his head out and shuts the door. His eyes are wide and the kids are frozen in their spots, staring at him.

Here we go. The torture.

"Someone got a bike!" he yells, and the kids shriek.

Nonna rolls her eyes and takes another small sip from her cup, but she loves this part, too. I can remember when Charlie, Olivia, and I—along with the Evil Joes—were withering against the wall just like the little ones are now.

Not to be outdone, Jake says, "Pretty sure I saw a dollhouse in there. A pink one."

The girls scream. Loudly.

My phone vibrates on the table and I flip it over to see a text from Margot.

MARGOT: What cup is she on?

I can't help but laugh.

ME: Halfway through the second one. The littles are going nuts.

MARGOT: Just like you did

ME: How's my niece this morning?

MARGOT: I just got back from seeing her. She's gorgeous and I fell apart because I can't hold her yet. Ugly cried. Now my boobs are hooked up to these pumps and like every other part of my body, they will never be the same.

ME: God, Margot, not the visual I need this early in the morning

MARGOT: The outfits are adorable. Of course Mom has a million questions about where they came from

ME: Sorry you had to lie to her

MARGOT: Small price to pay for the visit. Thank you for coming to see us. It was the perfect gift.

I scrub my hand across my face to brush away the tears that well up. Nonna watches me, then sets her cup down.

"I think I'm ready to go in," she says.

Within minutes, there are paper and ribbon and bows whipping through the air like they're caught in hurricane-force winds. It's chaos, but the absolute best kind. Nonna circles the room, commenting on each gift she sees and delighting in the pandemonium. She stops next to me and whispers, "Your mother sent over a few things. She didn't want you to be empty-handed this morning." Nonna points to a small pile next to Olivia.

I stare at the packages with my name on them for several minutes before I start opening them, trying not to get too emotional. She got me the phone case I've been wanting, along with a new pair of boots and an assortment of my favorites from Sephora. I pop the old case off my phone and start wrestling on the new one.

Aunt Kelsey's four daughters parade around the room in their new princess dresses while Denver and Dallas battle it out with Mary and Frannie with their new lightsabers. Uncle Sal's son, Banks, is testing out his new guitar while Webb, who still isn't wearing pants, is steamrolling over everything and everyone on his new hoverboard.

Olivia struggles to open the gigantic jar of bread-and-butter pickle slices. She gets a jar like this every year, and every year it's the first thing she opens. When Olivia was five, she ate an entire container of these pickles at Aunt Kelsey's house, so when Christmas rolled around that year, Aunt Kelsey gave her a huge jar of them. There's just something about getting this ridiculously oversize jar every year that makes her so happy.

She pops one in her mouth and says, "I'm seriously going to need a nap later."

"Yeah, maybe we can sneak away before lunch."

Olivia looks at the mess around me, then nudges a small box toward me with her foot. "You forgot one," she says.

Sure enough, there's a small package wrapped in brown paper with my name on it. I tear off the wrapping and open the plain white box.

Inside, there is a silver bracelet with something hanging from it. I hold it closer so I can see what it is.

"Ooh! Is that a charm bracelet?" Olivia says.

"I think so." And then it clicks. There are two letters hanging from it—an *S* and a *G*. Surely my mom would not have bought me this.

"There's a card in the bottom of the box." Olivia hands me a small square of paper.

Sophie,

Saw this bracelet while I was shopping with my mom yesterday and thought of you. I think these letters look good together, don't you?

Merry Christmas
Griffin

I show Olivia the card, and her face scrunches up when she reads it. "Not sure what to think about that."

I tuck the card and the bracelet back in the box because, yeah, I don't either.

Ugh.

Charlie walks toward us wearing a University of Arkansas hoodie he must have gotten as a gift this morning. Olivia throws up her hand. "We're banishing you from our club."

"I'm the president of that club, so that's not possible," he says, pushing her arm down and sitting between us. "Uncle Ronnie gave me this and I'm wearing it until Uncle Sal notices.

But I'm not the one you need to be worried about. Ask Sophie about some of the colleges she's applied to."

Olivia leans forward to look at me. I know she's thinking about our old LSU pact, the one I didn't think was even relevant anymore. "Where did you apply?"

"I've applied to a bunch of different places."

"Like Massachusetts," Charlie adds.

"You hate it when it gets too cold," she says.

Charlie holds up his hands and nods, as if he's thanking her for making his point.

"I haven't decided for sure," I say.

Olivia gives me a small frown, then gets up from the chair. "It's Christmas and there are still cinnamon rolls in the kitchen. Let's go eat."

We've hit the food coma stage of the day. Papa and my uncles are sacked out in chairs while the game plays on the TV in front of them. Nonna and my aunts are still around the dining room table, visiting and drinking their weight in coffee to keep from falling asleep. The cousins have taken over the family room, since the little ones don't want to stray too far from their gifts.

"I think this is the first time I've seen the Evil Joes look happy," I say to Olivia and Charlie. The three of us are squeezed together on one of the oversize chairs. Across from us, the Evil Joes are sitting on the couch next to their boyfriends, Aiden and Brent.

"There has to be something wrong with them. The guys," Olivia adds.

The guys are exactly who I imagine Aunt Maggie Mae would expect her daughters to date. Tall, preppy, handsome. But they also seem normal, which is why we're confused.

Charlie leans in close. "Maybe they're like those pod people. Regular on the outside but some weird alien life-form on the inside."

"Or maybe the Evil Joes are only evil to us. Or maybe we're the evil ones for not seeing them the way their boyfriends do."

Both Olivia and Charlie stare at me like I've grown an extra head.

"Do I need to remind you what happened at the beach?" Charlie says.

We need to tattoo *I'm never getting over it* on his forehead.

"We all remember what happened at the beach," Olivia says.

Charlie rolls his eyes. "It's not just that. There are lots of moments like that. Remember the water park in Dallas? Field day in sixth grade? The Easter egg hunt at church when we were seven?" His voice gets louder with each incident he recalls. Olivia and I shush him.

"Evil Joes are evil," he whispers.

I push up from the chair, leaving them to their speculations over Aiden and Brent, and head to the kitchen. Lunch is over and all of the food, except for the desserts, has been cleared away. I walk to the window and peer at Wes's house. He told us last night that he'd be at his grandmother's house for most of the day, but that doesn't stop me from checking.

I hear movement behind me and spin around, but it's only Aiden—Mary Jo's boyfriend. He's carrying a couple of empty glasses and a plate.

"Hey," he says, then moves to the sink to deposit the dirty dishes.

"Hey," I say back. I grab a cookie off the plate on the counter and slide into a chair at the kitchen table.

He starts to walk out of the kitchen, but then turns toward me. "MJ told me your sister had her baby early. Same thing happened to my sister a few months ago."

I perk up. "Are they okay now?" I ask

He moves closer to the table. "Yeah, they're both good. Let me show you a picture of my nephew. He was so little when he was born, but in just a few months, he's gained a ton of weight."

Aides scrolls through the pictures on his phone with one hand while pulling out a chair with the other. Once he's seated next to me, he shows me the screen and, sure enough, there is an adorable little boy with a double chin and fat, fluffy arms.

"Ohmygod he's so cute!" I squeal.

Aiden leans forward to swipe through several shots of him.

"What's his name?" I ask.

"John," he says. "After my dad."

"So how early was he?" I ask.

Aiden looks up at the ceiling. "Um, I think maybe four or five weeks? He was in the NICU for a week, but then he was okay to go home."

It feels good to hear this. Good to see this chunky baby who started out the same way Anna has.

We're both *ooh*ing and *aah*ing over his phone, so neither of us hears Mary Jo until she's right beside us.

"Ready to go?" she says in a sharp voice. From Aiden's expression, I can tell it's one he's heard before.

"Sure, I'm ready when you are," he says. He stands up and nods to me. "See ya later."

I nod back, then look at Mary Jo. Yeah, she's pissed.

Aiden walks away, but Mary Jo stays put.

"I would think you'd be too busy with all these dates to be so flirty-flirty with my boyfriend."

"Seriously, Mary Jo, we were just talking. He was showing me pics of his nephew. You're totally overreacting."

She rolls her eyes. "Yeah, I guess that's what us Evil Joes do."

Yikes. I didn't think they knew we called them that.

Before I can come up with a response, she moves to the board and picks up one of the dry-erase markers. "I won't be able to come by in the morning to write down what your date is, so I'll just do it now."

Oh no.

This won't be good.

Mary Jo writes:

6 pm
Dinner and a movie

Huh. That doesn't *sound* bad. But then she turns around and gives me a creepy smile. The same smile she had when she turned the lock on our condo, trapping Charlie outside in his underwear.

She walks away and I'm left staring at the words she wrote like there's some secret message there to uncover. There's no way it's just dinner and a movie.

No way.

I'm not sure how long I stand there, but eventually Charlie and Olivia end up on either side of me.

"It can't be that simple," Olivia says.

"Use the 'get out of date' card. Use it now," Charlie says.

"But there's still Aunt Maggie Mae," Olivia argues.

And then we're all silent, still trying to figure out what the Evil Joes have planned.

Saturday, December 26th

Blind Date #5: Evil Joes' Pick

Olivia and I show up to Nonna's after the slowest day of work ever to find the house bursting with people. I would have thought two days without any dates would have made the excitement wear off, but it seems to have had the opposite effect.

Since Charlie, Wes, and Olivia go to the same high school as the Evil Joes, they came up with a signal if they think I should use the "get out of date free" card: dragging a finger across their neck.

Obviously, Charlie picked it.

Aunt Maggie Mae is standing over the betting chart that's in the middle of the table. "Camille, why are you picking such an early time? Sophie won't be home that soon!" Aunt Maggie Mae has been pretty obnoxious telling everyone how wonderful this boy is and what a fantastic time we're going to have.

"It's dinner and a movie," Uncle Sal says. "I would think it's pretty easy to figure out how soon it will be over."

"I'm still in the lead for Best Date," Sara reminds everyone.

The Evil Joes are here, without boyfriends this time, so I guess this isn't a triple-date sort of thing. But I'm still a little nervous about being one-on-one with a guy they chose.

I decide to ignore them and check on Margot while I'm waiting.

ME: How's Anna today?

MARGOT: Same. Still stuck in that plastic box. And everyone wants to go in during visiting hours but there are too many of us so we have to pick and of course whoever I don't pick gets their feelings hurt and then there is so much time just sitting around waiting for the next set of visiting hours

Oh God. That sounds miserable. As much as I want to be down there, I'm glad I'm not.

ME: Need me to fake an illness that will bring Mom and Dad home? It would save me from my date tonight.

MARGOT: You should be worried about that date. Seems too easy. Have you checked to see what's playing?

ME: Yeah. There are a few good movies out so maybe I'm overreacting

MARGOT: I don't think so

ME: Oh by the way, Griffin showed up here on Christmas Eve and then left me a gift

MARGOT: Hmmmm . . . how did it feel seeing him

ME: Weird. Like he's so familiar but it's also like I don't know him at all anymore

MARGOT: Did you at least get something good?

ME: If a charm bracelet with our initials on it is good. Oh and he bought it AFTER we broke up

MARGOT: Ew. It's not

"Sophie, you need to get dressed. He'll be here any minute," Aunt Maggie Mae says.

I look down at my clothes. I've got on my comfiest pair of jeans, which belonged to Jake when he was in middle school and are worn out in all the right spots, and a T-shirt I stole from Olivia two years ago. It is safe to say I did not dress to impress.

"I *am* dressed," I answer back.

Her forehead scrunches up and I know she's dying to say something. Thankfully she refrains.

A loud cry from upstairs catches everyone's attention. We look up to see Mary, one of Aunt Kelsey's daughters, standing in the hall with tears racing down her cheeks.

"I can't find Hannah Head!" she squeals.

Those five words get everyone moving. Hannah Head is what's left of a doll our older cousin Hannah gave Mary for her birthday years ago. Mary named her Hannah, but then as she lost limb after limb, then finally the torso, Hannah became Hannah Head. The same head now accompanies her everywhere, and Mary likes to wrap the hair around her index finger so she can sniff it while sucking her thumb. Hannah Head has dried snot in her hair and one eye missing, but she's Mary's prized possession and we all know there will be no peace until she's found.

My family scatters, each searching a different part of the house. I head straight to the family room, where she was watching a movie earlier, and get down on my hands and knees to search under the couch. I see the head, pushed back toward the center, and have to lie on the floor and stretch my arm underneath to grab it.

Once I have Hannah Head in my possession, I hurry toward the stairs.

But instead of finding Mary and my family, I see a guy standing there, looking a little lost. After my meeting Aiden and Brent, he's exactly what I would expect one of their friends to look like. Very cookie-cutter—with the short brown hair, muscular build, and warm brown eyes—wrapped up in a button-down and khakis.

"Hey! I'm Sophie," I say.

He looks from the doll's head to me, and I can see the disgust there.

"Oh! This belongs to my little cousin. Hold on." I move to the stairs and call for Mary. She comes racing down and launches herself at me when she sees what I'm holding. Within seconds, that crusty brown doll's hair is wrapped around her finger, and her thumb goes straight to her mouth. I hear her take a big inhale as she walks away.

"That thing looked pretty nasty," the guy says.

It is, but I hate him saying it.

"She loves that doll," I say.

The rest of the family trickles back in and the Evil Joes push their way to us.

"Oh, Nathan! You're here," Mary Jo says. She pulls his arm, bringing him closer to me.

"Nathan Henderson, this is my cousin Sophie Patrick."

He nods. "Nice to meet you."

I nod back but don't say anything.

Charlie and Wes come up behind me and I turn to gauge their reaction.

Charlie stares at Nathan, then shrugs. Wes leans in close and whispers, "He's new. Moved here a few months ago, so we don't really know him."

Olivia steps in front of me. "Hey, Nathan. I'm Sophie's cousin Olivia. So where are you taking her tonight?"

He shrugs. "I thought we'd grab something to eat and then catch a movie."

"Sounds fun," I say, then motion for Nathan to head out the front door. The sooner this date begins, the sooner it will end.

Just before I'm out of the house, Olivia whispers, "We'll

see you at the movies." Charlie and Olivia are going to a movie, too, for backup. I'm not sure if they invited Wes or not.

I don't look back at her, but I nod, then follow Nathan to his truck, which is jacked up to a ridiculous height. He opens the door for me and helps me inside.

"Ready to go?" Nathan asks once we're both inside.

I nod again and realize if I don't start talking soon he's going to think I'm incapable of conversation.

"So," I ask. "I heard you're new. Where did you move from?"

"Dallas," he answers. "My dad got transferred for his job."

We ride in silence another few minutes. I glance around his truck, trying to get some idea of what he's like, and spot an air freshener with the Hooters logo hanging from the rearview mirror.

Um, okay.

He pulls into the drive-through lane of a fast-food burger place.

"Is this cool?" he asks.

I nod again, trying to keep the disbelief off my face. I'm not assuming he should take me to some five-star restaurant, but I was hoping at least I wouldn't be eating in my lap.

We drive up to the intercom, and a voice crackles through the system. "Can I take your order?"

Nathan leans out of the window and says, "I'll have a double bacon cheeseburger with everything, large fry, large Coke."

"Will that be all?"

He spins around to me. "What do you want?"

"Uh . . . I guess chicken nuggets."

"You want the meal?" he asks.

I shrug. "Sure."

He rattles off my order and drives to the window. Once we have our food, he's unwrapping his burger before we even get out of the parking lot.

"Here's yours," he says, handing me a bag.

So I guess we're not even going to pull over to eat.

He's trying to drive while chowing down on his huge burger, and mayo and mustard and bits of tomato are flying through the air with each bite he takes. I notice it's full of onions, too, so there's a really good chance I won't be breaking my good-night-kiss dry spell.

I keep one hand close to the center console in case I need to grab the wheel.

We talk a little, but it's the most basic form of small talk, and suddenly I hate that the movie theater is on the other side of town.

My phone dings and I take a peek while Nathan is slurping the last little bit of Coke from his drink.

MARGOT: I didn't get a pic of this one. Is he cute?

ME: Uhh kind of? We're not clicking though. This is going to be a long night

MARGOT: That stinks. You can always fake a headache and go home early

ME: Yeah, I feel something coming on

"Who are you texting?" Nathan asks. "Your ex-boyfriend? MJ told me all about him."

"No," I say pointedly. "My sister. She had a baby a few days ago and they're both still in the hospital."

I wait for him to ask me how they are, but nothing. Yeah, I definitely feel a headache coming on.

For the first time, I look out of the window and realize we're on some random road in the middle of nowhere. Oh my God. He's a serial killer and he's taking me to the woods to kill me.

"I thought we were going to the movies?" I ask.

"There's this cool drive-in movie place right outside of town. I think you'll really like it."

I've never been to a drive-in movie. It does sound kind of cool—if I were with anyone but Nathan—but I need to let Olivia and Charlie know we won't be at the regular theater in town. And give them directions, just in case he does dump my dead body in the middle of nowhere.

Just as I fire off a text to them, we turn off the highway onto a gravel road, under a vintage-looking sign that doesn't look restored. In fact, it looks like it's missing most of the bulbs.

Okay, so now I'm convinced I'm going to die.

I twist around in my seat, trying to get my bearings, when we stop at a small booth. There's a middle-aged guy inside who sells us our tickets.

"Tune into FM 94.3 to hear the audio," he says just before we drive away. There are a few other cars scattered around. I take a deep breath. I'm definitely just being paranoid. Right?

Once we pull into our spot, Nathan flips on the radio. Some cheesy elevator music floats through the speakers. The gigantic screen up ahead is blank. We're parked on a gravel lot, but the surrounding area is full of overgrown weeds and bushes. It's dark outside and a little creepy.

"So what movie is playing?" I ask.

Nathan makes a show of looking around. "I'm not sure. I think it's a Christmas one, though."

"Have you ever been here?" I ask.

He shakes his head. "No. MJ told me about it. Sounded cool."

I scan the area and see a gift shop on the far side of the lot. This is so bizarre. I check my phone discreetly, but neither Olivia nor Charlie has replied yet.

I scan the other cars. "Have you noticed all of the other cars only have one person in them?"

He turns and takes in each vehicle. "Well, maybe their dates are in the gift shop? Or in the bathroom?"

I turn back toward the gift shop. The building isn't much bigger than Nonna's kitchen. "It must be pretty crowded in there."

The music crackles and I see lights flicker on the screen. Here we go.

On the screen, two girls in elf hats and skimpy costumes are in a workshop surrounded by old-timey-looking toys.

"Those are some seriously cute elves," Nathan says, his eyes glued to the screen.

My upper lip curls.

"That one on the left, especially," he adds.

Okay, he's the worst date ever. I check my phone again, willing Olivia or Charlie to respond. I may not have to lie about this headache.

Then a very muscular Santa comes on-screen, wearing only pants and a Santa hat. There seems to be a great deal of oil lathered over his bare chest.

What is happening?

It only takes another twenty seconds to tell what kind of movie this is. The two elves start talking about how bad they've been, and in another couple of seconds, they're only wearing the elf hats and NOTHING ELSE.

Repeat: NOTHING ELSE.

And don't get me started on the sounds coming out of the stereo.

I whip around to look at Nathan, who has yet to tear his

gaze from the huge screen in front of us. At least he seems surprised.

"How did I not know about this drive-in before tonight?" he asks.

And that's the last straw. I jump out of the car and run to the gift shop, nearly tripping on every stick and rock in my path while I pull up the contacts in my phone.

Wes answers on the second ring. "What's wrong?" he says.

"Um, can you come get me? Please. Pretty please. Like right now." My voice is about two octaves higher than normal.

"Where are you?" he asks.

"I'll send you a pin. I'm okay, but I can't stay here and I don't want to ride back with him. There's a gift shop. I'll be in there. Oh, and Evil Joes are evil."

I end the call and send him a pin just as I push through the gift shop doors. My eyes are assaulted by posters and books and toys and, *oh my good God*, things I wish I didn't know existed.

There's a woman behind the counter who seems surprised to see me. She looks as old as Nonna, but her hair is an orangey yellow and it's piled a foot high on the top of her head. Her name tag reads *Alma*. She's got a cigarette in one hand, and smoke circles her like a halo.

"Hey, hon. What can I help you with?"

"Do you have a bathroom?"

She nods and gestures to a door on her left. I glance out of the window and see Nathan barreling toward the gift shop.

I point to him and say, "Tell that guy our date is over. I have someone on the way to pick me up." And then I race to the bathroom.

I can hear Alma relay my message, but it doesn't stop Nathan from banging on the bathroom door.

"Come on, Sophie. I didn't know. I swear. I'll take you home."

The bathroom is small and smells horrible. I stand in the center with my hands plastered to my sides so I don't touch anything.

"Go away. I have a friend picking me up."

He argues with me halfheartedly while I ignore him. I'm thankful he doesn't test the fragile lock on the door. Finally, I hear him say, "Whatever." Then it's quiet.

A few minutes later, there's another knock on the door.

"Hon? He's gone if you want to come out."

I hesitate, then open the door a crack. The woman pulls out a stool and puts it next to the counter. "Have a seat while you wait for your ride."

I thank her and keep my gaze trained on the floor as I walk over to the counter. I check my phone and see a text from Wes saying he's on his way. Relief flows through me.

"Want to talk about it, sweetie?" the woman asks.

I'm about to tell her no, but for some reason I start talking and don't stop. I tell her about Griffin and the dates and Nonna and Hundred Hands Harold and Wes and Margot and the baby. She doesn't seem shocked by my word vomit, just nods along and lights another cigarette.

"So this boy that brought you here . . ."

"Nathan," I say.

"Yes, Nathan. You think he did that because some evil person told him to?"

I let out a sharp laugh. "The Evil Joes. My twin cousins, Jo Lynn and Mary Jo. Evil Joes are evil," I say, mimicking Charlie. I will never doubt him again.

The woman nods along. "But the boy on his way to pick you up . . ."

"Wes."

"He's just a friend?"

I chew on my bottom lip. "Yes. Maybe more. Maybe not. I don't know for sure. I'm so confused."

She takes a long drag and I watch the fire burn halfway up the cigarette. "It's awful nice of that boy to come all this way to pick you up. Do you get to go on one of these dates with him?"

"That's really not up to me," I say. "Someone else has to pick him."

A frown crosses her face. "Well, that doesn't seem right."

Lights sweep across the front window of the small gift

shop, and I see Wes's truck. But before I can get off my stool, he's barging through the front door.

I can tell when he registers the contents of the gift shop, because he blushes slightly.

"Did he pick this place, or the Evil Joes?" Wes asks. "And where is he?"

"The Evil Joes, hon," Alma answers for me. "And that boy left just after your friend here locked herself in the bathroom."

He moves closer to me. "Are you okay?"

"Yes!" I can't hop off of the stool fast enough. "This is just so completely awkward." As we turn to leave, I stop and throw my arms around Alma. "Thank you," I say.

She hugs me back and whispers, "Maybe you should be the one picking your dates."

Once we're out of the shop, I stuff my hands in my pockets. "I don't even have words for this," I say in a quiet voice.

"I didn't know anything like this existed," he says back, gazing up at the ridiculously large screen.

I punch him in the arm and he looks back at me, blushing. Then I start laughing. Wes joins in and before long we're both doubled over.

Finally, we leave the drive-in and get back on the highway headed home.

"Okay, spill," he says.

I give him the rundown. "The funny thing is, I really think he was as shocked as I was. But even if he was, I couldn't ride back with him. I mean, I've never felt so uncomfortable in my life!"

Wes shakes his head. "I'm glad you called me. What do you think your grandmother is going to say?"

I was thinking about that almost the entire time I was waiting for Wes. "You know they'll just play dumb and say Nathan picked the movie. *Oh, Nonna! We had no idea!*"

"And then Maggie Mae will be like, *That boy is a card short of a full deck!*" Wes's imitation of my aunt's accent is dead-on, and I crack up all over again. He throws me his phone. "Open the group text and tell them your date is over. Everyone is going to flip."

I open the group conversation, and scroll through the texts where everyone is recounting the bets they made on tonight's date. The majority of my family seems to think I'll make it until at least 8:30 p.m.

"Seriously?" I say to Wes. He grins and shrugs. I turn back to his phone and type:

WES: This is Sophie. Date was over approximately 20 minutes ago.

His phone starts dinging immediately, but I toss it onto the seat.

After a few miles, Wes says, "I thought I was going to lose it the whole drive here. You scared the crap out of me."

"I'm sorry," I say. "I should have explained what was going on, but I was so freaked out. This is the second night I've ruined for you."

"It's all good. I'm glad you called me." He pauses a moment then adds, "You haven't ruined anything."

I turn and gaze out the window at the dark night blurring past us. If I'm not careful, Wes is going to completely ruin me.

❄ ♥ ❄

"They're here," Wes says as we pull up behind one of the Evil Joes' cars.

I walk through the front door with Wes right behind me. Mary Jo and Jo Lynn are sitting at the counter with Nonna. Each of them has a slice of apple pie and a scoop of ice cream in front of them.

I can tell they're here for damage control. But I can't let them win like that.

"Yum, that looks good! Can I get a piece?" I turn to Wes. "You want one?"

"Of course!" he says loudly, winking at me. "I never turn down Nonna's cooking!"

Okay, so we're not the best actors.

Nonna jumps up from her stool and starts fixing us a plate. "How was your date? You're back earlier than I expected. Was the movie good?"

The Evil Joes are poised and ready. I grin.

"I enjoyed it, but I'm not sure Nathan did. He got a little squeamish and had to leave, so I called Wes to pick me up."

Jo Lynn starts to say something, but Mary Jo elbows her in the ribs.

"Well, that's not good," Nonna says, and glances at the Evil Joes with a pitying look.

"So you really liked it?" Jo Lynn says. "We thought you would. We figured it would be just your kind of movie."

Okay, so they want to play dirty.

I cock my head to the side. "Actually, there were these two girls in the movie that reminded me a lot of you two. They were really close, and they dressed the same and liked the same things. Y'all should go check it out."

Wes lets out a sharp laugh but covers it up quickly.

Giving me identical withering stares, the Evil Joes move away from the counter in perfect unison and hug Nonna.

"We have to go, Nonna. Thanks for the pie," Mary Jo says.

"And the ice cream," Jo Lynn adds.

And then they're gone.

Wes and I take their spots at the counter, and Nonna puts a plate in front of each of us.

"So how was it really?" Nonna asks once we hear the front door close. "I love those girls, but they never come by without their parents. I felt like I was waiting for disaster to strike."

"Nonna, it was fine. Really."

Nonna passes by Wes and pats him on the shoulder. "Well, I'm glad she had you to count on. Thank you for picking her up." Just before she leaves the room, she says, "Camille stopped by earlier, if you're curious about tomorrow night."

Wes and I swivel around at the same time toward the board.

Show your team spirit because you've got tickets on center ice!
Shreveport Mudbugs vs. Odessa Jackalopes
Be ready at 2:30—Puck drops at 3!

"Oh wow!" I say. Then read it again. "Is that a hockey game?" I actually had no idea there was a hockey team in Shreveport.

Wes nods. "Those games are fun."

"Not gonna lie, out of all the dates I thought Camille would pick for me, hockey is the absolute last thing I would have guessed." Aunt Camille's complete and utter love of animals is a well-known fact, so I would have put money on this date taking place at a shelter.

"So do you go to their games?" I ask. I want to kick myself when I hear the breathless way I asked him that. I need to have a serious talk with myself.

"Sometimes. My dad's company is one of the sponsors." He looks at me a second and then adds, "Maybe I'll see if Olivia and Charlie want to go."

Before I can even think about how big of a distraction that will be, Charlie and Olivia come bounding through the back kitchen door. Speak of the devil(s).

"So you send a text that says your date might murder you, and then we don't hear *anything* until you text from Wes's phone," Olivia says. "Definitely going to need some details."

I hold up a hand and shush her. "Tonight has been . . . interesting."

"So what happened?" Charlie asks as he steals my plate and finishes off my pie.

Wes tells them everything before I get a chance. Charlie nods knowingly. "I told y'all. Evil."

"Yes, Charlie. I will never doubt you again."

"Of all the ways I thought 'dinner and a movie' could go wrong, that one never occurred to me." Olivia moves closer to the board, then spins around with wide eyes. "Oh yay! Let's go, too! Wes, get tickets from your dad," she says. "Maybe we can sit close together!"

Yeah. It's going to be very distracting.

Sunday, December 27th

Blind Date #6: Aunt Camille's Pick

The breakfast crowd has left, Nonna is upstairs getting ready for church, and Papa is taking a midmorning nap in his chair in the living room, so I thought this was the perfect, quiet moment to catch up with Addie.

"So Griffin dropped off a gift for me," I tell her.

"What was it?"

"Hold on, I'll send you a pic." I take the bracelet out of box and put it on so that the letters lie against my wrist. I snap a pic, then send it to Addie.

"Did you get it?"

She's quiet a second, then asks, "Is that y'all's initials?"

"Yep." I read her the note that came with it.

"Huh," she says.

"Is it weird?"

"Well, it's weird because it sounds like he got it for you after you broke up with him. And it's also kind of *ugh* that he waited until the day before Christmas to buy your gift."

I think about the wrapped gift under our tree at home

with his name on it that I bought three weeks ago.

The kitchen door opens and closes, but I don't get up. I'm shocked when I see Wes standing in the door of the family room.

"I'll call you back in a minute," I say to Addie, and end the call before she can ask why.

"Hey," I say. "What's up?" Is my voice too loud? I think it's too loud. Between eavesdropping on his conversation with Charlie in the car and his coming to my rescue last night, I officially feel awkward around him.

He drops down beside me on the couch and holds out a small tube of lip gloss. "I think this fell out of your bag. Found it in my truck this morning."

"Oh! Yes, that's mine!" Yep. Too loud.

I reach out to take it, and he glances down at my wrist. Before I can stop him, he holds my hand up high enough so he can study it. "Is this new?"

And I see the moment he realizes what the charm is.

"Yeah," I answer.

He lets my hand fall.

"Well, anyway. Just wanted to get that back to you. And check on Margot and Anna."

He's closed off now. I want to chuck this bracelet across the room. It's like Griffin marked me with this thing.

"Margot and Anna are about the same. I talked to her earlier and she sent a few more pictures," I say. "Mom said they'll be in the hospital a bit longer, but that's normal, since she's a preemie."

Wes nods and stares off into the distance.

"Were you able to get tickets to the hockey game?" I ask.

He nods, still not looking at me. "Yeah, Dad had some tickets they weren't using." He gets up from the couch and moves toward the door. "Well, I guess I'll see you there."

I want to say *Please come back* or *I think this bracelet is weird* or any number of things, but all that comes out is "Okay."

At some point while I've been staring at the door, Nonna turns up all dressed for church.

"Well, I'm off. Be back shortly."

I hop up from my chair. I need a distraction. "Wait!" I say, and Nonna stops at the back door. "Give me a few minutes to change. I'm coming with you."

The church is old and big and really beautiful. We squeeze into an open space three rows back from the altar. I stare straight ahead, waiting for things to get started, but Nonna twists around in the pew, checking out who's here like she's taking roll.

I lean closer and whisper, "Who are you looking for?"

Her gray hair tickles my cheek. "This is the perfect place to scope out boys. That's what you need, a good boy who goes to church on Sunday."

And now I want to run for my life. She's trying to set me up *in church*?

"Oh look," she says, loud enough to get everyone's attention in the rows around us. They all swivel around to see what she's pointing out. "Shirley's grandson is sitting with her, and he's grown up into a fine-looking young man." Nonna nudges me. "Sophie, what do you think about him?"

And now everyone is trying to check out Shirley's grandson. I cover my face with my hands so no one can see it turn bright red.

The woman sitting in front of us leans over the pew. "He's staying with her because he got kicked out of school for drugs," the woman says. She whispers the word *drugs* so quietly I can barely hear it.

"Oh, well, that won't do," Nonna says.

Peeking through my fingers to watch this train wreck, I see the woman stretch even closer. I'm afraid she's going to topple right over into our laps. "Have you seen my grandson, Thomas? He's a nice boy!" Her head nods dramatically to the guy sitting next to her, who looks as freaked out as I am. I give him my very best *I'm sorry our grandmothers are so embarrassing* look.

He nods and turns back around.

Nonna pats the woman on the shoulder and says, "Fine-looking boy!"

Thankfully, the organ music swells and fills the room, and the rest of Nonna's words are drowned out by the choir in the balcony above us.

❄ ♥ ❄

I'm at the kitchen table while Nonna stands at the stove, making a big pot of spaghetti, and it's the calm before the storm. By noon, everyone will be here for Sunday lunch.

"Those two are getting ridiculous," Nonna says, pointing to the date board. Uncle Sal and Uncle Michael are still fighting over who gets to pick the date for date eight. There is sticky note over sticky note, each of them trying to get his name on top.

"You're going to have to make a ruling on that, because I'm not going on two dates in one day."

Nonna clucks her tongue. "It'll work out."

She goes back to cooking and I go back to waiting for Addie to text me.

There's a soft *ping* when Griffin's name appears on the screen, and my belly does a flip. I haven't heard from him at all since Christmas Eve.

I swipe open his message.

GRIFFIN: Did you get the gift I left for you?

I started a thank-you text to him a dozen times but never pressed SEND. Mainly because I'm not sure what to think about the gift.

ME: I did. Thank you. When did you drop it off?

GRIFFIN: Drove back over Christmas Eve but no one could find you so I left it with your grandmother

We had probably already left to go see Margot and Anna. That must be why Nonna knew we were gone.

GRIFFIN: Just want to tell you again I'm ok with you trying to figure out how you feel but I'm also glad I haven't seen any more pics of you with other guys

I don't have a response for this. And then I can't help but laugh when I think about what a pic from my date last night with Nathan would have looked like. Maybe one of us in his truck with the fast food spread out across our laps and scenes from the X-rated movie playing in front of us? Or maybe I should have posted one of me and Alma with the array of adult toys behind us?

But what's really killing me about Griffin's text is the fact he's *okay* with me going on these dates. Part of me doesn't care if he's okay with it or not—this is about me, not him. And the other part of me wonders, if I were really in love with someone, would I be okay seeing them go on dates with someone else?

Thankfully, I'm saved from responding when Nonna asks me to take the garlic bread out of the oven.

Within minutes, people start streaming through the back

door, and the noise level increases by 1,000 percent. I've given some thought as to how I'm going to act when I see the Evil Joes, but I'm not prepared when Aunt Maggie Mae and Uncle Marcus come in the door with only Jo Lynn. I keep staring at the door, waiting for Mary Jo, but she never shows.

"Okay, something is weird," Olivia says behind me. "They are always together. Like, always."

"I know," I say.

"And I had this speech all worked out! I was going to really give it to them for what they did to you last night."

Before I can tell her not to worry, Charlie skids into the room and stops right in front of us.

"Wondering why Mary Jo isn't here?" he asks.

Olivia punches him in the shoulder. "Of course, spill it."

He leans in close. "Aiden broke up with her last night."

"Why?" Olivia asks in a shocked voice.

"From what I heard, she accused him of flirting with Soph. Lost it on him. It sounds like she does this all the time and he's over it."

"He was not flirting with me!" I say. "He was showing me pictures of his nephew." Oh God. I shouldn't feel bad for her, but a tiny part of me does. I know how awful a breakup feels.

"Stop it right now, Soph," Charlie says. "I see that look on your face and we're not feeling sorry for her!"

Nonna passes by and shoos us off, telling us to set the table.

"So do you think Nonna's gonna set up a date board for her?" Olivia asks a few minutes later as she sets down the plates. I follow behind her with the silverware.

"I have no idea!" I say. We move on to the extra table Nonna pulled out last week, which Olivia, Charlie, Sara, Graham, Jake, and I have claimed as our own. Jake calls it the OSFTBT (One Step From The Big Table) as opposed to the KT (Kiddie Table) and HCR (High Chair Row).

At last, Aunt Patrice notices the empty bar stool at the kitchen counter.

"Where's Mary Jo?" she asks.

Everyone at the OSFTBT stops what they're doing and looks up.

Aunt Maggie Mae spins around on her stool. "She woke up feeling poorly, so we told her to stay home and rest. She'll be right as rain before long."

"Does she honestly think she can keep anything secret in this family?" Sara whispers.

"You underestimate how scared everyone is of Aunt Maggie Mae. We'll all talk about it, but not in front of her," Jake adds.

Graham nods along. "I bet even Nonna doesn't say anything."

And now I feel even worse for Mary Jo. Even though I hated the attention from the blind-date board when it first happened, I can't deny that it's brought me closer to my family in a weird sort of way. It feels pretty nice to have so many people rooting for your happiness. And Mary Jo may miss her chance at a piece of that.

Of course the family stays after Nonna's spaghetti lunch to see who's picking me up for the hockey game. Well, everyone except Aunt Maggie Mae and her crew.

"I have to work late tomorrow," Uncle Ronnie says. "Somebody needs to FaceTime me during the pickup so I don't miss it."

Charlie is standing next to Graham by the staircase. He leans close and says, "Those hockey games last about two hours. If it starts at three, then the game would be over around five. And it's about a twenty-minute ride from the arena back here."

Graham holds up a hand. "But that's only if she doesn't bail halfway through like last night. I thought she'd at least wait until the end of the movie before she ditched that guy."

Jake won the bet last night—only because he heard *dinner* but not *movie*—and has been rubbing it in everyone's face all day long. Charlie and Graham are determined to beat him tonight.

I lean in close. "You want the inside scoop? Aunt Camille probably picked someone halfway decent, so I don't foresee leaving early."

Charlie and Graham smile as they scratch their names in at 5:25 and 5:30.

"But you owe me half if you win," I say before walking away.

"Hey," Uncle Ronnie squeals from across the room. "Y'all got some insider info the rest of us don't know about?"

Charlie shakes his head and rolls his eyes. "Please. Sophie's a wild card. Never know what she's gonna do on one of these dates."

I turn to Uncle Ronnie and shrug. "There's some truth in that."

Wes pops in just before the designated time for my date's arrival. "Hey," I say when he stops next to Olivia and me.

He nods to me. "Hey."

Before I can say anything else, the doorbell rings and a quiet hush falls over the crowd.

"This is getting ridiculous, people," I say as I push through my family to get to the door. Several family members scramble to finish placing their bets.

I swing open the door and am surprised to see a familiar face on the other side.

"Hey!" I say enthusiastically.

"Hey," Wyatt says as he steps through the door, giving me a quick hug. I met Wyatt last summer when Aunt Camille roped all of us into helping at the huge pet-adoption thing. Wyatt and I bathed all of the dogs before the event started so they would have the best chance of being rescued. He's a really nice guy, and we have at least one thing in common—the inability to tell Aunt Camille no—but mostly I'm relieved that this date should hold very few surprises.

"Wait! Foul!" Uncle Michael calls out. "They already know each other. Therefore this can't be a blind date."

Aunt Camille rushes forward. "Wrong. She didn't know he was the one she was going out with tonight. That is the very definition of a blind date."

Wyatt and I just stare at them. They've definitely gone off the rails, and it's only 2:30.

"We've only met once before," Wyatt says. "And we really don't know each other."

I hold up my hands. "If we don't leave now, we'll miss the beginning of the game. And since I've never been to a hockey game before, I *really* don't want that to happen. We'll see y'all later." I grab Wyatt's hand and pull him through the open door. "Oh, and don't wait up. We may stop for ice cream on the way home." I wink at Graham and Charlie. The uncles huddle together and whisper worriedly.

Aunt Camille waves from the front porch and says, "I'll see y'all there!"

"Is she coming with us?" I ask Wyatt on the way to his car.

Wyatt looks back over his shoulder, then to me. His complexion is super pale, so he can't hide the slight blush that spreads across his cheeks. "I have no idea. She asked me if I wanted to take you to this game, and I said of course. Then she handed me some tickets. That's all I know."

We catch up on the way to the arena. He goes to the same high school as Olivia, Charlie, and Wes, but he doesn't know them well because it's such a huge school. It's hard for me to imagine, since mine is so small. We chat about senior year and college selections, and before long, we're here.

Wyatt pulls his car up to the gate designated for season ticket holders. "Your aunt gave us a parking pass, too," he says.

This is blowing my mind. I never even knew there was a hockey team here. And now Aunt Camille is a major hockey enthusiast?

Once we've parked, I get out of the car and scan the area. "Why do all of these people have their dogs with them?"

Wyatt and I spin in a circle and, yes, almost everyone walking to the entrance has a dog on a leash. Small dogs. Big dogs. Everything in between. Suddenly Aunt Camille's choice of date is making more sense.

"I have no idea," he answers. Then he stops abruptly and points to a large banner hanging from the side of the building that reads:

BRING YOUR POOCH DAY!
All Dogs Welcome at the Game
(Owners optional)

"Oh wow," Wyatt mutters.

Wyatt hands our tickets over to be scanned and we make our way inside. The lobby area is full of tables from local animal rescue missions, pet grooming business, and veterinarians. There are even pets available for adoption. If I didn't think my mom would absolutely kill me, I'd totally be leaving here with something cute and furry.

Just before we enter the short tunnel that will take us to our seats, we see Aunt Camille at a table for the same pet rescue group we helped her with last summer. We stop and wave.

"Isn't this wonderful?" she screams from across the room.

"It's pretty exciting!" I scream back, a little worried about my volume. I shouldn't be, though—it's impossible to be heard over the barking.

Wyatt studies the tickets as we make our way inside the arena. The music is loud and fun, and the announcer is yelling about the Doggie Parade on Ice that will happen at the first intermission.

"Need help finding your seats?" a man with a Mudbugs T-shirt asks Wyatt.

"Please," Wyatt says, then hands the tickets over.

"Ah! You're in one of the boxes." The man points to several squared-off areas right next to the glass. In each squared-off area is a sectional sofa and a couple of big puffy recliners like the one Papa has. "You're in the one in the middle. Right at center ice."

"Okay, thanks," Wyatt answers. We exchange a big-eyed look, then I follow him to our seats.

Each area is enclosed with a short wall that is about the same height as the sofa with just a small opening to slip inside. There's also a coffee table in front of the couch, which holds a tray with a couple of bottles of water.

Wyatt walks up to the glass and says, "This is pretty cool. I mean, we're right here, practically on the ice."

I pick up a note propped against the bottled waters, which reads, *Enjoy the game! Love, Aunt Camille.* "I guess if there's a way to see your first hockey game, this is it," I say with a grin. It's cold in here, way colder than I expected, and I can't help the shiver that rolls through me.

Wyatt takes off his jacket and throws it around my shoulders.

"No, you'll be too cold without your jacket," I say, trying to give it back. He pushes my hand away lightly.

"I've got a long-sleeve shirt on under this pullover. I'm good."

I pull it closer to me and sit in the corner of one of the couches. This box is pretty cool, but it's an awfully big space for just the two of us. I look up toward the sea of faces—human and canine—that rise up behind us in the regular seats, and it feels a little like we're in a fishbowl.

"I feel like we'll be watched as much as the game," I say. Wyatt turns around to look up at the stands. Just then, Aunt Camille enters the box.

"So what do you think?" she says.

I'm not sure if she means the box seats or the four little puppies she's carrying.

"Oh my goodness! Look how adorable!" I squeal. I peel one of them out of her arms and bury my nose in its fur.

She hands Wyatt the other three and then motions to another woman, whose arms are just as full. "Bring them in here, Donna!"

Donna doubles the amount of puppies in our box. They crawl over the furniture, knocking down the bottles of water, and rolling all over each other across the carpet.

"Donna and I are going to spend the game gathering signatures to remodel the dog park, so we need somewhere for these fur babies to hang out."

"Oh, okay," I say. Wyatt has a puppy gnawing on his shoelaces while I have one clinging to the hem of my jeans.

"Just shut the gate and they'll be fine," Aunt Camille says, then she and Donna take off.

"We totally should have expected this," Wyatt says.

"We really should have," I answer.

The puppies explore the small square area, and we both notice one of them has already peed on the carpet.

"Do you think they can escape?" he asks.

I shrug. "Maybe we should help them?" I'm only half joking.

Just as Wyatt and I are able to clear a space on the couch

to sit, I hear Olivia scream from somewhere behind us, "Sooooppphhhieeee!"

I twist around and scan each row until I find her. They're on the very top row—basically as far away from us as possible.

Throwing my arm up, I wave and she waves back. I expected to see Charlie and Wes—both of them grin and wave at me from their nosebleed seats—but I wasn't expecting to see Sara, Graham, and Jake, too.

"Is that your family up there?" Wyatt asks.

I spin back around. "Yes. And I had no idea they were all coming. This date thing has moved to a really weird level where my family feels overly invested."

Wyatt laughs and sits down next to me. "I think it's cool you have a big family. Mine doesn't even fill up my mom's dining room table."

The lights dim and a spotlight shines on the ice, highlighting a girl in a fancy red dress and skates who sings the National Anthem.

Just as she finishes singing, Olivia says, "Hey!"

I swivel around on the couch. My family members are standing at the gate to the box, looking as eager to be let in as the puppies are eager to get out. Wes stands toward the back as if he isn't quite sure what he's doing here.

Wyatt must be able to read their expressions, too, because he says, "Y'all want to sit down here with us?"

Anyone listening can tell he's just being nice, but they immediately jump inside.

Charlie plops down on a recliner with one of the puppies in his lap. "Man, this is how you're supposed to watch one of these games." Graham and Jake are leaning over the short wall so they can chat with the girls sitting in the next box. Sara and Olivia sit on the floor, even though the carpet looks questionable, and both are completely covered up in puppies within seconds.

I've never seen a hockey game before, even on TV, so I spend equal time during the first period watching the ice and making sure none of the dogs escape. It's hard not to be mesmerized by the action right in front of us . . . as much as we can be while also wrangling eight puppies.

The announcer screams, "Power play!" and everyone cheers.

"What does that mean?" I ask to no one in particular.

Wyatt opens his mouth to answer, but Jake plops down on the couch next to me.

"Number twenty-three on the other team is in the box for slashing, so that means we have more players on the ice than they do," he says.

Graham sits on the floor in front of me and scoops three of the puppies in his lap. "It's the best time to try to score."

Players slam each other against the Plexiglas wall, and we're inches from the action. Thanks to the running commentary by

Jake and Graham, I now have a working knowledge of power plays, lighting the lamp, and breakaways.

Wyatt leans around Jake and says, "I'm heading to the restroom. Want me to bring anything back from the concession stand?"

Jake says, "Popcorn!" I elbow him in the side. "What?"

I give him a look. "I'm good, Wyatt. Thanks!"

Wyatt nods and leaves the box. Jake gets into a very technical conversation with Graham about some penalty the Mudbugs just got, and I slide off the couch and move closer to Wes. He's barely inside our area, sitting on the arm of the couch, with his eyes glued to the ice.

"Hey," I say.

He gives me a quick glance and says, "Hey."

"This is a good game!" I say with a tad too much enthusiasm.

He nods. "Yeah, they're having a good season so far."

"Well, I'm officially halfway through these dates," I say for lack of anything else. I'm not sure what he thought when he saw that bracelet, but I want him to know I'm still very much not back with Griffin.

He looks at me, and I can't read his expression. "I know you'll be glad when things can get back to normal."

I shrug. "I don't know. It's not how I was expecting to spend the break, but I have to admit, things have been better than I thought they would."

I feel like I'm talking in code. Why can't I be as direct as he was in the car with Charlie? *I'd rather be doing nothing with the three of you than anything with Griffin.*

"Yeah, I'm sure by now Griffin realizes he made a stupid mistake."

Before I can set Wes straight, the Mudbugs make a goal and the entire arena explodes in cheers. Most of the crowd throws small red plastic crawfish out onto the ice, and then these cute kids on skates pick them all up with shovels almost as big as they are.

Wyatt sits down beside me. "Looks like I got back just in time," he says, nodding toward the ice.

Wes hops up and moves to the couch with Charlie, Jake, and Graham.

"I'm sorry we got invaded like this," I say. And I *am* sorry. This isn't fair to Wyatt.

He shrugs. "It's okay. It's not like we don't have the room for them."

Aunt Camille shows up just as the first period is over. "Oh good! This will make things easier," she says when she spots the crowd in our box.

At this point, I get a little panicky anytime a relative who's set me up on a date says something I don't understand. "Makes what easier?"

"Each puppy has a person! So much easier for the parade."

On the ice, pet owners are lining up with their dogs. "Who Let the Dogs Out?" is playing over the speakers, and the dogs go nuts every time the singer makes that barking noise.

Aunt Camille starts passing around leashes. "Everyone pick a puppy and follow me!"

"What is happening?" Olivia asks.

Graham's eyes get huge. "Are we really going out on the ice with these dogs?"

"So what if one of them poos out there?" Charlie asks.

Wes laughs. "I guess if it's yours, you clean it up."

Aunt Camille leads us to a side door near our box and holds it open while we file out onto the ice. I've never walked on ice before and I only make it about two steps before I'm sliding. My arms flail around, trying to find anything to hold on to, but it's useless. I'm going down.

Seconds before I make a complete fool out of myself, someone grabs me by the waist and pulls me back to my feet. I expect it to be Wyatt, but it's Wes.

"Shuffle your feet instead of trying to walk," he says, then lets go of me. But I haven't caught my balance yet, and I start to fall again.

His hands tighten on my hips, anchoring me to the ice. "If I let go, are you going to fall?" he asks.

My breath catches. "I think I've got it now."

He whispers, "Remember: shuffle, don't walk," then he's gone.

I take his advice and shuffle my way toward the starting

line, my heart beating fast. Sara squeals, "Look at that cute little fluffy one wearing the crawfish costume!"

Olivia moves beside her, and they *ooh* and *aah* over the other dogs while I'm praying my feet don't fly out from under me again. My puppy doesn't seem to like the cold, so she's currently trying to sit on my feet. Not helping.

Wyatt slides up next to me and stays by my side as we make our way around the rink. "Everything okay?" he asks. I nod quickly, hoping my cheeks don't look too flushed. The barking echoes off the ice, and we pass more than one yellow spot.

Finally, we finish the lap around the rink, the Zamboni following slowly behind us, and get back to our box just as the game starts up again. Every time one of the Mudbug players smashes one of their opponents' faces into the glass in front of us, Graham and Jake bang on it. Those poor guys are getting beat up from both sides.

I make an effort during the second period to stick close to Wyatt. We try to talk over the action in front of us—the barking dogs and the fans screaming "You suck" every time the other team loses the puck—but I feel like we're fighting a losing battle. I'm more in tune to Wes's movements in the box than what Wyatt's saying right next to me.

By the time we get to the second intermission, I feel like this game can't be over soon enough.

"How are they going to top the doggie parade from the

first intermission?" Sara asks. She's back on the floor, covered in puppies, and I know she's already trying to figure out how to take one of them home.

A man skates out onto the ice once the players have left for the locker room. He's wearing a tuxedo and holding a microphone; his voice booms through the arena.

"Ladies and gentlemen," he says. "It's that time!"

The song "Kiss Me" starts playing over the speakers and red hearts bounce across the huge screen that hangs over the rink. My stomach drops.

"Here comes the Kiss Cam!" the announcer yells.

The camera stops on an older couple, and they smile and wave, then lean into each other for a quick kiss. The camera pans the crowd again, stopping on a couple who seem embarrassed. They bump heads and start laughing.

Several more couples kiss, and the song winds down. But then the announcer says, "We have a very special couple with us tonight! Sophia and Wyatt!"

And then, *oh my God*, there we are on the big screen.

"They're on their first date! Hopefully it's not too soon to get that first kiss!"

I want to crawl in a hole and die. People in the stands are yelling at us to kiss, and everyone in our box is laughing and taking pictures of us. Well, everyone except Wes. I can't help but think about how much I wanted him to kiss me the other night.

"Well, what do you think?" Wyatt asks. His cheeks are bright red.

I glance back at Wes and our eyes meet. Then he moves out of the box and is gone.

I look back at Wyatt and nod, not sure what else to do. He leans in. Just before his lips touch mine, I shift slightly and his mouth grazes the corner of mine. It's quick, and probably no one but the two of us know it isn't a real kiss. The crowd goes wild.

We pull away from each other and, thankfully, we're no longer featured on the screen.

"That was really awkward," he whispers.

I laugh. "I'm going to kill Aunt Camille," I say.

On the ice, kids are trying to shoot a puck into a goal from the center line for prizes. I scan the bleachers behind us to see if Wes went back to his seat. I'm dying to gauge his reaction.

But he's gone.

Charlie is almost pushing us to the car once the game is over.

"We're a half hour from my slot," he shouts. "Keep it moving, people!"

"Where did Wes disappear to?" Olivia asks.

"He said he ran into some guys he knew at the concession

stand. I think they were headed to some party," Graham answers.

Disappointment stabs through me. Is that all it was? Or was it the kiss he thinks happened but didn't? I shake my head clear, and Wyatt and I wave good-bye to the rest of the group.

Once Wyatt and I are in his car, he turns in his seat to look at me before cranking the engine.

"That date was pretty weird, right?"

I let out a laugh, relieved he's broken the tension. "Yes. The game was fun, but it felt like so much pressure being in that box. And then my family descended on us. I'm really sorry."

He smiles and starts the car. "It's okay. Don't take this the wrong way, but I know you'd rather have gone on this date with Wes."

My mouth falls open. "What do you— Wes and I are just . . . friends."

So much for being discreet.

"I could just tell there's something weird going on with you two. You seemed really interested in what he was doing, and it seemed like he was just as interested in you."

"I'm sorry. I should have been a better date."

He laughs. "It's okay. Really. Jake explained what was going on with you this week. Let's just say, I'm glad my family is small."

We make easy conversation the rest of the ride home until

we pull onto Nonna's street. Charlie has been tailing us the whole way back; I caught glimpses of his truck behind us every time we made a turn, and now I see him gesturing furiously toward the house in the side mirror. A glance at the clock shows I've got four minutes to get inside or he loses.

Wyatt parks the car in front of Nonna's, but I stop him before he cuts the engine. He seems surprised but recovers quickly.

"Did Jake also tell you about the betting?" I ask.

"Um, no, he didn't mention that part."

I quickly catch him up. He looks like he has no words for the madness I've just dropped on him.

"We're right in the middle of Charlie's time block. Want to make him sweat?"

He laughs. "Absolutely."

We finally reach for the door handles and get out of his car.

Charlie is pacing the front yard. "You're cutting it close, Soph," he stage-whispers.

Wyatt and I stroll at a leisurely pace up the front walk. Before we're even on the porch, the door swings open, and Uncle Sal and Graham stare at us.

"Do you have to be inside the house for them to call the winner?" Wyatt whispers.

I nod. "Another minute or so and my uncle Sal wins today's pot."

Wyatt links his arm with mine. "Charlie looks like he's about to crack. Let's walk up the stairs *really* slow."

We cross the threshold just before Charlie's slot ends, and Charlie lets out a loud whoop from the front yard. Uncle Sal throws his hands up in the air and heads back to the kitchen.

The other members of my family finally have the decency to let me say good-bye to my date in private. They move off to different parts of the house, grumbling about the betting sheet.

Wyatt leans in and gives me a quick, friendly hug. "Good luck with Wes."

I laugh and say, "We're just friends. Really."

He gives me a look, and I blush. Then, with a final wave, he heads out.

He's barely out of the door when I hear Uncle Bruce yell from the kitchen, "Soph, how do you feel about s'mores?"

I walk toward the kitchen and see a crowd gathered around the board. Aunt Maggie Mae is setting up tomorrow's date; I've already decided there is a high probability I will use the "get out of date free" card.

"Why?" I ask. I can't see past my uncles to read the board. But finally they step aside.

It may be chilly outside,
but this fire should keep you warm!
4 pm

And on the table next to the board is a small basket with chocolate bars, graham crackers, and those big, fluffy marshmallows.

"That's not much to go on," I say, scanning the room. I don't see Aunt Maggie Mae—or any member of her immediate family—anywhere.

"Yeah, you should use the card. Use it now," Olivia says. "And why does your date start at four o'clock? Something's weird."

Nonna is already shaking her head. "Don't do it, Sophie. At least see who she picks! What fun is canceling the night before?"

I spin around to face Nonna. "Because there is no way I want to go out with anyone Aunt Maggie Mae set me up with." I don't mention that whoever is picking me up was probably picked out by one of the Evil Joes, not Aunt Maggie Mae.

"You can still cancel in the morning. Don't make any decisions tonight," she says, then flees the kitchen before I can argue my way out of this.

Uncle Ronnie produces a white sheet of paper full of empty squares. He looks at the board, then back to the betting sheet. "I'm picking the four p.m. and the four fifteen blocks. I love a sure bet."

I escape upstairs and call Mom. I haven't heard much from her or Margot, but I know they've got a lot going on.

She answers on the second ring.

"Hey, Mom. How's Anna?"

"She's about the same. They're watching her oxygen levels closely." She sounds tired.

"Is that normal?"

"For a preemie, it is."

"And Margot?"

She hesitates a second before saying, "She's okay. Still very weak. She gets dizzy when she does too much, so we're trying to get her to rest."

"That doesn't sound good."

"She's just overdoing it," Mom assures me. "She's promised to take it easy."

We chat a few more minutes before Mom says, "It's almost time for us to visit Anna. I'll take a picture and send it to you."

"Okay. If you can, kiss her for me."

"Of course," Mom says, and then she's gone.

I hesitate a moment before heading back downstairs. I can't help but feel like things aren't as okay as she makes it sound.

Monday, December 28th

Blind Date #7: Aunt Maggie Mae's Pick

You wouldn't think a plant nursery would be busy the Monday after Christmas, and you'd be right. As much as Olivia and I try to talk her out of opening, Nonna's adamant that we keep regular hours.

Only half of the employees are on duty, and they're all just sitting around waiting for something to do. Olivia and I are at the front counter, praying a customer comes in to save us from the pit of boredom we've fallen into.

Nonna comes through into the front room. "Today all garden statues are half price. Hopefully we can get rid of all those ugly gnomes your grandfather bought from that salesman while I was out of town."

"Those things are hideous. I'm not sure we could give them away for free," Olivia says.

I look at Olivia. "I bet I can sell more than you."

She raises that one eyebrow. "You're on."

Nonna taps her index finger against her chin. "Well, I have

an extra gift certificate for Superior Grill left over. How about twenty-five dollars to whoever sells the most?"

Olivia and I high-five. It's on.

Two hours later, I'm in the lead. With one sale.

Olivia is currently trying hard to sell one to an old man who came in for some fertilizer.

"Mr. Crawford, one of these would look adorable in your garden!" she says with way too much enthusiasm.

He looks like a deer caught in headlights. There is no way he wants that ugly thing, but he's way too nice to say no to Olivia. Especially a persistent Olivia.

She finally wears him down and does a victory dance the second he leaves with a statue tucked under his arm.

"We're tied now!" she says.

"Yeah, but there's a good chance he was our last customer for the day."

"Then we should spend our time wisely—checking out the guys who work here. Papa has to pick someone for Nonna's party, and they're practically the only people he knows."

This makes me sit up a little straighter. I've been so worried about Nonna's pick on New Year's Eve, I haven't given any thought to Nonna's party. So now I'm scanning every guy who walks past us.

And because we're on a skeleton crew today, there aren't many options.

"Randy, Jason, Chase, and Scott are the only guys here

today, and two of them are married. And I'm pretty sure Chase is wanted by the law," I say. "You're going to have to talk to Papa. See if he needs help picking someone out."

"At least the whole family will be at Nonna's party. You probably won't even have to hang out with the guy."

I nod and pull out the schedule for the upcoming week to see who else is working. Olivia reads it over my shoulder.

"Wes and Charlie will be working on Tuesday," she says.

"I see that," I reply. Does she know things are weird between Wes and me right now?

Her chin rests on my shoulder. "Wes and his family are invited to the party, so it kind of makes sense if Papa picks him. But he probably knows y'all are just friends."

Yeah, she has no idea where my head's at with Wes. It's probably best I didn't mention the almost kiss.

"Are you worried about tonight?" she asks.

"A little. It's Aunt Maggie Mae. I mean, why is our date starting at four?"

She swivels around and around on her stool, and I get dizzy just watching her. The door chimes, and we both look up, excited that we may have an actual customer. But it's not a customer. It's Olivia's boyfriend, Drew, and Seth is with him.

"Looks busy today," Drew says, then laughs. "We were close by and thought we'd pop in to see y'all."

Seth leans against the counter. "Hey. How's your sister?"

"She's good," I say. "My niece, too."

Seth leans closer to me. "Good. I was worried when you told me what was going on."

"Yeah, me too."

There's an awkward pause. "Well, let me know if you've got any free time while you're still here," he says.

I wait for the excitement that should be rushing over me—or even a little bit of a blush—but there's nothing.

I think he can tell he's thrown me, because he adds, "But I know you've got a lot going on."

I'm relieved. Seth is a great guy, and I'd be dumb not to consider another date with him. But if he pressed me, I think my answer would be no, and I don't know why or what that means.

"Maybe we can all go out again after this date thing is over," Drew says. "Olivia said she's not letting Sophie disappear on her again, so it sounds like we'll be headed to Minden. Seth can come with us."

This isn't the first time they've mentioned this, and suddenly I can't take it anymore. "I didn't disappear on you."

Olivia gives me a funny look. "We text some, but we haven't hung out in months and months. Charlie says the same thing. You never want to come here, and every time we mentioned going there, you had some lame excuse. I'm not letting you get away with that when you go back home." She wags a finger between her and Drew. "You're stuck with us." And then she points to Seth. "And you might be stuck with him, too."

They laugh and Seth says, "Thanks for making this awkward."

But I'm still trying to digest what she said.

Drew and Seth get ready to leave, and Olivia walks Drew to the door. I pull Seth to the side.

"So I have a favor to ask," I say. "Is there any chance I can talk you into buying one of those garden gnomes?"

I point at the creepy little statues against the wall, and he looks stricken with fear at the sight of them.

"They look possessed."

"They're harmless. But Olivia and I have this bet going. Don't let her see you with it until you're out the door, or she'll make Drew buy two of them."

A few minutes later, Seth and Drew are headed to their car while Olivia and I watch them from the front porch.

Seth gets into the passenger seat of Drew's car. Just before they pull away, he rolls down the window and holds up the gnome.

"What? No fair!" Olivia yells at him.

"Looks like I'm up by one!" I do a victory dance.

We head back inside—me at the counter, Olivia arranging the remaining gnomes—and within seconds my phone chirps.

"Oh no," I say.

"What's wrong?" Olivia asks. "Is it Margot?"

"No. I've been tagged in a post and I'm terrified to look at it."

Olivia rolls her eyes. "Oh. That was me."

My eyes get big. "I'm sitting right here. You didn't want to show it to me first? Or, God forbid, ask me if I wanted you to post it?" My voice has gone to that awful screeching level.

"You would've said no," she says with a huge smile on her face. "And I felt like we needed a distraction."

"What did you do?"

Olivia shrugs and then squeals, "Oh! Here comes Mrs. Townsend! She'll buy anything." And then she's gone, chasing after a little old lady who is wandering down the front walk.

I take a deep breath and swipe open my phone so I can see what kind of damage she did.

And there it is.

It's a picture of the giant screen from the hockey game yesterday with the caption: *Hot enough to melt ice! Hope @mudbugshockey can skate on water!* And then there's like ten flame emojis. Wyatt only kissed the edge of my mouth for point-two seconds, but the photo makes it look like we're lip-locked for eternity. We're framed by a big red heart on the giant screen, with lots of tiny little hearts all around the edges. If Wes didn't see it in real time, he'll for sure see it now.

Ugh.

And just like every other post, Griffin has been tagged in the comments more than once.

"Olivia!" I scream across the store. She gives me a quick

wave before dragging poor Mrs. Townsend to the greenhouse out back.

I wait for a text from Griffin, but nothing comes.

Just as Olivia and I are leaving, my phone vibrates in my hand. I almost ignore it until I catch a glimpse of Mom's name on the screen.

"Mom?"

"Hey, Sophie." Her voice sounds wobbly.

I sink down on the front steps and Olivia drops down beside me. "What's wrong?" she whispers. I hold the phone between us so she can hear, too.

"It's been pretty rough today," Mom says. "Just wanted to keep you up-to-date with what's going on here."

I haven't even heard what's wrong yet and I already feel like I'm about to vomit. "Tell me everything."

Mom takes a deep breath. "Anna's oxygen saturation is around eighty. That's not good."

"Oh God! So what are they going to do?"

"Well, they're going to sedate her and put her on a ventilator. Her little body needs to rest to get strong, and the machine will breathe for her for a while."

A muffled cry escapes. I feel like I got punched in the stomach.

"Sophie, it sounds worse than it is, I promise. The doctors think if they give her some time, she should be okay.

Hopefully, she'll only be on the vent for a day or so, and then they'll start weaning her off."

"Should," I squeak out. "That's the best they can say? She *should* be okay?"

"Well, they can't make any guarantees right now, but they feel very confident."

I swallow the lump in my throat. "How's Margot?"

Mom takes another deep breath, and now I'm bracing myself for what's coming.

"I told you last night that she's been really weak and dizzy. She lost a lot of blood when she delivered and hasn't bounced back the way she should have. Her hemoglobin is at six, which is really low. She's probably going to need a blood transfusion. The doctors are in with her now, so we should know shortly what they're going to do."

Olivia clutches my hand. My heart is thumping so hard right now. "Mom, are they going to be okay?"

"I know I'm hitting you with a lot right now, but I promise you, the doctors have assured us that it's not unexpected. Everyone fully expects both of them to get past this and hopefully be on their way home soon. It's like a bump in the road."

More like a mountain.

"Should I come down?" I ask.

"No, sweetie," Mom says. "Stay there and I'll keep you posted. Once Margot and the baby are home, we'll come back for a visit. You can't see Anna right now anyway, and Margot needs to rest."

"You'll call me and let me know everything that's happening, right?"

"Yes, of course," she says. "Oh, and as much as I hate it, I don't think we'll be back for Nonna's birthday party. We just can't leave here until we know everything is okay."

"How's Dad? He's texted me a few times but I haven't really talked to him."

Mom lets out a quiet chuckle. "He's climbing the walls. He hates that he can't fix this." Her voice drops to a whisper. "Brad's dad keeps trying to sell him insurance."

I can't help but smile when I picture Dad stuffed into one of those uncomfortable hospital chairs while Brad's dad drones on and on.

"So he's basically miserable."

"Pretty much. I'll let you know about Margot. Don't worry, okay?"

"Okay."

When we hang up, Olivia hugs me, then pulls me up. "C'mon, let's head to Nonna's. Your date should be there soon."

Tonight's date is the absolute last thing on my mind. There's no way I'm going. I'm heading south to check on Margot and Anna.

I throw my clothes into a bag upstairs. I can hear everyone downstairs, just like last night, laughing it up and chatting. It makes my stomach hurt.

Mom's name flashes across my screen and I grab my phone.

"Hello," I say.

"Hey, sweetie."

"How are they doing?" I ask immediately.

"The doctors say a few units of blood will help Margot bounce back. While I wish she didn't need a transfusion, I'm glad there's something they can do for her to make her better."

"I don't like this. I feel like everything is falling apart."

"It's just another bump in the road. I'll keep you updated. As scary as it sounds, it won't take long to do the transfusion. Anna seems to be resting well. They'll check her oxygen levels in the morning. Tomorrow will be a better day."

I talk to Mom a few more minutes, then she ends the call.

Yep, not waiting until tomorrow.

I'm digging under the bed when I hear that familiar thump of the basketball next door. I crawl over to the window and there he is, standing in his driveway. Wes is dressed in jeans and a hoodie, and he looks really good. He's not shooting the ball, just bouncing it while looking out toward the street.

What's he looking at?

No matter how hard I press my face against my window, I can't see more than ten feet in front of him. I'm just about to give up and get back to packing when the car pulling into the driveway stops me.

Wes walks up to the driver's-side window and leans down. I can't see who he's talking to and it's killing me. He stays like that for a few minutes, then straightens and moves to the passenger side. Just before Wes slides into the seat, he glances up at my window. I hit the floor.

I count to ten. Slowly. Then lift up just enough to peek out of the window. I get a glimpse of the driver just before the car moves out of sight.

It's Laurel.

I slide back down and lean against the wall under the window. He's leaving with Laurel.

"Sophie!" Olivia says, popping inside the room. "It's ten to four. Are you going to come down?"

It takes everything in me to heave myself off the floor. "I'm done. I'm driving down to check on Margot and Anna."

Olivia looks at the bag in my hand. "Want me to go with you?"

"No. I may stay there until the break's over. I haven't decided." I gather up all the clothes off the floor and shove them in the bag.

"Okay. Are you going to tell the family? Or are you just going to leave?" I don't miss her tone. She thinks I'm being rude or cold or whatever, but I just want to be with my parents and Margot and Anna right now.

"I'll call Nonna from the road. I don't want her to stop me." I pause on the way to the door. "Do me a favor? Put my bag in my car for me so she doesn't ask questions?"

We look at each other for a long moment, then she finally takes my bag and leaves the room without another word.

I follow her downstairs, still wearing the jeans and T-shirt I had on for work today. My hair is in a messy ponytail, and I have zero makeup on. I just need to send this date away and get on the road.

Uncle Charles takes one look at me and turns to Charlie. "Go change my bet. Pick the four spot."

Uncle Ronnie laughs from across the room. "Too late. Already took it."

Right on time, the doorbell rings, and Sara sprints to it, swinging the door open wide. The entire room falls silent.

"No way," Charlie mumbles.

Standing in the open doorway is Griffin.

Charlie steps in front of me and says, "Uh-uh. No way. Not happening."

Griffin moves forward. "Sophie, just talk to me for a second. If you don't want to go out with me, I'll completely understand."

"What's going on?" Uncle Sal whispers behind me. "He looks like a nice enough guy."

Banks says, "That's the ex-boyfriend."

"Oh," Uncle Sal responds, drawing out the sound.

I look at Aunt Maggie Mae, who's smiling. "Sophie, Griffin reached out to me and practically begged me to pick him."

Nonna comes up behind me and puts an arm around my waist. "You don't have to go, sweetie."

Griffin's eyes are pleading with me. "Talk to me for just a few minutes before you decide. Please."

I nod, only because I need to get out of this room. But I turn back just before I leave.

"I'm using the card," I say, then shut the front door behind me.

We walk out to the front porch for some privacy. When he comes to a stop, I turn to face him, keeping several feet of distance between us. "Your aunt is right," he says. "I called Mary Jo to ask who was picking your dates for the rest of the week, and she gave me her mom's number."

Oh, I'll bet she did. Out of all my cousins he could have reached out to, that's the one he picks?

"I can't go on a date with you tonight," I say. I see his mouth open—probably to argue with me—and I cut him off before he can start. "This has nothing to do with you. I'm actually canceling the rest of my dates and heading down to the hospital. My sister and niece aren't doing well, and I need to be with them."

"Then I'll drive you," he says.

"You don't need to do that," I say as I walk down the front steps toward my car.

He catches up with me. "You're upset. It would be safer for me to drive you down. Then you can ride back with your parents."

I stop in the middle of the front walk and look at him. "You'll drive me. Just like that, you'll drive me three hours to see my sister? Then what?"

His head tilts to the side. "Whatever it takes. If I need to wait there with you, I will. Or if you want me to leave, I'll drive back."

I stare at him a few seconds and then nod toward his truck. "Okay."

We head toward the curb just as the front door opens. Charlie and Olivia step outside.

"Let me grab my bag," I say to Griffin.

I head toward my car, and Charlie and Olivia meet me there.

"Are you going out with him?" Olivia asks.

Charlie's head swivels back and forth between Griffin and me.

"Not going on a date," I say. "Griffin is driving me down to the hospital."

Olivia flinches. I know we're both remembering her offer to go with me not ten minutes ago.

I pull my bag out of the backseat. "Look, I know you offered to take me, but I'm sure you've got other things—"

"Just when I think we're good again, you shut me out," she says. "Just like before."

I whip around. "Excuse me? *I* shut *you* out? Are you kidding me?"

Charlie steps in between us. "Hold on, hold on," he says, his hands extended. "Let's not say anything we're going to regret."

"Maybe we should have said something two years ago when she ran away from her family," Olivia says to Charlie. "Maybe she wouldn't have totally disappeared if we had this out with her back then."

"Oh my God, are you kidding me?" I want to scream.

Several of our family members have come out onto the front porch. Nonna is halfway down the stairs.

"I never ran away from my family," I say. "I wanted nothing more than to be with you and Charlie. And Wes. But that's hard to do when y'all pulled away from me. You have no idea what it was like when I had to leave every Sunday, knowing you three would still have each other every day. You had other friends I didn't know. And clubs I wasn't a part of. And parties I wasn't invited to. And you never really tried to make me feel like I was part of it. You think I disappeared? Y'all were the ones pushing me away."

I'm on the verge of tears by the time I finish. I can tell they're shocked.

Griffin is hovering close by. "Let me grab your bag for you," he says, picking it up off the ground next to me.

"Look, I can't do this right now. We'll talk when I get back," I say, moving past them.

I follow Griffin to his truck, where he stops in front of the open passenger door. Before I climb in, Laurel's car is turning into Wes's driveway just a few feet in front of us.

I can see his face as he looks between me and Griffin, before the car zips down his driveway and moves out of sight.

Yeah, I need to get out of here. "Let's just go," I say to Griffin.

Griffin walks around the front of the truck and hops in. I don't look back as he pulls out of the drive.

We've only been in the truck for ten minutes, and the silence is awkward. Finally, he asks, "Want to talk about it?"

"No. Not really."

"Are you ready to come back home now? I know how tired of your family you get when you're stuck over there."

I cringe, my argument with Olivia still too fresh. "Actually, it's been good for me. I didn't realize how much I missed them." *And Wes*.

He lets out a grunt. "Yeah, looks like it's been a great time," he says sarcastically. "So who's that guy that lives next door? You were in one of those pictures with him. Did y'all go on a date?"

I take a deep breath and blow it out slowly. How could I

have been with Griffin for a year and never told him about one of my oldest friends?

"I grew up with him. We've been friends since we were little, and he's Charlie's best friend. And, no, I wasn't on a date with him."

I feel like I should know everything there is to know about Griffin, but I'm not sure what that slow nod means. I squirm in my seat, unsettled by how familiar yet strange it feels to be back in his truck.

Thankfully, he turns up the radio and a country song chases away the silence.

It's actually one of the songs Olivia was making fun of on my last road trip.

"This song is like a Lifetime movie," I say, hoping to lighten the mood.

He looks at me like I've said the dumbest thing ever. "What does that mean?"

I start to explain, but I can tell by his expression he doesn't get it. "Never mind."

Four songs later, we start talking about school, the only subject that feels safe and familiar.

"So I got some good news last week," he says.

I turn to the side so I can look at him a little easier. "Oh, yeah?"

He nods. "Got an early acceptance to TCU."

My eyes get big. "That's huge! I didn't even know you were

applying there." And why didn't I know that? We've talked about Texas schools, but he never mentioned TCU. It's not even on my list.

"Yeah, well, I didn't want to say anything in case I didn't get in."

"So is that where you want to go?"

"If I can get the money, then yeah. That's my first choice."

Another ten miles pass in silence.

"What did you have planned tonight?" I ask.

He smiles. "I picked an early time so I could take you back home. I thought we could hang out at your house like you originally wanted to do this week. Just you and me. And then we could swing by the field later. Eli and them are having a bonfire tonight."

I give him a big smile, but the more I think about it, the faster my smile disappears.

He looks from the road to me. "That is what you wanted to do this week, right? That's what you said. I'm just trying to give you what you want."

"That is what I said." But why couldn't he give it to me before?

He lets out a frustrated breath. He puts on the blinker and takes the next exit. "I need some gas."

We pull into the station and I wander around the store, looking for snacks. Griffin joins me and we each get a drink and a bag of chips.

When I'm back in the truck, my phone buzzes in my pocket. It's a notification that Griffin has tagged me in a post.

I glance at him, but he isn't looking at me. I swipe open my phone and see it's a selfie he just took of us while we were standing in the checkout line. He's got the phone held up high and he's looking at the camera, but I'm looking at my phone. The caption reads: *Glad I can be here for my girl.*

What the . . . Did he seriously stand two feet from me, take this, and then post it without telling me?

I wait until we're back on the interstate before I say anything. I hold up my phone and say, "Not going to lie, this is a little weird."

"Are you mad I posted it?" he asks.

"I don't understand. We're in the gas station on the way to the hospital to see my sister and niece. I'm not even looking at the camera. Why did you post it?"

His face darkens. And now I'm second-guessing his motives for driving me down.

"It's just a picture," Griffin says. "Don't make this a bigger deal than it is. God, I don't know why things can't just be easy with you."

"'Glad I can be here for my girl'? First, I'm not your girl. We're broken up. And second, if you were really here for me, you wouldn't use what's going on with my family as a stupid caption for your post."

His hand grips the steering wheel. "This is what I was

talking about with Parker. Things are always so serious with you now. You didn't use to be like this."

I let his words sink in. I'd thought I'd lost my family and my best friends, and I'd tried too hard to fill that gap with Griffin and the Inspiration Board and everything else that wasn't what I really wanted. "You know what? You're right. I didn't use to be like this. This last week has showed me just how much of myself I lost."

His face is incredulous. "So it's my fault you're boring now?"

I let out a frustrated laugh. "No. That's on me."

The truck goes silent, and I think we both know that after this ride, we're done. I lean my head back against the seat, trying to figure out when my life got so twisted around. And I think about everything Olivia has said to me in the past week—about losing me, about feeling like they'd just gotten me back.

Maybe I wasn't the only one hurting.

"This is it, isn't it?" Griffin says eventually.

"Yeah," I say. "It is."

When he pulls into the hospital parking lot, he doesn't even put the truck into park. He hits the unlock button and says, "I hope they get better."

"Thanks for the ride," I say, grabbing my bag.

And he's driving off before I even get to the hospital door.

I make my way through the same corridors, elevators, and escalators as before, but this time I head straight to Margot's room. I hit a waiting room on the way and stumble right into Mom, Dad, and Brad's parents. Both of my parents jump to their feet.

"Sophie!" Mom shrieks.

"What are you doing here?" Dad yells.

But then they're hugging the breath out of me.

"I had to come," I say. "There's no way Margot was going to go through this without me being here."

They hold me for a really long time before finally letting me go. We sit down, Mom's hand clutching mine while Dad's arm rests on the back of my chair.

"So tell me the latest," I say.

Mom starts. "They're giving her the transfusion now. Brad is in there with her. It's a really simple thing, actually, and she should almost be done. They have to get all the blood in within a four-hour period or the blood in the bag goes bad or something like that."

"They said she'll be at full speed within twenty-four hours," Dad adds.

"And Anna?"

Mom smiles. "She's doing better. They just checked her levels, and everything's looking good."

"Did you drive down by yourself?" Dad asks.

"Griffin drove me," I say. Their eyebrows shoot up.

Mom looks around the room. "Well, where is he?"

"I guess he's on the way back home. We decided on the way down that it's really over between us." I feel an unexpected sense of relief saying the words out loud.

Dad pats me on the shoulder. "You okay with that?"

I nod. "I am."

Mom's about to ask me something else when we hear a loud noise coming from around the corner.

"I said take a left at that last turn."

"We *did* take a left at that last turn."

"So now we need to take a right!"

Seconds later, my extended family has taken over the waiting room. Nonna and my aunts and uncles take turns hugging Mom and Dad. Olivia, Charlie, Jake, and Graham are here, too.

Olivia almost knocks me over when she hugs me. Then Charlie is hugging us both. She pulls away just slightly but clutches both of my hands. Charlie has an arm slung around each of us.

"We talked about it the entire way down, and I never looked at it from your perspective. I didn't realize how hard it was for you. We've missed you so much. I should have made sure you knew that," she says.

"Yeah, it's not the same without you," Charlie says. "And no matter what, you're not going to school in Massachusetts."

"I should have told you I was feeling left out. I've missed

y'all, too." I look around the waiting room. "How did this happen?"

"Well," Charlie says, "as soon as everyone heard where you were going and why, we started making plans to come down, too."

"Not everyone could come. Some had to stay behind and watch the littles," Olivia says.

Dad, who usually looks stunned when surrounded by the family, seems relieved that there's someone else willing to sit and talk insurance with Brad's dad. Mom and Aunt Lisa are sitting down, their heads are bent close together, and Mom seems to be catching her up.

The three of us move to the chairs across from them. Aunt Lisa gets up and gives me a hug.

"I can't believe y'all came," I say to her.

She gives me a confused look. "Why? As much as you want to be here with your sister, we all want to be here with *our* sister." She sits back down next to Mom, their hands linking together.

I didn't even think of it like that.

"Where's Griff?" Charlie asks.

"On the way home." I grimace. "Let's just say this road trip wasn't as fun as the last one."

Charlie gives me his shocked face. "You mean, Griff isn't as much fun as the three of us? Say it ain't so!"

I push his arm. "Ha. Ha."

A woman in blue scrubs stops in the middle of the room. "Oh my," she says. "Lots of family."

Mom and Dad get up, along with Brad's parents, and they talk to the doctor for a few seconds. Then Mom motions for me to follow them down the hall toward Margot's room.

I'm not sure what I expect her to look like when the door opens, but she looks . . . just like regular Margot.

"Hey!" she says when she sees me. I rush to her bed. The parents stay back, giving us some space.

"You scared the crap out of me," I say. "Are you okay?" I can't help the tears flooding my eyes, and I have to force myself not to jump in the bed with her. But no matter what, it was so worth the drive down to see a little color in her cheeks and hear the strength in her voice.

"I'm good. So much better now that there's a little more blood pumping through me. They want me to take it easy for the next few hours, but if my blood pressure lowers, I'll be able to get up and move around."

We visit for a few minutes, then Mom starts rotating us in and out so all of the family has a chance to see her. As soon as I leave her room, I grab Olivia and Charlie and go look at Anna through the glass wall.

"I don't like seeing all that stuff attached to her," Charlie says.

"Yeah, but she's gorgeous," Olivia says with a sigh.

"I'm in love with her," I say.

As the family trickles out of Margot's room, they all end up with us at the glass wall looking at Anna. I take this chance to sneak away and get a little more time with Margot.

Mom is the only one in her room when I get back. She makes an excuse to go find some coffee, and then it's just me and Margot.

I crawl into bed with her just like I did a few nights ago.

"Did you go see her?" she asks.

"Yes. She has the biggest fan club ever. All the other babies are jealous."

Margot laughs. "I can't believe all of you drove down here. It's really so sweet."

"Both of you are really loved."

"And we love you. Mom told me about Griffin. Are you really okay?"

I nod. "I really am."

"Well, good thing, since you have a few more dates to go. Have you figured out who Papa is setting you up with for their party?"

I give her a funny look. "I'm here. I'm not going back until Mom and Dad do."

She pulls away so she can look at me. "As glad as I am to see your face, you don't want to stay here. I'm good. Going to be great by tomorrow. And the doctors are going to start weaning Anna off the vent."

"I can't leave you," I whine. And I can't go back and see Wes with Laurel.

"I'm hoping we're out of here in a few days. Then you can come back and stay as long as you want. You'd be miserable in the hospital. And I am dying to see how these dates end. Go finish it for me."

I rest my cheek against her shoulder. "Only because I don't feel like I could tell you no right now," I say.

I walk back out to the waiting room a few minutes later and stop in front of Nonna. "Margot thinks I should go back and finish the dates."

Nonna claps her hands together. "Well, of course!"

Uncle Michael pulls out a fresh sheet of paper. "Anyone have a pen? We can start the bets for my date right now."

Uncle Sal perks up from across the room. "But it's my day tomorrow."

"Nonna . . ." I say.

She holds up her hand. "We'll figure this out when we get home."

An hour later, we're all saying our good-byes. Nonna, Olivia, Charlie, and I pile in Michael's car. I just have three more dates to get through, I realize. Then Christmas break will be over and everything will be back to normal.

Just what I wanted when all this started.

So why am I dreading it all ending?

Tuesday, December 29th

Blind Date #8:
Uncle Michael's/Uncle Sal's Pick

The first thing I do when I open my eyes is check my phone. I slept with it in my hand in case Mom called with news about Margot or Anna, but obviously I was out of it, because I didn't hear the notification of the text she sent about an hour ago.

MOM: Margot is so much better this morning! She's up walking around. Getting ready to go see Anna. Will call you a little later. Love you.

I sink back into the bed and let out a big sigh of relief. Margot is better. Now we just need Anna to get off that vent.

I pull up the conversation with Margot and send her a text.

ME: Mom said you're feeling better!

Her response is instant.

MARGOT: I'm so much better today! I feel like I could run a marathon

ME: You've never even run to the end of the driveway

MARGOT: Ok so clearly I'm exaggerating but you get what I'm saying. I feel really good. Now I just need my baby girl to start breathing on her own and maybe we can get out of this hospital.

ME: I'm coming back to visit as soon as you're home and I'm going to hold Anna for like ten hours straight

MARGOT: Haha can't wait

Sometime later Olivia busts in the room and jumps on the bed.

"Why do you have so much energy in the mornings?" I ask her. "We just got home a couple of hours ago."

She fluffs her pillow, then turns toward me. "It's a gift, really." She watches me a few seconds. "So what happened with Griffin?"

I fill her in on our road-trip breakup. She gives me that one-brow-raised look I envy.

"Are you sure you're okay? I know how much you liked him."

I let out a deep breath. "I did, but I'm really okay that we're not together."

She nods. "Well, today is a new day and Uncle Sal and Uncle Michael are both downstairs."

I rub my hands across my face. "They're going to make me pick, aren't they?"

Olivia pulls me until I'm out of the bed. "No idea, but let's go see!"

Not only are Uncle Michael and Uncle Sal here, but so is half of the family. Nonna has a full breakfast buffet set out on the counter, and every chair and place at the table is taken.

Uncle Sal and Uncle Michael are both sitting in chairs in front of the board where my dates are written, drinking cups of coffee.

"Ah! There she is," Nonna says. "Well, this is what we're going to do. Sal and Michael will each write down the date they have planned, and then we'll take a vote. For those who aren't here, Charlie is getting their vote by text."

Charlie is at the counter, looking half asleep.

"We're all voting?" I ask.

Nonna gives me a look. "Of course! We're all invested at this point, so it's only fair. Remember, you're doing this for Margot!"

"Uh-huh. I knew you'd find a way to use that against me." Then I give her a hug and say, "Bring it on." There's really no use fighting this anymore.

Olivia and I squeeze in between Aunt Camille and Charlie's mom, Aunt Ayin.

Uncle Sal hops up from his chair and moves to the

whiteboard. There's a black line cutting the board in half, and he starts writing on the top part.

When Uncle Sal steps away, we all read the board.

Heating it up in the Kitchen!
2 pm

"So I guess this is a cooking date?" I say. There's a lot of whispering throughout the room.

Uncle Sal sits back down, and Uncle Michael shakes his head. "*Heating it up in the kitchen*? Is that the best you could come up with?"

"Well, let's see what you've got," Uncle Sal answers.

Uncle Michael makes a big production of getting a rag and wiping away the already clean space below the black line. Then he stares at the blank surface, his fist sitting under his chin as if he's in deep thought.

"Get on with it, Michael," Nonna says from her chair.

He writes each letter so slowly I want to groan with impatience. Finally, he steps away, looking very pleased with himself.

Sophia Patrick will be a member of House Lane-ister
We'll be Livin' on a Spare because We Don't Give a Split!
So Strike a Pose and be ready at 6!
It'll be Gutter-licious!

"I know who I'm voting for!" Aunt Camille shouts.

Uncle Sal turns to look at her. "Really?"

She shrugs. "That's just too cute, Sal. And you know it."

I read the board three times.

"So . . . this is a bowling date?" I ask.

"Yes! And because you're on my team, House Lane-ister, you'll need to dress accordingly."

"Is that a *Game of Thrones* reference?" Charlie asks.

Michael's expression shows us just how dumb he thinks Charlie's question is.

Olivia starts jumping up and down. "I want to go! Pleeeeease!" she whines, then looks at Uncle Sal. "Sorry. Yours looks fun, too."

"We're full, but I might be able to get you a spot on I Can't Believe It's Not Gutter," Uncle Michael says. "You have to dress like you're on the cover of a romance novel, though."

Now I'm really confused. "What does that fake butter have to do with romance covers?"

He looks at me incredulously. "Because Fabio, the guy from the romance novel covers, was in all those fake butter commercials." All he left off was the *duh* at the end of his sentence.

"Sign. Me. Up!" Olivia squeals.

"How are you on a bowling team when you don't even live here?" Uncle Sal asks Michael.

"Just because I don't live here doesn't mean I don't have friends here. There's this thing called *social media* where people who live far away from each other can still keep in touch. Maybe you've heard of it?"

Uncle Sal rolls his eyes. "Whatever. My date will be fun, too!"

"Well, they both sound like fun dates! But we still have to vote." Nonna stands up in front of the board. "Raise your hand if you vote for the cooking date."

Of course Uncle Sal raises his hand along with half of his kids. Aunt Kelsey's four daughters' hands shoot up, but I'm not sure they even know what they are voting for.

"Raise your hand if she should go bowling!"

It only takes a second or two to scan the crowd before Nonna says, "Okay, so pretty much everyone picks bowling."

Charlie holds up his phone. "Unanimous over here for bowling."

Olivia stands. "Uncle Michael, do you need help picking a date for her? Because I might have a suggestion."

He shakes his head. "I've got it covered!"

I pull on her sleeve. "Who is your suggestion?"

She leans forward and whispers, "I've been watching you." She pauses a second and then nods toward the back door. "And I've been watching him, too."

Wes is standing at the back door. He sees Charlie and moves to the bar, sitting down next to him on a stool Banks just vacated. Wes turns toward the room, searching it. When his eyes land on me, he gives me a small smile.

"Yep. Watching you two," Olivia says again.

Nonna gave us the day off, since we're tired from our late-night road trip and we need to go shopping. Once it was decided I would go bowling, Olivia pulled Charlie, Wes, Graham, Jake, and Sara aside. As of thirty minutes ago, they've called the bowling alley and added their own team. They went back and forth for a while, but finally decided on a *Grease* theme with Pin Ladies and T-Balls. We all head to the secondhand store to see if we can find something that will fit the theme, girls in one car, guys following behind.

We're wandering through the racks when Wes and Charlie come up on the other side.

"Hey, guys," Olivia says a little too loud. She's looking at Wes, then me, and then back at Wes. She is not smooth. Not at all.

Wes and I haven't been around each other since he bailed at the hockey game. He nods when we make eye contact.

I smile and nod right back. "So, you excited for bowling tonight?"

"Yeah. Seen any cheap black leather-ish jackets?" Wes says.

"Because we're the T-Balls," Charlie adds, and then dissolves in giggles. He's such a little kid.

"I'll help you, Charlie. Come over here," Olivia says, pulling him to the men's section on the other side of the store. "Wes, you watch *Game of Thrones*. Help Soph find something to wear."

Then she winks at me.

Definitely not smooth.

"I haven't seen you in a couple of days," I finally say to break the awkward silence.

He nods. "Yeah, it's been a little crazy. Charlie told me what happened yesterday with Margot and Anna. I'm glad they're both better."

"Yeah, me too. That was super scary."

He nods. "He also told me about the conversation y'all had before you left with Griffin."

I let out a laugh. "Conversation is a pleasant way of putting it!"

He grins. "Yeah, I guess. But, Sophie, seriously, I hate that we made you feel like we didn't want you around. If I knew that's what you were thinking, I would have . . ." He trails off.

"What?" God, why do I sound breathless? I've got to pull it together.

"I would have made sure you knew how much we wanted you with us."

I'm blushing. I can feel it. I turn around and start digging through the rack behind me.

"I think I'm going to dress up like Arya Stark, even though I'm supposed to be a Lannister."

He laughs. "Michael will love that." Just before I get too far away, Wes says, "Looked like you finally got that kiss."

I stop. My back is to him, and I'm staring at Olivia helping Charlie find a jacket, debating whether or not to turn around and answer him. Finally, I work up the nerve.

"Yeah, I guess so. But it wasn't the one I wanted."

I'm shocked I actually said that. He seems equally surprised.

"How was your ride down last night?" he asks.

"It was the closure I needed." And now I'm killing it with the confidence.

He nods again, and I see a small smile play across his face. "I'm glad. You look happy."

I'm hoping he'll tell me what's going on with him and Laurel, but he doesn't.

"Wes, see if this one fits you," Charlie yells from across the store. Wes gives me one last long look and walks away.

Olivia edges back over to me.

"Can we finally talk about it?" she asks. We both know she's talking about Wes.

I shrug and pick through the pile of shoes in front of me. "I've been so confused this week. And things were still so fresh with Griffin. And I have no idea if he thinks of me like that. And I worry it's too soon to like someone else."

Olivia rolls her eyes. "First off, it's not like Wes is some rando you just met. You've known him your whole life. You were in love with him for half of it."

I open my mouth to deny what she's saying, but she holds up her hand. "I know you didn't pursue it with him because of me. And I feel bad that maybe y'all wasted all that time because I liked him for five minutes."

"It's probably a good thing," I say. "We were fourteen. It wouldn't have lasted. Especially since we live in different towns and go to different schools. Look what it did to our friendship."

She gives me a small frown. "I wish we could have a redo."

I shake my head. "We're good now. That's all that matters."

"But the timing makes sense now. You're almost eighteen, and you're both headed to the same college . . . you are planning to go to LSU, right? You aren't still planning to go somewhere a million miles away, are you?"

I shove her shoulder. "LSU was the first school on my Inspiration Board, so I think it's a strong contender."

"So . . . when you finally admit you want to go to school with us, the two of you will live in buildings that are literally next door to each other. And we'll be roommates. And everything will be perfect."

"I don't know. Is it too weird? I mean, it might be weird.

And it might not be up to me. He was with Laurel two nights ago."

"Or it might be incredible. But you won't know until you take a risk. And he was with her for like half an hour. Her grandparents got him a gift for Christmas because they're clueless, so he rode with her to go pick it up, and then she brought him right back home."

Oh.

By the time we check out, Olivia has pink jackets for her and Sara, while I have the closest thing I can find to dress up like Arya Stark. After scouring all of the images on Google, I decided to mirror her look from the later episodes and was lucky enough to find a pair of dark olive-green fitted pants and a brown leather jacket. All I need is a sword.

Olivia and I stop next to my car, and Charlie moves toward Wes's truck, but Wes lingers.

"So I guess I'll see you tonight," he says.

"Yeah, I'll be the one with the sword." And then I shake my head. "Okay, maybe I won't be the only one with a sword."

He laughs. "Well, I'll be the one who has ruined a perfectly good fake leather jacket by writing the word *T-Ball* in white paint across the back."

Wes is close enough that if I wanted to, I could reach out and touch him. And I really want to slide my hand into his.

But I don't, and he doesn't reach out for me. And then he finally walks away.

Once I'm back in the car, Olivia laughs. "You two are killing me."

❄ ♥ ❄

The crowd is back at Nonna's to see who picks me up for the bowling date. And the stakes are especially high, since the bets from last night rolled over to today.

I never thought I'd get tired of going on dates, but I'm officially there.

The Pin Ladies and T-Balls are looking quite good, and I have to force myself not to be sad I've got a sword instead of a shiny pink jacket.

Uncle Ronnie studies the betting squares, looks at me a minute, then looks back to the betting squares. "So which one from that show are you dressed up as?" he asks.

"I'm dressed up like Arya. When it's my turn to bowl, I'm going to repeat the names of all my dates this week over and over like she does with the people she wants to kill."

Uncle Ronnie's head pops up.

I give him a big smile. "Just kidding!"

He backs away from me slowly.

Uncle Michael flies down the stairs. At least I don't feel so out of place now. He looks exactly like Jaime Lannister, except with black hair instead of blond. He's even sporting the "gold" fake hand.

"You going to be able to bowl with that thing on?" Charlie asks.

Even though Charlie looks good with his hair slicked back and that white T-shirt on under his black jacket, I know him well enough to know he has costume envy. When we were little, he dressed up like a pirate for four years in a row just for the sword.

Uncle Michael slides the fake hand off and back on. "Don't worry about me," he says, then looks me up and down. "We're Team Lane-ister! Did you not look at any of the pics I sent you?"

I smile. "I did but decided I was feeling a little less Cersei and a little more Arya."

"Whatever." Uncle Michael stands in the open doorway, scanning the street. Maybe this guy will be a no-show, I think optimistically.

A few minutes later, he throws his hands in the air and yells, "Finally!" to the guy walking up the front path.

"I had to circle the block three times trying to find a place to park!" the guy says. "Someone must be having a party or something."

Oh, just wait until he sees who's waiting inside to meet him.

He steps through the door and Uncle Michael says, "This is Jason Moore."

Jason moves closer. His hand is outstretched and he's smiling wide and he totally mistakes Sara for me.

Before she knows what hits her, Jason is shaking Sara's hand. "Hey, it's nice to meet you!"

He has stars in his eyes, and she looks equally charmed, if confused. I wish I could push them out the door and let them have this date.

"Um, you too, but I'm Sara. Sophie's cousin." She nods her head to the side. His eyes leave her and land on me. And yeah, the stars are gone.

"Oh." Reluctantly, he lets go of Sara's hand and reaches for mine. "Sophie. Nice to meet you."

The family starts whispering. Charlie pulls the sheet out and starts adjusting bets. Uncle Michael looks panicked.

"So about how long does this thing last?" Uncle Sal asks.

Uncle Michael shakes his head. "Not telling."

Uncle Ronnie leans in close to Uncle Sal and says, "Michael picked the ten-to-ten-fifteen spot."

"Well, we'd better get going," Uncle Michael says, and all but pulls us through the door.

Just before I leave the house, I turn to Sara and mouth, *Want to ride with us?*

For a split second I think she's considering it, but she finally shakes her head. "I'll see you there," she whispers.

Maybe Nonna isn't the only matchmaker in the family.

Jason, Michael, and I get in Jason's car. I wasn't expecting us to ride together, but at this point in the dating game nothing surprises me.

Jason and I chitchat on the way to the bowling alley, and I find out he's a junior at the same school as Olivia, Wes, and Charlie. He has Media Arts with Charlie, and I hear story after story about the bizarre things Charlie does in the name of entertainment.

Wish I could say any of it surprises me, but it doesn't.

I can tell when we're at the right place because every person in the parking lot is in some kind of costume.

"We're not the only *Game of Thrones* team, are we?" I ask Uncle Michael.

"Nope," he says. "There's House Bowl-ton." He points to a group of guys walking toward the door wearing black jeans and T-shirts with the "flayed man" picture on the back. "And then there's Lords of Pin-terfell." He looks me up and down again then adds, "I guess you should be bowling with them, dressed like that. And there's A Team Has No Name. But we were the first!"

I turn to Jason and ask, "Have you ever done this before?" I've yet to find out how Uncle Michael knows him.

"No. But my brother is on Michael's team, so I've heard about it. The stories don't do it justice."

"Do y'all dress up every time you get together?" I ask Uncle Michael.

"Nope, just for the end-of-year bash."

We get inside, and Jason and I have to rent shoes. We're the only ones who need to. Everybody else not only owns their own shoes, but it looks like they also have their own bowling balls. And in most cases, their team's theme has been worked into the design of the ball.

We sit side by side, pulling on the blue-and-red shoes, when a pack of half-dressed guys walk in. It's almost like there's an invisible fan in front of them, blowing their hair back perfectly.

"Olivia is going to be bummed she's not on that team."

Jason laughs. "I would think being oiled up like that would make bowling difficult."

And oiled up they are. They're practically glistening under the fluorescent lights.

While Michael and his teammates program everyone's name into the overhead scoreboard, Jason and I people-watch. There's a group in the lane next to us dressed up like priests and nuns named the Holy Rollers. We've also seen Team E-bowl-a, who are a bunch of doctors in their scrubs, some redneck-looking guys in Team Gutt-er-done, and the stoners of Team Smoke-A-Bowl.

But my personal favorite is Team Spare Wars.

"I'm kind of bummed they don't dress up like this all the time," I say to Jason.

"Okay, now that we're all here, it's time for a team picture," Uncle Michael says. He gathers everyone together and puts Jason and me front and center. "Since we're the Lane-isters, I want to see arrogance and smugness." He glares at my outfit yet again. "Or we could all aim our swords at the traitor in the middle?"

"Ha. Ha," I say.

After some discussion, Jason and I cross our arms across our chests and get back-to-back, then turn our faces toward the woman taking our photo. She's wearing a black pencil skirt, white blouse, and black glasses, and her hair is in a bun.

"What team is she on?" I ask.

"Team Ballbarians," Jason's brother, Hank, answers. "Nothing hotter than a librarian who bowls."

She takes several shots, then Uncle Michael uploads it to all of his social media accounts, tagging everyone in the group.

My phone lights up with notifications, and I swipe it open. The first thing I see in my feed is a picture of Griffin and a girl from the grade below us named Sabrina. They're sitting in two folding chairs in front of a bonfire with their faces side by side.

There isn't a caption, only a string of fire emojis.

It's super lame.

And thankfully, I feel nothing when I see it.

The Pin Ladies and T-Balls finally arrive, and they're assigned to the lane about four down from ours. Olivia is trying to get them together for a group pic.

I rush over and say, "Want me to take it?"

She hands me her phone and then gets between Charlie

and Wes. Looking at my family and Wes on the screen, I've never wanted to be a Pink Lady more.

I take several, then hand Olivia back her phone.

"Wait," Wes says. "Let's get one of the four of us."

"Yes!" Olivia squeals.

Olivia and I get in the middle, then Wes stands beside me. His arm is around me, and he pushes in close. I know my smile is ridiculous, but I can't help it. It feels like we're the Fab Four again.

"Oh, I should have been on that team," Olivia says once we're done with pictures. She's finally spotted Team I Can't Believe It's Not Gutter. I laugh.

"Sophie," Uncle Michael calls. "You're up!"

After two rounds, it is obvious I am not a good bowler. In fact, after two rounds, my score is still zero.

Zero.

Jason isn't much better, but at least he's in double digits.

"How many games do we play?" I ask.

"Two," everyone on my team answers at the same time. They're trying to be nice to me even though my score is dragging our team down, but I see one guy bury his head in his hands.

Is it bad I'm watching the game four lanes down more than my own? Probably. But I'm not the only one who can't stop looking at the Pink Ladies and T-Balls. Jason has glanced over at Sara a dozen times.

When it's my turn again, I can almost hear every member of my team groan as I line up at those dots in the floor.

"You need to take your first step with the same hand you hold the bowling ball with," Wes says beside me. He's got an imaginary ball in his hand and he steps forward on his right foot at the same time he swings his right hand forward. "It's got to be done in the same motion."

"Are you helping the other team?" Charlie yells. We both ignore him.

Wes nods to me. "Try it, but don't let go of the ball, yet."

I hold my ball in front of me and try to re-create what he just showed me, but my timing is all wrong. I back up and try it again, but the result is the same. And then he steps in behind me, putting his left hand on my hip and his right hand on my elbow.

"Okay, let's try it one more time," he says in my ear.

I nod because words have completely failed me at this point. He tugs on my elbow just as I step forward with my right foot and he follows me through the swing.

"Now go for it," he says.

I take a deep breath and get back on the starting line. And then I'm off. The ball bounces twice on the lane before it starts a very slow roll toward the pins. I spin around and look at Wes.

"I can't stand it. Just tell me how it ends."

He laughs while he watches the slow progress of the ball

behind me. My teammates are still smiling, so it must not be in the gutter yet.

Wes is nodding his head and murmuring, "Keep going . . . keep going."

When I hear the sound of pins dropping, I twirl around in time to see seven of the pins fall.

I jump up and down, then throw my arms around Wes's neck. "I did it!"

His hands grip my waist and he pulls me in close. "You're a natural," he says in my ear.

Wes releases me, nudging me to get the ball for my second try. Of course, this time I go straight to the gutter. But I'm on the board!

Wes walks back to his group, and I take a seat by Uncle Michael.

"So I picked the wrong guy for you for tonight, didn't I?" he says, with a grin. "Now I get why Olivia offered to help."

I shrug. "Jason's nice. I'm glad I met him." Then I nod to where Jason and Sara are talking behind us. "He's going to be just fine, I think."

"Yeah, I suck at this." Uncle Michael laughs. "Does neighbor boy feel the same way?"

"I don't know."

"He's been staring at you all night."

I hit Uncle Michael in the arm. "Seriously?"

He laughs again and nods. "Seriously."

Wes doesn't come back to our lane for the rest of the game, but we get busted watching each other more than once. And in the end, when all of the team scores are tallied, the Lane-isters are actually not dead last. We're close . . . but not at the very bottom. We take it as a win.

Jason and I take our rented shoes back to the counter. "This was fun," he says while we wait for the girl to bring us our own shoes. "Even though it didn't go quite the way I thought it would."

I hug him briefly. He is a really nice guy and any other time I would be lucky to be on a date with him.

"My grandmother's birthday party is tomorrow night at Eastridge." I look at Sara, then back at him. "All of my family will be there. You should stop by."

He grins. "You're a really cool girl, Sophie. And I would very much like to come to your grandmother's party."

He gives me another quick hug, then heads toward the door.

"Did he just ditch you?" Olivia says behind me.

I spin around. My whole family is standing there, looking like they're ready to go to battle for me.

"No, it's not like that. We decided to go ahead and end our date here."

Charlie looks at his watch. "Dang! I missed it by half an hour!" And then he's on the phone, presumably noting the end-of-date time on the group text. "Uncle Ronnie won again. How is that even possible?" he mumbles to himself.

"But I do need a ride home," I say. I'm avoiding looking at Wes, because I know my feelings are written all over my face.

Olivia throws an arm around my shoulders and turns me toward the door. "Of course. But let's go get some pizza first."

Jake hobbles in front of us, since he's still wearing that boot on his right leg. "Let's get sushi," Jake says. "We get pizza all the time."

"My vote is Whataburger," Graham says, but Olivia strikes it down.

"We're not going to Whataburger."

Graham shakes his head. "For once, I'd like to pick."

The arguing continues into the parking lot. I can't pry the smile off my face.

Olivia's arm is still around me, and she's slowed down so there's some distance between us and the rest of the group.

"Are you really okay?" she asks.

I nod. "I really am."

Olivia's mouth lifts up on one side. "I saw that whole *Let me show you how to bowl* move. Classic." I snort and elbow her.

Charlie and Wes are standing by Wes's truck, and the rest of the family is next to Graham's SUV. Olivia pulls me to Wes's truck.

He opens the passenger door and asks me, "Ready to go?"

"I sure am."

Wednesday, December 30th

Blind Date #9: Papa's Pick

"Good news," Olivia says. "We only have to work a couple of hours this morning, then Papa is giving us the afternoon off so we can go with Nonna to get her hair and nails done for tonight's party."

This perks me up. "Are we just hanging out with her while she gets pampered, or do we get pampered, too?"

Olivia's eyes light up. "He said as long as we don't blab to all the other cousins, he's treating us, too. I told him we know we're the favorites and we've kept that info locked down for *years*. No need to start worrying about us talking now."

I slide out of the bed. "Not going to lie, a pedicure sounds pretty fantastic right about now. But you know Nonna's going to put up a fight."

"She already is, which is why Papa is sending us with her. Otherwise, he doesn't think she'll go."

When we get to the kitchen, Nonna is at the sink. I check out the board, not surprised when I see:

Nonna's Birthday Party!
7:00 pm!

"Happy birthday, Nonna!" I say. She spins around from the sink, and Olivia and I give her giant hugs. "Do you know who he's setting me up with?"

She shakes her head. "I have no idea. But it should be interesting!"

We grab muffins off a platter on the bar, then head to Olivia's car.

It's slow at the shop. Painfully so. Olivia has ditched me and is walking through the greenhouse with Drew. I'm sure they're making out behind the azaleas. Papa has Wes and Charlie busy out back, deciding which plants are going to be used as decorations for the party tonight.

My phone dings with a text from Margot. I've been careful not to bug her, since she's got so much going on, but I've really missed talking to her.

MARGOT: Good news! They started reducing the amount of oxygen Anna was getting from the vent last night and right now she's only getting 25% from the machine and she's doing great! Hopefully the tubes will be out tomorrow!

ME: THAT IS THE BEST NEWS!!!!!!

ME: I'm so relieved!!!

MARGOT: You have no idea. It's awful to see your tiny little baby with so many machines attached to her

I wish I was there to hug her. And Anna, too.

MARGOT: So I hear you're as bad as Nonna with the matchmaking

ME: This family has a serious gossiping problem

MARGOT: I hate we're missing Nonna's party. Any idea who Papa picked?

ME: No. And I'm a little concerned

Nonna walks through the front of the shop, her hands clasped in front of her.

"Well, I've got good news," she squeals.

She must be waiting for a reaction from me, but we just stare at each other. Finally, she says, "I found your date for tomorrow night!"

"Just now?" I ask. "You've been at the nursing home visiting Gigi."

"Yes, I know! Funny how things work out. It was meant to be."

And then she dances off toward her office, and I'm left wondering who in the world she saw at the nursing home.

It's close to lunch before I see Wes. He looks really cute

today in his jeans and Greenhouse Nursery T-shirt. He leans against the counter while Charlie drops down on the stool next me. Charlie's covered in potting soil.

"Did you have an accident?" I ask.

He brushes off the loose dirt. "Let's just say I went two rounds with a sago palm and the palm won."

Wes laughs. "I didn't think it was possible for someone to get into a fight with a potted plant, but Charlie proved me wrong."

"That plant weighed about forty pounds! And I didn't see that last step," Charlie says.

Olivia drops her phone inside her purse and says, "Well, boys, y'all can have it. We're out of here."

Charlie jumps up. "What? How'd you get the rest of the day off?"

Picking up my bag off the floor, I say, "We're taking Nonna for hair and nails."

"Totally unfair. I would be willing to run Nonna around all day."

Olivia and Charlie bicker all the way to the front of the store about who is the favorite and why, but I hang back to talk to Wes.

"Any chance you were at Garden Park Nursing Home this morning?" I ask.

I can tell the answer by his expression before he even says it.

"No. Why?"

I shake my head, hoping my disappointment doesn't show. "No reason. Never mind."

Olivia yells from the front door. "Help me get Nonna in the car! She's saying she doesn't want to go."

"I'll see you later," I say to Wes, then hurry outside to help Olivia. We all but bully Nonna to get in Olivia's car.

"It's ridiculous to spend the entire day at the beauty shop," Nonna says once she's finally in the passenger seat. "I should be at the club helping them set up for tonight."

Her party is being held in one of the banquet rooms at Eastridge Country Club. Nonna wanted to keep it small, but even just our family is a crowd, so we needed the space.

"Mom and all the aunts are taking care of it," Olivia says. "They want to surprise you."

Nonna lets out a *pfff* sound but finally stops complaining.

"Has Papa told you who he's setting me up with yet?" I ask her.

She shakes her head. "No, and I've been after him all morning about it. I mean, who does he know that isn't related to you?"

I let out a sharp laugh. "I can ask you the same thing about my New Year's Eve date!"

She glances back at me and winks. "That date will be the best one. You just wait!"

I don't even try to hide the groan.

My phone dings and a smile bursts across my face when

I see Margot's name. Four pictures of Anna appear one right after the other. I pass the phone to Nonna so she can see her. It's pretty awful to see that big tube going into her little mouth, and she's still sedated, but she's a healthy rosy color. I'm taking that as a good sign.

Nonna passes the phone back to me. "Won't be long before she's as fat and happy as the rest of y'all were."

"I hope so."

MARGOT: The doctors are going to start weaning!! Her oxygen saturations levels are looking good. Fingers crossed!!
ME: Crossing fingers and toes and anything else I can manage!!

At the salon, we talk Nonna into having her nails painted a soft pink with a touch of glitter. Olivia and I choose the same color. They wash and style her hair, and there's even a woman who applies her makeup.

By the time we're headed back to Nonna's, we only have about an hour or so to get dressed and get to the club.

Olivia has her change of clothes with her, so we share the guest bathroom and help each other with our makeup.

"As many bad dates as I've had this week, I shouldn't be worried about who Papa picked, but I am," I say while Olivia carefully runs black liquid eyeliner across the edge of my upper right lid. Applying liquid eyeliner takes a skill I don't possess.

"Shhh, or I'm going to mess this up," she says. "And it

won't matter. You can ditch whoever it is, since we'll all be there. It's wreaking havoc with the betting, by the way. Everyone is fighting for the ten-to-ten-thirty spots."

I'd roll my eyes if I could, but she's got one of the lids stretched too tight. "I'm going to blow everyone's chances and stay out with whoever it is past midnight."

Olivia steps back and looks at me. "Really? Do I need to change my bet?"

"Oh my God, no," I say.

Since everyone is scrambling with last-minute duties for the party, the front hall is blessedly empty, except for Nonna, Papa, Olivia, Charlie, and me. But judging by the way Charlie is glued to his phone, I have no doubt that everyone in the family is getting a play-by-play.

"Papa and Nonna, y'all are looking pretty hot," Olivia says. And they do. He's in black slacks and a crisp white button-down shirt under a sea-green pullover sweater. She's wearing dark charcoal fitted pants with tall black boots and a silvery-looking top.

"You two look smashing!" Olivia says in the worst British accent ever.

"We clean up nicely, I think," he says, looking at Nonna. She looks back at him, her eyes crinkling, and I feel myself grinning.

The doorbell rings. Papa clasps his hands together, and his face lights up with utter joy.

But I'm just shocked when the door swings open and Wes is standing there.

I can't hide the smile that spreads across my face. "Wha—"

"Wes, what are you doing here?" says Papa. "Where's Peter?"

And then disappointment hits me like a hammer. Peter is a guy who works at the shop. He was in the group of possible candidates Olivia and I had narrowed down.

"Peter got sick at work right as we were closing up. Really sick. He threw up all over the break room." He gives me a confused smile. I realize he can read the disappointment on my face, and I want to rush to tell him that he's wrong—that I wanted it to be him.

He looks back at Papa and continues, "So I told him I would come over here and let you both know."

Papa looks crushed. "Oh, Sophie! I've let you down."

I rush to his side and give him a hug. "Not at all, Papa. It might have been weird to have a date at Nonna's party, anyway. This was meant to be, I promise."

Papa hugs me back, then turns to Wes. "Well, maybe not all is lost! Wes can escort you. I know you're only friends but . . ."

Before Papa can finish, Laurel walks in behind Wes. "Hey!" she says to us, then turns to Wes. "Your mom told me you walked over here. I'm ready when you are."

Wes is bringing Laurel to the party. The realization hits me like a gut punch. His eyes flick to mine for a second or two, and he looks like he wants to say something. Instead, he turns to Papa. "We'll see you there, I guess."

And then they're gone.

According to Charlie, who is currently in the backseat of Olivia's car, there's a great debate over the winner of tonight's bet. Some are saying that whoever had the closest spot to seven wins, while others think it's null and void since there wasn't an actual date.

"Just roll it over to tomorrow and the winner gets double the usual pot," Olivia says.

He passes that message along, then says, "Okay, everyone's cool with that."

"Why was Laurel with Wes? I thought that was over," Olivia asks Charlie.

"I don't know, but that's the first thing I'm going to ask him when we get there," he answers.

Olivia turns around so she can face me from the front seat. "I'm sorry. He said they were done . . . and he never mentioned he was bringing her tonight."

I shake my head. It isn't Olivia's fault. I was the one who read too much into every little word and gesture. But what does it mean that seeing Wes with Laurel hit me harder than seeing the post of Griffin and Sabrina?

Charlie looks at us. "Why are you apologizing to her? What am I missing?"

"Nothing!" I say. I don't want to keep secrets from Charlie, but I also don't want Wes to know I'm upset.

"I'm sorry she got stood up," Olivia ad-libs. "And that Wes wasn't free to step in."

Thankfully, Eastridge isn't far from Nonna's, so I'm spared any further conversation about Wes and Laurel. As we get out of the car, I take a deep breath. Since the Fab Four is back together, I'm going to have to get used to being around Wes, no matter how bad it sucks.

I guess this fall at LSU will look a little different than Olivia described.

Olivia laces our fingers together and squeezes my hand. We're a few paces behind Charlie. "I *am* so sorry," Olivia says quietly. "I really thought they were over."

"I saw what I wanted to see," I say. "He was being a good friend and I made it into more than it was."

Charlie stops and points to a big palm tree in the corner. "That's the one that almost killed me."

The plant is missing half its leaves, and the pot has a huge crack down the side where dirt is dribbling out onto the floor. "It looks like it put up a good fight," I say.

"I think every plant from the shop is here," Olivia says as we walk through the entrance to the club. It definitely feels like we're inside a garden.

We walk into the main ballroom and it's packed. There's a band set up on a stage with a dance floor in front of them. Round tables with white tablecloths are scattered through the room, and the buffet runs along the back wall. Each table has fresh pink and white flowers in the center, and there are lots of blown-up pics of my grandmother through the years propped on easels everywhere I turn.

Nonna and Papa stand near the entrance, where there's a huge line of people waiting to tell her happy birthday. As much as she likes to grumble about the attention, I can tell she's happy everyone is here.

We move through the room, looking for the tables set aside for the family, and almost every person we pass stops us to say hello and ask, "Which one do you belong to?" By the time we make it to the other side, I've been hugged and kissed and pinched on the cheek enough to last me a lifetime.

Uncle Ronnie and Aunt Patrice are on the dance floor doing some weird mash-up of grinding and swing dancing, and there's a small crowd off to the side.

"That saying *dance like no one is watching* should be *dance when no one is watching*," Charlie says. "And how can they even dance like that to old-people music?"

Olivia and I stare at them with horrified expressions. It's too early in the night to be moving around like that, especially with this crowd of grandmas watching.

"Let's get some food," Olivia says.

"I'm not sure I have an appetite after witnessing that display," I answer as she drags me to the buffet line.

To no one's surprise, most of the food spread out on the table in front of us is Italian. There are big pans of lasagna, and spaghetti and meatballs, and mini muffulettas and pasta salad. And while it's all pretty good, it doesn't compare to my grandmother's cooking.

We sit down at the table with Jake, Sara, Graham, and Banks. As hard as I try to not look for Wes and Laurel, that's exactly what I find myself doing.

They're sitting nearby, just separate from our group. Several times, I've seen her sitting at a table by herself, scrolling through her phone, while Wes hangs out with Charlie near the dance floor.

Neither of them seems as aware of each other as I am of them.

Thankfully, Nonna pulls us out on the dance floor as soon as we're done eating, and the band starts playing songs I actually know. I finally quit worrying about Wes and Laurel and just enjoy dancing with Nonna.

And Nonna can *move*! It's not long before the lights are dimmed and everyone crowds that small wooden square. We dance and dance, having long ago abandoned our shoes to the pile right off the edge of the stage. I've never been so glad to be dateless. I take pictures and short videos throughout the night and send them to Mom and Margot.

My grandparents dance to the same song they had their first dance to at their wedding, and there isn't a dry eye in the room.

It's getting late, and I'm scanning the table full of different flavors of cannoli, when Wes appears by my side. I saw Laurel leave a half hour ago, but it's the first time Wes has approached me all night.

"Which one are you going for?" he asks.

"Well, it's between the chocolate one and the peanut butter one," I say. "Or I might get both."

He laughs. "You should definitely get both."

We each fill a plate with desserts, and he follows me back to the table. I put my plate down and start to pull out my chair, but his hand on my arm stops me.

"Let's dance first," he says.

The band is playing a slow song. There are several couples on the dance floor, including Jason and Sara.

"Okay," I say, and follow him to the dance floor.

We face each other and he puts his hands on my waist, pulling me close. Really close. Close enough that it takes nothing for me to slide my hands over his shoulders and around his neck. We move with the music, and I don't dare look around the room to see which of my family members are watching us. I wish more than ever that we were somewhere else. Somewhere that we weren't the subject of no less than five different conversations right now.

"Did Laurel go home?" I ask, and then want to beat my head against the wall. Why am I bringing her up? So stupid.

"She went to meet friends," he answers.

"Oh," I say. It's a lame response, but it's all I can muster when what I really want to do is grab him by the shirt and shout, *Tell me everything.*

And I can tell he wants to say more. He actually opens his mouth, but no words come out. Finally, he says, "Her parents and grandparents were also invited tonight. They were all here earlier. She asked me the other night while we were at her grandparents' house if we could go to this together and figure things out between us. We talked on the way over here, and we both agreed we want different things. She bailed as soon as her family did so she could hit another party across town. I guess you can say we've gotten closure."

"Closure," I repeat. This feels big. But am I reading too much into it? Is he just talking this out with his friend?

"When I drove Peter home and he told me he wasn't going to make it to your date, Laurel was already on the way to my house."

Oh God. I can read a thousand things into what he's saying. A million.

"It worked out for the best. I'm not sure how good of a date I would have been with all of my family here," I say.

"Peter was pretty bummed." He gives me a small smile. "Just like I was when I couldn't step in for him."

Before I can say anything, Charlie pops up next to us, one hand on Wes's shoulder, his other hand on mine. I want to scream.

He looks at Wes. "Two choices: one, we take all those plants back to the shop first thing in the morning like we planned, or two, we do it tonight after the party and won't have to be at work until ten."

Wes finally looks away from me to Charlie. "Tonight. I'd love to sleep in tomorrow."

"Same!" Charlie says, patting us both. "This thing is almost over, so let's get started on the ones outside. I'll pull the truck up."

And then he's gone.

The song ends as if on cue, and Wes's hands slowly fall from my waist. I drag my hands away from him, although that's the last thing I want to do. Just before he walks off, he says, "One more date and then you're done."

It feels like it takes ten trips from the car to Nonna's house to bring in all the leftovers that Eastridge packed up for us, but it's better than what Wes and Charlie are doing. The last I saw Charlie, he was circling that giant palm like a gunslinger at a shoot-out.

My money is on the palm.

Nonna plops down in a chair and massages her bare feet. "I knew those boots were a bad idea."

Olivia and I have to rearrange everything in the fridge just to get the extra food to fit inside. Papa shuffles in carrying a huge flower arrangement and sets it in the middle of the table. He comes up behind me and wraps me in a hug.

"I'm sorry the date didn't work out, Sophia," he says quietly.

I spin around and hug him back. "I had a blast! The party was fantastic, and I'm glad I could just hang out with the family."

He seems pleased with my answer. Papa moves to Nonna and kisses her on the top of the head. "Happy birthday, my sweet girl."

She holds his hand in hers, then brings it to her mouth, kissing his knuckles. "Thank you for my party."

Papa heads upstairs and Nonna sinks into her chair. "I may sleep right here. I'm too tired to stand up."

"Well, I'm pretty sure I ate my weight in meatballs. The second I close my eyes I'm going into a food coma," Olivia says.

Nonna claps her hands together.

"Oh, I almost forgot!" She goes to the board and starts writing.

Dear Sophie,
A treasure to be sure!
Let me just say I've enjoyed your stay
Like your mother, you are a sweet soul!
And there's one more date until you're done—
So be ready by 2 p.m.!!

"That's pretty cryptic," I say.

Olivia studies the board and repeats Nonna's words quietly to herself.

"This is the weirdest one yet," she says.

Nonna shrugs, blows us a kiss, then heads to bed.

"Well, you know how Nonna is," I say.

Olivia tilts her head from side to side. "I feel like she's messing with us. There has to be a clue buried in there somewhere."

"I wouldn't get your hopes up. Whatever it is, it has something to do with some random guy from the nursing home."

Olivia moves toward the stairs and mutters, "It may take me a minute, but I'm going to figure it out."

Thursday, December 31st

Blind Date #10: Nonna's Pick

As bad as Nonna is at keeping secrets, it's impressive how tight-lipped she is about today's date. Olivia has pestered her so much that Nonna sent her to the store for supplies just to get a break from her.

Charlie and Wes got here about an hour after we did. We're only open until noon on New Year's Eve, and as expected, the shop is a ghost town. The only thing people buy on New Year's Eve is food, alcohol, and fireworks . . . not plants.

So here we sit, watching the clock.

"It's too quiet in here," Charlie says. "I'm going to see if Randy and Chase are playing cards in the back greenhouse."

And now Wes and I are alone.

Charlie is right—it *is* way too quiet in here. Wes is parked in a chair close to the break room door while I'm sitting on the stool near the register. I pull out my phone just to give me something to do. Last night is still too fresh, and I don't want to read too much into that dance. Now that it's just the two of us, I have no idea what to say to him.

"Who do you think Nonna picked for you tonight?" he asks.

I shrug and look down at the floor. It's too hard to maintain eye contact with him and not blurt out every thought swimming through my brain. "No idea."

"I wish it was me," he says quietly, and my head shoots up.

"You do?" I ask.

He gets up from the chair and moves slowly toward me. "I wish all the dates had been mine." Then he laughs. "Okay, maybe not the drive-in porn. Or the Nativity thing. But you know what I mean."

I'm going to melt right off this stool. I let out a nervous laugh. "I wish they were with you, too."

His hands land on the counter behind me, one on each side, effectively boxing me in. I fight the urge to touch him.

"I also wish I could have been the first one to give you a good-night kiss," he says, "but Kiss Cam boy beat me to it."

I shake my head. "Um. Not really."

"What do you mean? I was there. And I saw the pic Olivia posted."

I smile. "I turned my head. You couldn't tell from the angle of the picture."

His eyes light up. "Not even when you were with Griffin?"

I roll my eyes. "Not even close."

"Well, this is unexpected." And then his brow creases. "But there's still one more to go."

"I can tell Nonna I don't want to go and—"

He's shaking his head. "No, don't do that. Nonna would be bummed if you didn't go on her date."

I nod. There's no way I can disappoint Nonna. I'm glad he gets that.

"But I'll be waiting for you to get home. And after this last blind date, it's my turn."

I bite my bottom lip so I don't say something stupid like *Yes! Please!*

The front door chimes, and Wes pushes away from me. It's Mr. Crawford, carrying that ugly gnome Olivia talked him into buying a few days ago.

He puts it on the counter. "This thing won't quit staring at me. Every time I go outside, his little beady eyes follow me around the garden. And it scares away all the birds."

I hear Wes laugh behind me. I don't dare turn around, or I'll lose this straight face I'm working so hard to keep.

"I understand, Mr. Crawford," I say. "Would you like to exchange it for something else?"

As I help Mr. Crawford pick out a statue, Chase calls for Wes to help with a delivery.

Business picks up a little after that, and finally Olivia and I are flipping the CLOSED sign and locking the front door. Before we leave, I look for Wes one last time, but I haven't seen him since he disappeared with Chase. I square my shoulders as we head toward the car. *One more date to go.*

✻ ♥ ✻

MARGOT: Anna is officially off the vent and breathing beautifully all on her own!!

I let out a loud gasp. Nonna and Olivia turn to look at me.

"What's wrong?" Nonna says, concern all over her face.

I open my mouth to answer, but Olivia throws up her hand. "Wait! Make her tell you what the clue means first!"

"Olivia, really," Nonna says. "Is it bad?" she asks me.

I shake my head. "No! Not at all! Anna is off the vent!"

Olivia and Nonna both squeal. Nonna says, "This calls for a special treat!" And then she's pulling bowls and mixers and sugar and flour and other things I can't identify. She slips a bright red apron over her clothes that reads: CAUTION: HOT!

Nonna gets to baking and I get back to the text from Margot.

ME: This is wonderful news!! So will you get to take her home soon?

MARGOT: Maybe as early as tomorrow if she keeps doing this well. I can't believe one minute she's got all these machines hooked up to her and then the next we're getting ready to leave, but they tell me this is more normal than I know.

ME: I know you're ready to get out of there

MARGOT: Yes! And how about you? Ready for this last date?

ME: I guess. I have no idea what we're doing or who it's with so it's kinda hard to get excited

MARGOT: Any chance Nonna picked Wes?

ME: No. We talked about it. But he said he'd be waiting up for me when I got home.

MARGOT: Okay my heart melted a little

ME: I thought the same thing!! So I just have to get through tonight and then I guess we'll see where it goes

MARGOT: Text me when you figure out where you're going tonight. There's a separate side bet on what this date is. Brad put $20 on dinner at the Steakhouse.

ME: Are y'all on that dumb group text, too?? And I know y'all are old and have a kid now but who eats dinner at 2 pm?

MARGOT: He's obsessed with the group message and I said the same thing about dinner. I googled things happening in Shreveport today so my money is on this interactive art exhibit at Artspace. You know how much Nonna loves that place.

That actually makes sense. Nonna does love that place.

ME: Well, then I should be home early!

MARGOT: Have fun! And send pics!

Nonna is still busy at the counter whipping up something delightful, so I motion for Olivia to follow me into the family room.

"What?" she asks.

I open the internet browser on my phone and search for the event Margot mentioned. When it pops up, I show it to Olivia.

"This has to be it, right?" I ask.

She reads the screen and squints. "I guess it could, but how boring is that? I'm expecting more out of her than this."

I glance at the clock at the top of the screen. "Well, we'll know soon enough. My date will be here in an hour."

Forty-five minutes later I'm brushing mascara over my top lashes, trying to psych myself up for the date. I've been listening to the steady thump of Wes's basketball next door, and any lingering thought that he was in on some grand surprise has disappeared. He's in shorts (but no shirt!) and seems to be taking his frustrations out on that poor orange ball.

And I may have verified his shirtlessness several times just to make sure.

Olivia sprints into the bathroom, barely making the turn into the doorway and hitting the door with a loud thud.

"I figured it out!" she screams.

My eyes get big. "What? Where am I going?"

She pauses dramatically. "You're going to Dallas!"

I side-eye her. "Texas?"

She nods and then holds up her phone, showing me a picture of the clue Nonna left on the board.

I read it again:

Dear Sophie,
A treasure to be sure!
Let me just say I've enjoyed your stay
Like your mother, you are a sweet soul!
And there's one more date until you're done—
So be ready by 2 p.m.!!

"How do you get *Dallas* out of that?" I ask.

"Look at the first letter of each sentence," she answers.

And I do, and sure enough: D-A-L-L-A-S.

"What's in Dallas?" I'm trying not to panic. Dallas is three hours from here. Presumably we'll drive home tonight, because there's no way I'm staying in Texas with someone I don't know.

"I tried googling it, but since it's New Year's Eve, there are a thousand things going on. But this has to be it." She looks at her phone once more. "Five minutes. Let's go see what it is."

I follow her downstairs. My hands are sweating. What if this guy is a creep and I'm stuck on this road trip with him? I'm going to have to refuse to go, even if it hurts Nonna's feelings. There's no way I can do this. She's asking too much!

As expected, my ENTIRE family is here—even the Evil Joes. Olivia and I have to push our way through the crowd to the front door, where Nonna is sitting in a nearby chair, as regal as Queen Elizabeth sitting on her throne.

We're all staring at the door, waiting.

"There's a car pulling up outside!" my cousin Mary screams.

There's a mad rush to the window. Outside, Wes has stopped dribbling and is holding the ball against his hip. The car is a huge limo-size SUV with tinted windows, and it seems to be idling at the curb.

This is painful.

"Is he getting out?" Jake asks.

"Nice ride," Graham says.

Nonna coughs loudly behind us.

"It seems it's time for the date to start," she says. Everyone turns from the windows. Nonna looks right at me and says, "Come here, Sophia." I'm a little worried that she's used my full name, but I move closer to her.

"When you showed up on my doorstep in tears more than a week ago, it broke my heart. And I wanted to do anything I could to fix that. You've been a good sport through all of these dates, even the ones that weren't very good." She looks over my left shoulder and gives Aunt Patrice *the look*.

I nod along. Where is she going with this?

"Thank you for going along with all of this. That beautiful smile is back and that's all I wanted."

I lean forward and hug her. As bizarre as this experience has been, I feel good. I feel happy. And reconnecting with my family was worth any heartache I had from my breakup with Griffin.

Nonna has a white envelope, and she pulls out what looks like several tickets. "Tonight's date is something I hope you'll like. It won't be just you and your date. I thought it would be more fun if you had some company."

She looks past me. "If you are between the ages of seventeen and nineteen, please step forward."

The crowd murmurs and everyone starts shuffling around. Within a few minutes, Charlie, Olivia, Graham, and the Evil Joes are standing next to me.

Nonna stands up and passes two tickets to everyone standing in line, except me. Olivia takes one look at them and shrieks, "No! Way!"

I look over her shoulder. "No. Way."

Nonna has scored us tickets to Deep Ellum's New Year's Eve music festival. The lineup of bands and musicians is to die for.

"Each of you has two tickets, and you're welcome to invite someone to go with you."

She's still holding four tickets in her hand. I'm assuming two of those are for me and whoever she picked to go out with me, but not sure what she's doing with the other two.

"How'd you score tickets for this, Mom?" Uncle Michael asks.

"How'd you even know this existed?" Jake asks. "And why can't we go?"

"This nice gentleman I met while I was visiting Gigi got

me these tickets because his company is one of the sponsors. The poor thing is in town to visit his mother, and she's not doing well. When I told him all about Sophie, he offered to hook me up. Plus, you boys already have big plans. I've heard you talking of nothing else for the last three days."

I nod toward the front door. "Is my date ever coming in?"

Nonna cocks her head to the side. "There is someone out there, but he's not your date. That's Randy from the shop. He's driving y'all over to Dallas. He'll go visit his brother while you're at the concert, then he'll drive you home. Did you know he works as a chauffeur on nights and weekends?" she asks excitedly.

I shake my head. "So where's my date?" I ask.

"We've all chosen your last nine dates. But tonight is different." She hands me four tickets. "Tonight it's your choice. Two of these tickets are for you and your date. The other two are for the other couple already in the car. Have a wonderful time!"

For a moment, I can't catch my breath. Then I throw myself in her arms, hug her hard, and dash for the front door.

Wes is still in the driveway, staring at the car at the curb. He turns in my direction when he hears my footsteps.

He drops the ball. "What's going on?"

I hold up the tickets. "Nonna got tickets to a music festival in Dallas. And I get to pick my date and—" I draw in a breath, suddenly feeling heat prickle all over my body, despite the chilly air. I look him in the eye and finally say what I've been wanting to for all these days. "And I pick you. I hope you say yes."

Wes's eyes move over me and a slow grin spreads across his face. "Yes." He pulls me in close, his hands on my waist. "Do I have to wait until the end of the date to kiss you?" he asks. "Because I've been waiting a really long time to do that."

I close the distance before he can say another word. My lips land on his, and my arms wrap around his neck. It doesn't take him long to catch up. His hands push my hair back as I melt into him.

"Sophie, your grandmother is seeing this," Jake yells from the front porch.

I pull slightly away from Wes, then hide my face against his neck. "They're all watching us right now, aren't they?"

"Yep."

I push him. "Go get dressed. We have places to be."

He starts to walk away but then pulls me back in and kisses me quickly on the lips. "Be back in five minutes."

Randy opens the back car door for us, and Addie and Danny yell, "Surprise!"

I throw myself into the car and give her a big hug. "So this is why you haven't returned my calls all day!"

She laughs. "I knew if I talked to you I would spill everything. Radio silence was the only way to go."

I hand her their tickets, and Wes and I crawl into the backseat. He took a shower in record time and now we're on the way to pick up everyone's plus one. Well, everyone but the Evil Joes' dates. They accepted the tickets from Nonna but opted to drive themselves in case *they want to come home early*. Whatever.

Charlie keeps turning around in the middle-row seat and looking at us with a confused expression. He finally faces Olivia and points back at us. "Did you know about this?"

She lifts that eyebrow. "Not as soon as I should have."

I'm a little nervous. This is Wes who I've known my whole life, but this is also new.

Wes links his hand with mine and tilts his head close. "We have lots to talk about, Soph."

"Good thing we have a couple of hours until we get there."

He smiles. "Freshman year. October. The haunted corn maze," he says.

I nod. I have no idea where he's going with this. "Um . . . Yeah?"

"Do you remember that night?" he asks.

I blink. "Kind of."

He gives me a small smile. "I had been there the week before, and there was this hidden space I found. I told you to take the first three right turns."

"I remember. I thought you were telling me a shortcut, but I got lost and thought I was going to die in the maze. Were you waiting for me?"

Wes nods. "For over an hour. I was going to make my move. But you never showed. And by the time I finally gave up, you and Charlie were getting popcorn from the concession."

My eyes get big. "I had no idea. I thought you liked Olivia."

"And I thought you didn't like me. That night at the corn maze wasn't the first time I tried to tell you I liked you. But it just never worked out the way I planned."

"I really had no idea."

He laughs. "I know that now, but I was a dumb fourteen-year-old who had no idea how to tell you I liked you. And then I tried to make it work with Olivia, but we all know what a disaster that turned out to be."

I bite my lip and glance at Olivia, but she's in deep conversation with Drew. "We both liked you, but she swore she liked you more, so I stepped back for her."

He tilts his head forward until his forehead is resting against mine. "So we were both dumb fourteen-year-olds."

"It seems like we were."

"One last confession," he says in a whisper. "My favorite cookies are those Key-lime-pie ones you made with Nonna, and I was the one who wrote you that love letter when we were in middle school."

"That was you?" I shout.

Charlie and Olivia turn around. "What was him?" Charlie asks.

"The love letter," I answer. "The one I thought was from Ben down the street."

"Oh, man, you've had it bad a long time," Charlie says in a pitying voice.

Wes looks at me. "I have."

Wes and I spend the entire trip tucked into the backseat catching up on every little thing we've missed over the last couple of years. When we arrive in Dallas, this is already the best date I've ever had.

The music festival is held in a huge warehouse downtown, and there are six bands slated to perform up until midnight. We dance and sing along and eat and talk and I never want this night to end.

We see the Evil Joes throughout the night, and we all really try to get them to hang out with us, but I don't think we'll be the Fab Six anytime soon. I can't help but notice Aiden and Mary Jo are back together. I hope this time it works out for them.

We're all sitting around one of the tables, hot and a little tired. Randy is supposed to pick us up right after midnight, and the clock is winding down.

When a slow song starts, Wes pulls me to my feet. We sway to the music, his hands running up and down my back.

The lead singer stops singing and starts the countdown.

With each number he yells, Wes rains kisses across my neck and cheeks.

When the singer gets to "one," Wes's lips fall on mine. It's soft and sweet at first, but it deepens as people shout "Happy New Year!" all around us.

The band starts playing another slow song, and Wes pulls me in close. "So what's your New Year's resolution?" he asks.

I tighten my arms around him. "No more blind dates."

Friday, January 1st

By the time I stumble to the kitchen, it's past lunch.

"It's about time you woke up."

My head jerks up and then I'm running straight into my dad's arms.

"When did you get here?" I ask.

He hugs me, then ruffles my hair. "Last night. After you had already left for your date."

"There's my girl," Mom says as she walks into the kitchen.

She squeezes me and I squeeze her right back. God, I've missed them.

Dad nods toward the table. "Have a seat. Want some coffee?" he asks.

"I'd love some."

"So tell me about that," he says, pointing to the blind-date chart.

Mom sits down across from me and I tell them everything. Most of it they already know, thanks to that group message and Margot's big mouth, but Mom says it's not the same unless they hear it from me.

Of course, I gloss over the drive-in movie date.

"You've had a busy break," Mom says. "How do you feel about it? Are you still sad things are over with Griffin?"

I shake my head. "Actually, no. That was for the best. He just recognized it before I did."

Dad takes a sip of his coffee, then sets it down gently on the table. "And what's going on with Wes? Nonna said you picked him last night."

I blush. "Wes has been my friend for a long time. And now we're going to see if there's anything more."

Both of his eyebrows shoot up. "Not too much more, I hope!"

"Dad," I say. "Quit being weird."

The back door opens and Wes walks in. His hair is sticking straight up, and he's still in the same shirt he wore last night.

"'Morning," he says, waving to us. "How's Margot and Anna?"

Mom gives him a recap, but Wes never moves from beside the back door, near the wall where the date board is.

"You want some coffee?" I ask.

He shakes his head. "No, I just came by to do one thing." Wes grabs a rag off of the kitchen counter and then erases

Nonna's cryptic message from yesterday. Then he picks up the dry-erase marker and writes:

New Year's Day Meal
Cabbage = Riches
Black-Eyed Peas = Luck
Dinner Next Door at 6:00
(But I want to hang out with you way before that)
(Just let me shower first)

He turns around. I can tell he feels a little awkward with my parents watching him. But he winks at me and says, "Catch up with you in an hour?"

I nod and hide my smile behind my coffee cup, and then he's gone.

"Well, that's the cutest thing ever," Mom says.

"Will his parents be home while you're over there?" Dad says.

I get up from the table and kiss them both on the cheek. "I'm going to jump in the shower. Love you both."

Just before I leave the room, Mom says, "You seem really happy, Soph."

I give her a huge smile. "I really am."

Three Months Later

Anna's crying voice fills my car over the Bluetooth and I can barely hear what Margot's trying to tell me.

"What?" I say for the third time.

I hear some shuffling and then a loud smacking sound.

"Okay, sorry," she says in the blessed silence. "She acts like she's starving to death when I just nursed her an hour ago, but I guess she's a greedy little girl."

"Ew, Margot. TMI. These are details I don't need."

I'm on the interstate, headed to Shreveport, just like every Friday for the last three months. Margot and I still text all the time, and thankfully now the only pics she sends are the ones of my beautiful niece, who is as round as a butterball. Hard to imagine she's the same tiny thing who didn't even weigh six pounds when she was born.

But this is our time to chat. A solid thirty minutes that's only interrupted when Anna needs to eat.

"So y'all are coming down next weekend, right?" she asks.

"Yeah, Mom is letting me check out early so we can be there by dinner."

"Okay, we can't wait to see you. And that outfit you sent Anna is adorable, but she's growing so fast she'll probably be too big for it in another month."

"That just gives me an excuse to buy her something else."

We chat until I pull up in front of Nonna's.

"Okay, I'm here. I'll text you later," I say.

"Have fun and send me pics so I know what y'all are doing," Margot says before ending the call.

That week and a half I spent here at Christmas changed everything. I realized I needed my family . . . and that cute boy next door . . . in my life, so now I'm here every Friday night and I work with Wes, Olivia, and Charlie at the shop every Saturday. And most times, Olivia, Charlie, and Wes come back to Minden with me on Saturday and we hang out with Addie and all of my other friends.

Whatever this is I'm doing with Wes doesn't have a label. He's not my boyfriend and I'm not his girlfriend. We're best friends who kiss. A lot.

And every Friday is date night.

We're both happy with this arrangement since we don't live in the same town. But we're both talking about how things will be when we're at LSU, living in dorms that are right next to each other.

And I can't wait. I bound up the front steps and yell hello when I open the door. It's chaos as usual, with kids riding scooters and skateboards down the hall. I can smell something delicious coming from the kitchen.

Nonna has on her *Of course you have room for dessert* apron that Aunt Kelsey had specially made for her.

"Hey! How was school this week?" Nonna asks.

I give her a quick hug and kiss on the cheek. "Senioritis has kicked in. I just don't see the point anymore."

"You're almost done! Finish strong," she says. I walk to the board to see what's waiting for me. I smile when I read the words in Wes's handwriting.

There's a big arrow pointing down to a blanket and several of those movie theater–size snacks.

Weather is just right for a
movie in the park
Be ready at 8:00

"Oh! Fun! I wonder what's playing?" I ask.

"Well, you'll have to wait and see, I guess."

At first I dreaded what was on this board, and now it's something I look forward to. Wes isn't the only one who puts our plans there. Sometimes it's Olivia, sometimes Charlie, and sometimes I call ahead and have Nonna write something there for me.

But there is always something on the board on Friday night, and unless someone is out of town, like I will be next weekend, we're all together for whatever is written there.

But before the date, it's always Family Dinner.

And just like clockwork, everyone starts filing through the back door.

Olivia and I set the table while Charlie chases down Aunt Kelsey's daughters, trying to get them in their high chairs. Nonna has enough food for an army, and Uncle Ronnie side-eyes the plate of cannoli like they're plotting against him.

It's chaotic and wonderful and I love every minute of it.

"Hey," Wes says from behind me.

I spin around, then we're closing the distance between us. It's a pretty PG greeting, since my entire family is in the room, but he still manages to squeeze me tight and press a few kisses along the side of my neck.

"You're early," I say.

"I couldn't wait," he answers.

Yeah, we waited a long time to get here. But, as I lean in to press my lips against his once more, I decide it was totally worth it.

Acknowledgments:

As always, thank you to my agent, Sarah Davies, for your continued support. This book surprised us both!

A huge thank-you to my editors, Laura Schreiber and Hannah Allaman. I really appreciate all of the love and support you give me. I'm lucky to have you! And to the fantastic team at Hyperion: Dina Sherman, Melissa Lee, Holly Nagel, Elke Villa, Danielle DiMartino, Guy Cunningham, Mary Claire Cruz, and Jamie Alloy. Thank you all so much for your hard work.

To Elle Cosimano and Megan Miranda, thank you for being the absolute best critique partners a girl could ask for. Love you both.

To Dr. Stephanie Sockrider, thank you for answering all of my questions about what would and could happen to Margot and the baby. Any and all mistakes made and liberties taken are fully on me.

To my family: I know you are all trying to guess who is who in this book, but just know you are all Charlies and Olivias to me. I had the best childhood and some of my favorite memories are portrayed in this book, especially Christmas morning. Could Mamma drink her coffee any slower?! I'm so lucky to be related to all of you.